Advance Praise for *Baby Jack*

"Schaeffer updates the God of G. K. Chesterton, who struggles against self-absorbed Sarah and Todd, characters as memorable as Updike's Rabbit. Boarding schools and elite colleges will ban this novel; it cuts too true about post-9/11 American upper-class society."

—**Bing West**, co-author of *The March Up*

"I had to read *Baby Jack* in private because it wrapped me up emotionally and left me wrung-out. Frank Schaeffer writes about duty and honor without irony, but without self-righteousness too. He draws a stark portrait of modern America, where most give none, and some give all. It's inspiring, poignant, and painful, because it's true."

—**Nathaniel Fick**, author of *One Bullet Away: The Making of the Marine Officer*

"Frank Schaeffer's *Baby Jack* is a passionate elegy to the fallen dead of America's wars and to those who mourn them. A scathing social satire as well as a tragic love story, Schaeffer tells a tale that is heartbreaking, redemptive, and surprisingly funny. . . . *Baby Jack* is a highly original literary achievement where God makes a brief appearance, as does the Puritan poet, Anne Bradstreet. This timely novel addresses one of the most important themes in American life today: who are the individuals who fight America's wars and who are the ones who do not."

—**Charlotte Gordon**, author of *Mistress Bradstreet: The Untold Life of America's First Poet*

"'*I am the repentance that can find no forgiveness*.' Searing, heart-shattering, Baby Jack plunges the reader into the crucible of a son's sacrifice and his family's agony . . . It is a chronicle of the brutal madness that attends grief, and the relentless imperative to discover grief's meaning. In the end, neither death, nor time, nor God himself are as once imagined.

"Above all else, the novel bears witness to undying love, and its power eventually to redeem even our worst atrocities."

—**Kimberley C. Patton**, Professor of the Comparative and Historical Study of Religion, Harvard Divinity School and author of *A Communion of Subjects: Animals in Religion, Science and Ethics.*

"This is a highly original novel devoid of clichés, on a subject—a Marine and his doubting dad—about which Frank Schaeffer knows firsthand. It's also a near hallucinatory tale about God and the afterlife—about which Schaeffer, eerily enough, also seems to have special insight. If you think 'supporting the troops' means a yellow ribbon on your car, read this book."

—**Max Alexander**, author of *Man Bites Log*

"Families of American servicemen and women deployed overseas should be heartened and comforted by this unique and compassionate novel."

—**Carolyn See**, author of *Making a Literary Life*

"Frank Schaeffer . . . has captured brilliantly the emotions both of those who serve and the families who love them. . . ."

—**Cathy Franks** (Mrs. Tommy Franks), active-duty military wife for thirty-four years

BABY JACK

Other Books by Frank Schaeffer

Fiction

The "Calvin Becker Trilogy":

PORTOFINO

ZERMATT

SAVING GRANDMA

Nonfiction

KEEPING FAITH: A Father-Son Story About
Love and the United States Marine Corps
(Co-authored with Sgt. John Schaeffer USMC)

FAITH OF OUR SONS: A Father's Wartime Diary

VOICES FROM THE FRONT: Letters Home
From America's Military Family

AWOL: The Unexcused Absence of America's Upper Classes
From Military Service—And How It Hurts Our County
(Co-authored with Kathy Roth-Douquet)

frankschaeffer.com

BABY JACK

A NOVEL

FRANK SCHAEFFER

CARROLL & GRAF PUBLISHERS

NEW YORK

BABY JACK

Carroll & Graf Publishers
An Imprint of Avalon Publishing Group, Inc.
245 West 17th Street, 11th Floor
New York, NY 10011

AVALON
publishing group incorporated

Library of Congress Cataloging-in-Publication Data is available.

ISBN-10: 0-7867-1716-5
ISBN-13: 978-0-78671-716-3

9 8 7 6 5 4 3 2 1

Interior design by Susan Canavan
Printed in the United States of America
Distributed by Publishers Group West

For Jennifer Lyons, my friend and agent

Part I

1

A few weeks after Jack turned seventeen he invited a Marine recruiter to our home. I was stunned by the intrusion. Sarah didn't say much at first but her face looked tight. Up till that moment the talk about the Marines had been just that, talk. Worse, Jack broke the cardinal rule and invited him midmorning when he knew I'd be painting.

The man claimed he was a sergeant. He sat bolt upright at the kitchen table. He was wearing a kind of glorified doorman outfit. An enlisted man, not even an officer; officers need to have some sort of college. Even I knew that.

The recruiter brought these little packs of plastic cards with him, the sort of prop a second-rate child psychologist might use to coerce evidence from an eight-year-old in a molestation case. The cards had words like "motivation" and "discipline" stamped on them. They reminded me of the bible memorization cards my father used to leave by my bedside in his effort to interest me in the "things of the Lord." He gave up after I worked them into a collage of centerfolds stuck to a sheet of plywood dashed with sperm and blood donated by my friends at the Boston Museum School. It was my version of *Piss Christ*. Only I called mine *Sticky Jesus* and no one paid attention.

"Pick the word that is the reason you want to join," said the sergeant.

I cringed. How could *my son* have become someone who, after his exposure to the life within our home, after he and I had been such friends—after I allowed him to change high schools—even joke about joining this collection of victims?

Jack picked "discipline."

I asked the recruiter what Jack would have after they were done with him.

"Have? I don't understand you, sir."

"Please call me Todd. What I mean is what benefits will Jack gain?"

"He'll be a United States Marine, sir."

"Todd. The name is T-o-d-d!"

"Yes, sir."

"Todd!"

"Yes, si—Todd."

"Will Jack get to call everyone he meets 'sir'? Is that the benefit?"

"There are other benefits. There's the GI Bill. But," the recruiter looked around our kitchen taking in the Subzero refrigerator, granite surfaces, the recessed halogens, and cherry wood cabinets, "I assume that getting money for an education isn't why Jack wants to volunteer."

"Maybe he wants the sort of challenge I found at Harvard Law," said Sarah.

"Jack, why do you really want to do this?" I asked.

"You and I have been through it."

"You can do a lot better. There are all sorts of ways you can stick it to me!"

"Maybe you want to go ROTC," said the recruiter.

"No, I want to go enlisted."

"We need to talk about this more amongst ourselves," said Sarah.

"Maybe this is a good thing for somebody who would otherwise be in jail or pumping gas, but this is not for you," I said.

"I'm joining the second I turn eighteen so you might as well sign the fucking paper!" shouted Jack.

There was a dead silence. Even the recruiter looked embarrassed. He shot Jack a disapproving glance.

Up to that moment Jack hadn't said he would outright defy me. That he did this in front of a stranger made me feel as if, literally, I was falling. Sarah turned a bright pink. The recruiter began to speak but I cut him off.

"Don't raise your voice to me, Jack!" I yelled. "If you want to mingle with Bible-thumping white trash then just get a job at Wal-Mart in Seabrook! You must find lots of your recruits there, Sergeant."

"Sir?"

"Todd!"

Sarah looked angry. But she's a big believer in the Rutherford decorum. So she tried to smooth things over.

"A Rutherford cousin did serve in the Navy in the Korean War. Maybe Jack's thinking of him."

"You never told me," said Jack sullenly.

"What does that have to do with anything?" I said.

"There are plenty of parents who object to their sons and daughters joining," said the sergeant. "I have two children and I want the best for them. When they graduate high school I'm not going to push them one way or the other but service is a good option."

"How old are your children?" asked Sarah.

"Seven and nine, ma'am."

"Jack," I said, ". . . What the hell is going through your brain?"

• • •

By the time Jack said he wanted to join the Marines, and everything went to hell, we'd been in our house so long that if I got up in the night to take a leak I didn't even bother to turn on the lights. The paths between furniture, the objects on the shelves, the dusty undisturbed places, were familiar as sunlight. We'd made our home our universe. We were settled.

Coffee first thing, then again mid-morning, lunch together on the days when Sarah worked via computer from home, dinner with the children—the "children" having dwindled to Jack when Amanda left. Sarah was still my model from time-to-time. And I was still seducing her in the studio from time-to-time.

Each room had its own season. Christmas belonged to our living room, full of overstuffed, dusty furniture. Sarah and I stood beneath the cracked plaster of the low ceiling, gazing through the windows as the sky behind the maples turned gold and made the bare branches into stark, black silhouettes. Thirty miles north of Boston the sun sets early in winter. Then from late December to late February Sarah would go to her office in Boston almost every day. I painted alone under the skylights in the barn.

Those winter months aged us. The air was cold, dry beyond the help of a humidifier. But sunrises in the kitchen turned Sarah into a golden reincarnation of herself, returned her to who she was on some long ago summer morning in New York as we ran side-by-side along the path around the reservoir in Central Park.

By April grim thoughts receded in proportion to the shoots of green emerging from the tired grass. The green brought the narcissus.

By early May there came a day that almost seemed like a good imitation of summer. Swathed in bulky sweaters we'd eat our first outdoor lunch on the screened porch.

In summer we concentrated on sun-ripened tomatoes and fresh mozzarella salads.

By late October we took our coffee out of doors, had it any-where, even on the rocks at the bottom of the garden overlooking the marsh. Days were warm, the mosquitoes dead since the first frost.

A day or so after the recruiter episode I was forlornly leafing through our family albums. My many snapshots of Sarah were a reminder of how quickly time had gone by. Amanda moved back to New York and sent photos from NYU. I felt cheated. I'd never figured out how to be a good father to her, and by the time I had a clue she was gone.

Somewhere, I was sure, in our childhood pictures of Amanda and Jack I'd find the reasons as to why Jack was doing this. I thought I'd learned from my mistakes with Amanda, paid attention. I put work second, and curbed my temper. I was there for Jack. I spent half a life patting him to sleep. Whereas Amanda cried for three minutes or so then went down. I didn't mind patting Jack. He was comforting to touch.

When Jack was four I set up a miniature easel next to mine and invited him to paint. Amanda was eleven and jealous. I had never allowed anyone except Sarah in the studio. We were still in New York so it meant Jack got to go to Williamsburg and Amanda didn't. I was too stupid to see how much this pissed her off. At the time it seemed natural. Amanda was musical and Jack loved to draw. If I had to do it over again I would have asked Amanda if she wanted to practice her cello in my studio.

I cut up small plywood panels for Jack and gave him a set of sable brushes, and his own paints, not acrylics, but the oils I used, thirty-dollar-a-tube pigments. Sarah asked why. She thought at four Jack should have been using something less toxic, but I told her that future curators would be thanking me for steering the young Jack Rutherford Ogden to materials almost as permanent as granite.

One of the family snapshots was of the three of us standing outside the Metropolitan Museum of Art. I asked some stranger to snap it as if we were tourists. I'm sure it was taken before we went in. Afterward I was too annoyed with Amanda to have bothered with a picture.

Every January a group of volunteers—mostly middle-aged and elderly ladies working under the direction of the museum's conservancy department—pack away the Neapolitan eighteenth- and nineteenth-century terracotta and wood silk-clad figures that decorate the Met's "Angel Tree." Thirty feet high and lavished with over one hundred and fifty, fifteen-to-twenty inch figures: beautifully painted faces gentle and innocent; swirling robes of silk, rich as thick smoke curling heavenward—a nativity scene to break even my pagan heart, angels, the holy family, wise men, shepherds and travelers. The volunteers put up the tree in November, then pack the figures away after cleaning each with sable brushes and special vacuum cleaners. The figures are kept in a temperature-controlled environment, held by supports, stored in heavy crates. Their creators would be pleased.

I watched the dismantling of the tree with Jack and Amanda. They were five and twelve. (Sarah was supervising the packing up. We were about to move to Salisbury.)

"Art survives because each generation protects it, loves it, values it, tries to make time stand still, or at least slow down," I said. "These ladies are my heroes, guardian angels protecting art made by men who are now dust."

"Will they take care of your paintings when you're dead?" asked Jack.

"I sure hope so," I answered. "You make sure someone does if I'm not around okay?"

"I will," said Jack.

"If you want them to take care of your work you should paint something nice," said Amanda with a laugh. "Why don't you ever paint things that are beautiful, Dad?"

"Don't be such a smart ass."

"Dad's pictures *are* nice!" said Jack.

My defender shot Amanda a furious glance.

How can my defender defy me? Who *is* he? I thought I knew.

Tall, tender, tough, smart, funny, kind, polite. Jack hated school. I would always imagine him moored to a desk, longing to sail away. And yet when he painted with me he never moved concentrating with a white hot intensity. By the time he was fifteen Jack was reading books about Eastern religions and could quote the sayings of Lao-tse.

2

The article in the *New Yorker* wasn't even about Dad. It was mostly about Lucian Freud, Wayne Thiebaud, and Steven Hawley. Dad got just a few paragraphs. He framed them.

Todd Ogden's work represents an outstanding late addition to the Modern Movement which is in the process of being reassessed. When we look at American painting in the 19th century, we see that there were already overlapping attitudes toward the notion of the real. Its greatest exponent was Eakins in a painting like *The Champion Single Scull* 1871, which provides a reflection of reality that would seem perfect but for the fact that it is so consciously disciplined. But Todd Ogden gives us something else as well—he conveys surprise at what he sees, as opposed to what we expect to see.

Some of his smaller paintings such as *Virgin and Frozen Peas In Front of Old Painting* 1983/4 produce this feeling of astonishment not just in the viewer, but

one senses in the artist himself. For the majority of
spectators the most familiar picture in this exhibition is
probably the *Female Nude in the K-Mart Parking Lot
1989/90*. Did the normally outspoken Ogden actually
intend the nude female facing the viewer to be a "blas-
phemous" Christ icon? . . .

Was that the bullshit they'd carve on Dad's headstone? I
wanted mine to say: "Jack Ogden, Marine." We look for meaning
because whatever peers out from our eyes isn't happy to be bound
up with a mortal body. We want to live forever. If life means something then maybe our hope that we're more than a sack of blood
and bones is evidence of an immortal soul rather than insanity.

I needed to cut out smoking weed, even on the weekends—
didn't want to pop the piss test. I heard the recruiters sometimes
sprang a surprise.

When Dad lost his mind I'd play along. "Just smile and nod."
But then I was just tense enough to fight back, not just pretend to
listen and then do my own thing. I was angry enough to fight him.

When he started in about how "dumb" the Marines were, I
told him that William Manchester was a Marine. End of discussion. At least for me.

My seventeenth birthday party—Dad, Mom, Jessica and guests
were on the new dock. Amanda called from New York.

Everyone was overdressed for the hot day so there were jackets
hanging off the cast iron lawn furniture. People always dressed up
for Mom's parties. And of course Mom looked cool and collected
in her pale yellow linen dress, and one of her big floppy hats.

The lawn was just cut so the garden smelled good. There were lots of boats on the river. Dad's boat was one of the biggest so people slowed down and stared at it and the lawn stretching up from the riverbank to the sprawling house. Plus, Mom hired a band. So there was some pretty good jazz floating out over the water.

Anyway, there were about fifty people milling around. It was my party but they were mostly Mom's friends. And because I left St. Martin's early and blew off their track team mid-season, there was only Jessica and three fairly decent guys from Chandler.

Mom's "friends" were people she always used this sort of occasion to get close to for her "causes." That day she invited four Salisbury selectmen and their wives because she was working on getting an easement to build a gazebo too near marsh, and the mayor from Newburyport was there, because Mom was raising money for the courthouse restoration.

Dad and I were arguing, or as close to it as Dad would get, being it was my birthday and he really was trying hard to be nice. I pointed out that lots of artists, writers, political leaders—the sorts of people he respected, had served.

"They were drafted," said Dad, "and that was a different time."

"No they weren't. Okay, some were but lots volunteered too."

The only other thing he could come up with was that I was meant to do "great things" and that the president was an asshole.

Then he started messing with Jessica, as if somehow he disapproved of *her* now! I'll bet if I had been headed to Harvard I could have been out all day, night and weekends with any girl and he would have loved her. And he had been busting my chops because

I was smoking. I know I could have smoked three packs a day and he never would have said a word if I wasn't saying I was headed to Parris Island. He called it "low class," but never said that about his agent, let alone the guy who came up from the Met to see his stuff and smoked the whole time. And he knew Alice and me were going at it like crazed rodents when I was fourteen and she was seventeen and he didn't give a shit! Back then I was winning track meets. I was sailing his boat. I was in a school he thought was great.

"Why would you want to only be a soldier when you could be so much more?" he asked.

I answered him like it was sort of a joke. But he knew, I knew, he knew, we really were fighting. So I was laughing and so was he, but we were staring at each other.

"First off, I'm not going to be a soldier but a Marine! Second, just because your generation screwed up Vietnam doesn't mean history stopped. Third, even a paranoid can have real enemies."

"To succeed in life you need to finish what you start," Dad said in a phony relaxed voice.

"Track just seemed stupid," I answered.

"'Stupid?' What's *stupid* is the way you're hanging around with that girl. Is she the reason you quit track? Did she get you to start smoking?"

Now the gloves were off but he hadn't got the balls to go after me on the Marine thing, not on my birthday anyway, so he settled for picking on Jessica.

"I didn't even meet her till after I left St. Martin's."

"Why would you go for some mousy little girl?"

"And you are a controlling bastard," I said more and more

mightily pissed off. "If I find her interesting, what's your problem?"

" '*Interesting?*' Where's your passion?"

Before I could stop him, Dad turned to Jessica. She was standing on the dock about fifty feet away talking to Mom where they were setting up the table for my birthday cake the caterers were fooling with. Dad and I were on the boat.

"Jessica!" he yelled.

"Yes, Mr. Ogden?"

"Come over here."

Jessica boarded. She didn't know you take off your shoes on a boat so right off he snapped at her and she seemed a little embarrassed as she kicked off her shoes.

She looked so beautiful in that long gray skirt and white blouse even if it was way too hot. Her black hair fell down her back almost to her waist. She reminded me of a Filippo Lippi Madonna, only with no pearls braided into her hair and she wasn't blonde. Jessica's blue eyes look directly at you, and were never cast down demurely Madonna-style, but she seemed to know the same secret those Lippi Madonnas knew. That's what reminded me of the Lippis, Jessica's inner peace, as if she was from someplace less noisy.

The way Jessica kept smiling even though Dad was being rude was brave. She sparkled and was about as far from "mousy" as you can get. She was different from the other girls at Chandler, not afraid to love ordinary things. Everyone else was into being extraordinary. Jessica *was* extraordinary but didn't know it. She talked about Sandy Point, and the way when the tide is out it looked as if you could walk across the bay to Crane's Beach, and how she had always wanted to do that. And when I told her about the Marines, she didn't look shocked or disappointed, just scared. And she liked Anne Bradstreet.

As Jessica stepped into the cockpit Dad started in.

"Let me tell you both about how I met Jack's mother," said Dad.

"C'mon Dad!"

No use.

"There was nothing rational about the experience. She seemed to have a shimmering outline around her as she walked through the gallery door. It was autumn and her cheeks were flushed. She wore one of those ratty Afghan coats everyone had in the seventies. It looked good on her! Her slacks were so tight you could've counted the change in her back pocket. And she was *so* beautiful! Her face is what got to me—those high cheekbones that pale Victorian coloring."

"That's it Dad! Okay, Jessica, let's go!" I said.

He grabbed her arm.

"Jessica *wants* to hear the end of the story, don't you?"

"Why not?" said Jessica and smiled.

She was cool as a cucumber and looking right at him. Dad turned away first. Then he talked even louder.

"I grabbed Sarah and kissed her before I even knew her name. Hell! I had her on the desk before I knew her name!"

He looked at us and smiled wickedly.

I dragged Jessica away. She laughed.

I spent the rest of the afternoon trying to explain Dad to her. I don't think she got his, I'm-a-genius-so-I-can-say-anything routine.

"I'll work him into a poem sometime," she said.

Jessica was wonderful. People find hope in beauty. If there's no meaning, if there's no soul, just eyes reporting to a brain, then our desire for there to be more is our madness.

3

We were at the start of the last summer before the Marine Corps. And I was preparing for the worst though still hoping he wouldn't go. I needed Jack more than ever. He had defied me and time was running out. And not being from a military family I had no sense of proportion. All I knew was that Marines got killed in Korea, killed in Vietnam, and killed in Beirut.

Jack was a writer, a philosopher, and a real artist! After we moved to Salisbury, I set him up to paint in my studio—a barn by the house, both built in the 1830s. Jack painted muddy little landscapes of our marsh and river views in a wobbly eight-year-old hand, and several good pictures of me at my easel.

Then there was the Duccio craze, when he copied a Duccio Madonna and even used gold leaf. He was eleven. I never enjoyed anything more than watching Jack paint.

Jack wanted to know all about the Duccio panels in Siena. After I showed him my slides he painted crucifixions. And he made me tell him the whole story of Jesus' life and death and resurrection because of those slides.

Jesus was a subject I had steadfastly resisted. It—"He"—gave me the screaming willies. But after explaining Jesus to Jack I began to incorporate Christ figures into my own work again. And those were the pictures that finally got me into the Met.

Cimabue, Duccio, Giotto, Uccello, Ghiberti, Masaccio, Brunelleschi, Donatello, Fra Angelico, Fra Filippo Lippi, and Botticelli, we looked at them all, in books and/or at the Met. And Jack must have had cadmium yellow on his fingers. I was furious and screamed at him. There are still little yellow fingerprints on my Illustrated Vasari.

After Duccio came Sister Gertrude. Jack loved her self-taught "primitive" art, painted on just any old board or piece of cardboard with childish daubings of color—happy angels, bible verses, and of course those famous self-portraits as the bride of Christ riding to heaven with Jesus in his airplane. Sister Gertrude painted herself dressed in white, her wedding veil flying in the wind behind her, her dark brown face set with big eyes, as she headed to paradise with her white Jesus.

We listened to a recording of her chanting apocalyptic gospel messages accompanied by her tambourine. She'd given up playing the guitar after the Lord told her not to play anymore. Later she gave up painting when he told her to stop.

"Why was the Lord so crazy?" asked Jack. "Did he hate art?"

I didn't know what to say. I don't believe in God so that meant I'd have to say Sister Gertrude was nuts. So I changed the subject and talked about how ironic it was that the only reason we knew about Sister Gertrude was because a Jewish art dealer took her Christ-promoting art seriously and made it—and Gertrude Morgan—into an American icon.

I'd talk about all sorts of bullshit while we painted.

• • •

When Jack was thirteen he finally came face-to-face with Duccio's paintings in the little museum inside the unfinished wing of the Siena Duomo, the cathedral's vast expansion that was never completed after half the population died of plague. By some miracle the Duccio room had no other visitors. Jack and I were alone with the figures of Christ and his disciples, the throngs of Jews, the Romans, the high priest, all painted in slightly green flesh tones and surrounded by the languid Tuscan landscapes, gold, strong faces and exquisite pastel coloring. Jack stood, staring at the panels.

"So *somebody* made something perfect!" Jack practically shouted.

After we got back from Italy we spent three months working at the marina—nights and weekends. By late October we were working under a tarp warming our hands over the butane heater every few minutes. Jack spent hours on his back reinforcing the connections between the hull and the deck. We added layers of fiberglass and strengthened the deck-attachments for the cables to support the mast. The two of us were planning to sail to Bermuda in the summer.

I carry pictures in my brain:

We were off Cape Hatteras with a lot of wind—the starboard rail was underwater then came up, foam gushing back into the ocean. The self-steering mechanism kept us on course. We were racing straight downwind and Jack's long sandy hair whipped around his smiling face.

I had growing confidence in Jack's seamanship and he had absolute trust in me. We alternated three-hour watches.

I had no worries when Jack took watch. I even slept. Jack and I worked on radio fixes, dead reckoning, current effect, we looked at Jupiter—I taught him what I remembered about coastal navigation.

Bright blue sky, clouds mirrored in Jack's lovely wide-set eyes, a dusting of freckles over his nose was growing more pronounced every day—sun burnt shoulders—Jack's seriousness about doing every job I gave him and doing it well—my absolute satisfaction that for once something was going as well as I hoped for.

We sat, heads back watching the sky and ocean slide past. Jack's back was warm from the sun as he leaned against me.

After Amanda graduated high school and left for New York, first for a child care job then NYU, Jack was like an only child. I almost never heard from Amanda. When she called she mostly talked to Sarah. I'd get snippets; assurance from Sarah that school was going well. It wasn't that I didn't love Amanda; just that I could only concentrate on what was in front of me—my work and Jack.

He draped his long arms over my shoulders when we walked off soccer fields. And that was when he was fifteen and tall as me, a time so many sons seemed embarrassed to even acknowledge the existence of fathers.

• • •

The Jack-and-the-Marines debacle started on September 11, 2001 when Jack was just sixteen. Thirty-seven of my works on paper were destroyed. As I watched the endless replays of the Twin Towers crumbling I imagined my art burning. Certainly this was insanely petty. Who gives a shit about art when a man and woman hold hands as they leap to their deaths? But who can visualize "thousands killed?" Who can grasp the end of the world?

I was mentally prepared to accept my fate: over time my art will forgotten. "Over time"—comforting words denoting centuries of gentle corruption, paper yellowing through eons, paint cracking, colors fading, not the entire *Sarah Pregnant* series soaked in jet fuel going up in flames as the gallery at the top of Tower Two was destroyed!

Amanda called from New York and told us she was fine. She was a senior at NYU. There was dust in the dorms.

Jack's reaction was odd. He said he wanted to enlist. At first I humored him.

• • •

One afternoon, a few months after the disastrous visit by the recruiter, Jack came into the studio and sat down. I paid no attention. That was our way while I was working. And he was back to keeping the old rules, at least that day. He sat still for a good twenty minutes till I was done and turned.

Looking at Jack made my heart feel pinched. I was so damn angry and sad too. But I didn't know how to express the sorrow. I just knew that I had failed.

"Dad," said Jack in a quiet serious voice.

"Yes, Jack?"

"Dad, I'm really going to go through with it."

"There's still plenty of time to work this through."

"I've done my thinking."

"What if I said, if you join the Marines we will not speak again?" I said.

"I'd say, okay if that's how you want it," he answered calmly.

I took this as a challenge, one that had to be answered.

"Maybe I will," I said.

"Okay."

Jack regarded me steadily. His voice was quiet. I was trying to use my most reasonable tone. I smiled again. He still didn't smile back so I stopped. I felt as if an icicle was being rammed up my spine.

"Why are you so ready to shit all over me?" I asked.

"You're the one that sees it that way. Not me. But I'm going down there."

"You're just going to sit there and defy me to my face?"

"Call it whatever you want."

"Then fuck you!" I bellowed.

Jack just gave me a hard look.

"*If you go down there I'll never speak to you again*!" I shouted.

"Fine," Jack said, in an infuriatingly calm voice.

"I mean it!" I screamed.

"Fine," said Jack. "We'll never speak again."

I knew he was bullshitting, at least I hoped so. Jesus, I knew *I* was bullshitting! It was gamesmanship. I wasn't man enough to call it off right then and there.

We left it at that. I hoped he'd forgotten the threat as the days passed. But nobody backed down, nobody unsaid anything. And then we stopped arguing about the Marines—for a while.

I was hoping that if I didn't bring it up again the whole idiotic topic might just fade away, that maybe he'd just not go. And I'd pretend to not notice and let him back down gracefully.

Sarah was filling in college applications and leaving them in Jack's room regardless of his rebelliousness. She was still begging him to go for early decision at Harvard.

And I was left wondering just why Jack was able to get to me so thoroughly and painfully. I'd climbed out of a crappy background to a good place. And somehow I guess, I'd always assumed my kids would do even better.

I hoped he knew that after he got back from boot camp we'd speak again even if I couldn't back down before he left. I figured he'd know it was like the times when he was little and I sent him to his room and said he had to stay there all day. After about a half an hour I'd come upstairs, relent, and release him from house arrest. I was counting on him knowing I was full of shit.

4

I was sick of always having the easy way handed to me, the ambitious Ogden/Rutherford nonsense where every step's just a petty calculation. I was going "open-contract." I didn't sign up for a specific MOS (military occupational specialty) but would do whatever the Corps needed.

My recruiter said I'd probably be in admin or motor-transport; a glorified truck driver or some poor jerk with a clipboard loading supplies. But like they said: every Marine a rifleman. We all have to qualify at five hundred yards, almost twice the distance to the target that the Army makes soldiers shoot. And the point was becoming a Marine, any Marine.

I didn't want a job that summer since I'd be working solidly for the next four years. I wanted a last vacation without a care in the world. As a graduation present my parents gave me $1,000 and told me I didn't have to get a job, to take a break and enjoy myself. It was *Dad* who said this. He also said he wasn't going to speak to me again if I went to PI. But the $1,000 told me his threat was bull-shit, as usual.

I was driving Dad nuts by refusing to back down. On the other hand he'd lose control whether I pushed or not, flipping-out had always been his way of dealing with stress. I was tired of backing down and giving in to his whims.

Dad was pissed when I reminded him he hadn't exactly followed in *his* dad's footsteps.

He dropped in on me just before I went to bed a few days after he threatened to never speak to me again. I think he was sort of trying to make up. But he wouldn't come clean. I decided to see if I could push him over the edge. A good way was to needle him about his wacky religious childhood, something "we never talk about."

"You don't love Jesus anymore, do you, Dad?"

"What?!"

"Well I think I'm going to be a born-again Christian like your dad."

"Don't go there."

"I want to call up your mom and ask her if she'll teach me how to love the Lord. How soon is Jesus coming back?"

"Cut it out!"

"But Dad, I'm feeling this call from God to preach about Jesus. Is he going to come and take us away? Are we going to be left behind?"

"Shut up!"

"I thought you always said that everything should be on the table."

I could tell he was about to explode but he contained himself and walked out.

Eventually he did sign the papers though. He had to. I'd been bugging him endlessly. He got so sick of me interrupting his painting he signed them and literally threw them at me after I'd asked about a hundred times. Anyway he knew a few months later I'd turn eighteen.

And once it was settled he even put up a pull-up bar by the barn and got in my face about training for boot camp! He wanted to control everything, even what he was against!

Dad and Mom acted as if they were foreigners. They never talked about America except when they complained about the president, what an idiot he was. But who were Mom and Dad going to call when the shit hit the fan? What was wrong with wanting to serve my country?

5

Jack is angry with Todd. Now he's furious with me too it seems. I'm not anti-military, just anti-Jack joining. Several members of our family served in World War II. And there was at least one Rutherford in Korea. So Jack is quite wrong. We *have* done our bit.

I even admitted to him that perhaps there is something valuable about military discipline, something like the Native American right of passage, alone in the woods for two weeks to become a man. But I think all-male societies are one-dimensional. I know they tolerate women in the military now but Jack is joining the Marines and they train the women separately. What does that imply? I'll try to get Jack to reread *On the Beach* and *All Quiet on the Western Front*.

Why on earth did Chandler School include that trite William Manchester muck in humanities? Education is such a mess these days. If they wanted to study war they should do something systematic, do the Romans before the Second World War for God's sake. Jack read Marcus Aurelius and missed the point! I had no idea that a certain type of male might be so vulnerable.

About half way through this dreadful post-graduation summer

I asked Jack to go for a walk. We went down to Graff Road and strolled along the edge of the woods. The marsh looked lovely by the Parker River. The smell of the woods, especially the woodchips from a freshly cut hickory, was sweet. People were canoeing. Everything seemed normal, cheerful, just like any other summer in New England. And yet Jack was in some obdurate delayed adolescence stalking along, not his normal easy-going self. I don't think he was noticing our surroundings. I was very much hoping the walk would somehow remind him of just why he should stay.

"Don't misunderstand me." I told Jack, "I do know people for whom the military could be a constructive experience. There was a former Marine at Harvard Law and I believe he's a judge now. However, who wants to actually kill or be killed? I don't understand your logic."

I took his hand and we walked along. He had nothing to say, though he did hold my hand very sweetly.

"What are your needs?" I asked him. "What needs are propelling you into the military?"

He had no answers. I was at my wits' end. What does one do with stony silence?

"You should aim to work at the cabinet level if you want to emulate your grandfather," I told Jack, "if you want to serve, work to develop *real* leadership, to make a *real* difference. Why don't you try politics? I'll call Robin and I'm sure she could fit you in as an intern on Kennedy's next campaign."

No interest whatsoever! Silence!

"Jack," I said, "I've always been uncomfortable near people who are dogmatic about their truth."

No answer. We walked back to the car. I wonder if Todd is right about this Jessica person. Perhaps she *is* the new ingredient that's driving a wedge between us all. Is she making my child happy? I know nothing about her people.

"Stay out of it as much as possible, Mother," Amanda said, after I called to talk over the situation. "You always end up lecturing."

"You're wrong," I told Amanda stung, "I *never* 'lecture' Jack. The kiss of death is to become a schoolteacher parent. Look where it's getting Todd!"

For whatever reason Amanda just wouldn't talk, she seemed angry with me. Now I have two angry children!

What's been the source of Amanda's bitterness? At Wellesley I majored in fine arts and philosophy. It was not a "jumped-up finishing school," as Amanda sometimes claims. It was a top college about excellence and doing things well, pursuing reason, thinking things out for oneself.

What *is* wrong with Amanda? I'll make allowances for her being distressed because of Jack's wild talk. But I think it is something deeper. My sister and I were lucky there was no son. My father treated us as "sons." Maybe it's better for a woman if there is no brother in the home. That's always been one of Amanda's problems. Jack got all Todd's attention.

And Todd is being so damn inconsistent! One minute he tells Jack he'll never speak to him again if he joins and then he goes out and puts up a pull-up bar! He told Jack he needs to get in shape for boot camp. For God's sake!

6

Office: 10th Floor—Editorial—Letters Department, rooms 1055 and 1056. Title: "News Assistant." Job description: One of the six persons responsible for producing the letters to the editor section of the *New York Times*.

The place radiates history but in a quiet way. The offices and most of the people I see in the elevators have an unmade bed quality. Everything is a little worn out and shabby. Since I was a little girl I've read the letters section of the *Times*. Well, they all came out of these offices on the 10th floor *where I work*!

Every letter Dad ever wrote that has *not* been printed—in other words all of them—came to these hallowed rooms. I thought the offices would be rather grand and imposing, marble columns, and high ceilings or maybe a modern version, high-tech chrome and glass everywhere. The newsroom on the third floor is more like that, big, with lots of cubicles, but up here on the tenth it's like the main building upstairs halls and principal's office at Chandler. We even have a dowdy little library in a big open area I walk around to get to the Letters office. It has a wood partition and the hall runs around the partition so when I walk from the elevators to our office I'm skirting what looks like a section of the Newburyport library.

Jason, our Letters editor, is in one room and his desk is across from his second in command, Susan. She's been here twenty-three years and *is* the Letters department. Jason has been here four years and before that was in the news department. They are all nice people, very academic and tweedy—very dedicated.

My fellow peons: Picture the younger faculty at the Chandler School, men in khaki pants, blue and white shirts with ties every which way and women who look as if they would be a lot more comfortable with a book sitting on the porch of some house in Kittery—lots of nondescript wool slacks, skirts and mauve blouses, the sort of women who wear shawls. The word "sexy" does not describe anything or anyone here.

The office I'm working in is about the size of the smaller sitting room in Salisbury. I sit looking out at a yellow/rust brick wall and some big air ducts. Our windows are large and the room has plenty of light. Next to us peons is the door that leads into Jason's room. The door is always open. Next to the door is a two-foot tall pile of past *Times* letters pages. The papers are held down by a brick somebody sent to us with the words "Convict Criminal Clinton" stenciled on it—but as Jason commented dryly: "This doesn't reflect my political philosophy, it's just one of the stranger objects we've been sent." As for the letters, these days they're mostly sent by email.

The papers under the brick are turning yellow from the bottom of the stack up. A chemist could illustrate a lecture on the acidity of paper from this slowly yellowing stack. The top pages are white and on the very bottom, about two feet down, the pages have turned pumpkin color. Actually the way the white gradually fades all the way to pumpkin is sort of pretty. It shows why Daddy always insists on using acid-free paper even for his most casual sketches.

I come to work at about nine—stay till six. The way we keep ourselves from going crazy is to download all the letters then sort by topic. We can use a key word, say, "Iraq," and then everything on the war goes into one pile. We print up hard copy and arrange all the piles on a little table next to the door leading to Jason's office. Then we do what we call the first sweep of the day by around ten. We do a second sweep by one and a last sweep by five or six, after that is the cutoff.

Most of our mail is in response to something by our columnists so I told Dad he has a much better shot of getting a letter in about a news story than a column. And we don't print rants so if he is serious about something he should cool his jets.

We're here to reflect the views of our readers fairly. And since most of our readers are smart enough to be of the left that's how the page comes off. In fact it's the conservatives who get the break because say we get one hundred negative letters about a Brooks column backing the president, and we get seventeen conservatives writing who liked it and say we publish four letters, two negative and two positive, it would appear to our readers that a half of the letters were positive but they weren't. So Jason is right, "You can't read the letters as a sort of opinion poll." We don't see ourselves a performing a watchdog function. That isn't our job. As Jason says, "The letters are another voice representing the news from another angle."

My position is the most junior. Everybody here is Ivy League.

(Everyone but me, that is, unless they count the fact that I got *accepted* at Harvard.) Most everyone got their job because somebody in the paper recommended them. That's how I got in. You have to have good computer skills—and a good grasp of the language—but above all you have to know somebody.

I was at NYU when Jack quit track and left St. Martin's. Dad called me and I was shocked. He'd been the star player on his junior high basketball team, and then at St. Martin's he was drafted to run on the senior track team after just one tryout. He started winning right away and kept winning all the way up to the state championships where he won the 400-meters. We all got used to seeing Jack win. Then suddenly he just didn't want to run anymore. But Dad didn't get it. I think it was Jack's way of telling Dad to get lost. I did the same thing by taking the au pair job in New York. I got to move out ahead of schedule.

The irony was that the people I worked for that summer were even more self-involved than Mom and Dad. They made them seem positively laid-back. I mean there's lax then there's indulgent. She-who-eats-her-young is a freelance contributor to the style section at the *Times*. He-who-is-terrified-of-his-wife is a plastic surgeon. After the little boy repeatedly socked me in the shins with a bat, "she-who-eats-her-young" said that I was to never say "no" to one of her children, but to find "creative and positive ways to redirect their creativity."

I lived in at the au pair job at 86th Street and 5th Avenue across from the Met. *Très chic*! (Though I felt I had somehow betrayed my roots on the Upper West Side by moving to the other side of the park.) Then I moved into the NYU dorm, then, after I graduated, moved to my place on the Upper West Side and started my job at the *Times*. After I graduated from NYU "she-who-eats-her-young" got me my job at the paper, she's related to the publisher—God's third cousin, whatever.

Mom drove me down to the au pair job. Dad was furious because he hadn't wanted me to take the job. And then she came back at the end of that summer and helped me settle into the dorm. Then, four years later, Mom stayed after graduation. (Dad headed straight home.) She stayed because I needed help moving into my studio apartment on West 102nd Street.

I picked a place not too far from where I grew up. It was nice to be "home." I never did feel like I belonged on the North Shore—too white and the East Side is well, the East Side. The Korean lady at the store across from the 103rd Street subway station remembered me from when I bought fresh orange juice there on the way home from school as a kid.

I still get that sense of relief every time Mom calls me with an update. The relief is that I'm here and not there. Dad seems to really be coming apart over the Marine thing. And now Mom says he's pissed off about Jessica—the new girlfriend. The sooner Jack's out the better for us all!

Jessica is not good enough for Dad. Just like my au pair job wasn't good enough. He doesn't say so but I think (I KNOW) it's because of Dad's weird sense of self. I called to ask him why he is being so hard on Jack.

"Some social experiments are not a good idea," Dad said.

"Are you saying Jessica isn't 'worthy' of Jack?"

"Will you be happy seeing your brother pumping gas?"

"Don't change the subject."

"Answer my question!" Dad snapped.

"What's wrong with pumping gas?" I asked.

"Nothing if you don't have potential."

"Maybe he'll be a general or something," I said trying to laugh.

"The second raters go into politics and the third raters are in the military."

"And the artists are the only 'first raters?'"

I was still trying to jolly him along.

"First raters are people who don't settle for less, who *finish what they start*!"

"So we're back to Jack quitting track? Jesus Dad!"

"No. But that's a good example of a character flaw."

"Dad?"

"Yes?"

"In the sixties, you weren't talking about winning track meets, were you?"

"I know you're being sarcastic but in fact the sixties were all about achieving our potential."

"While stoned?"

"It was about new beginnings, about moving beyond the cycle of violence based on the illusion of economic growth."

"From what I hear it was mostly about fucking."

"What's wrong with fucking?"

"And *that* is why you don't want Jack to be a Marine—not enough fucking?" I said and laughed.

"Your brother is throwing away his life." Dad paused. "He is also destroying my peace of mind, my ability to work!"

He is SO transparent! Poor Daddy!

"Daddy, not everything revolves around you."

"It only takes one generation to destroy everything. Think about the first family member of some German family who decided to join the Nazi Party."

"Jack isn't joining the Nazi Party!"

"I created a space where you all might thrive free of everything I grew up with, the prejudice, the narrow outlook, the stifling mentality. Jack's throwing it away."

What could I say? I told Dad I had to get back to work from my lunch break, which I actually did.

Later I called Jack and told him that I honestly think his joining the Marines is absolutely insane and he shouldn't do it just to spite Dad. He *could* find less drastic ways to stick it to Dad. But Jack says he really does want to join, although he won't get into why. "I just do," is all he says.

So I called Mom.

"I think Jack is just sick of all the selfishness," I say.

"Whose selfishness?" asked Mom.

"Yours, Dad's, aren't you sick of it?"

"He's just a young man trying to distinguish himself from the crowd," said Mom.

I don't know how Mom sticks with Dad. I just get it over the phone and can't take Dad for more than two minutes. I can take Mom for maybe three.

7

I was at Chandler for the last two years of high school. That's why Jack and I were first drawn together. We were both the new kids in a class that had had its own cliques already. He had been going to St. Martin's Prep but left after he quit their track team. I won a scholarship and transferred from public school the same year.

Even at Chandler, where people don't dress up or flirt in the usual overt teen manner—they're into being "natural" in a sort of granola-laid-back-but-pretty-intense way—Jack stood out as especially hot. The girls, even the nerdiest ones who were "above" ordinary teen stuff, didn't pretend they weren't looking at him. And the guys liked Jack too because as Dad said, "Jack's a regular guy."

After we'd been in school together about a month he started to ask me what movies I liked, if I ever read P. G. Wodehouse, how I liked school, what I was writing in my journal. I'd never read Wodehouse so Jack brought over some books. And Jack also brought over videotapes of old movies like *Being There*, *All That Jazz*, and *Full Metal Jacket*, his favorites.

And then Jack started wearing a Marines T-shirt. People

freaked out. The teachers told Jack they didn't think it was "appropriate." Some parents complained.

The T-shirt became a topic at a school meeting called to discuss this "free speech issue." We met in the school theater where the weekly meeting was always held. Three girls read an open letter about needing a new dress code that respected the sensitivities of other students. They said the T-shirt made them feel "uncomfortable."

Someone called it a "diversity issue" because of the "don't ask, don't tell" gays-in-the-military policy. Jack answered that if kids could wear "Nuclear Free Zone" T-shirts he could wear a Marines T-shirt. And, he said, that since Congress passed the law about gays in the military people who had a problem should petition Congress not blame the military. Then he looked around at everyone and asked them if they were saying that because the military isn't perfect did that mean we no longer need a national defense.

Then one teacher said that the military was homophobic. Jack answered that maybe it was but that; "On July 26, 1948, President Truman ordered the military to desegregate signing Executive Order 9981, which states," Jack pulled a note out of his pocket and read, " 'It is hereby declared to be the policy of the President that there shall be equality of treatment and opportunity for all persons in the armed services without regard to race, color, religion, or national origin.'" Jack put the note away and smiled at the assembly then said, "The military *followed* that order even though there were *plenty* of racists in the military just like there were in the rest of the society. So do you think it's fair to blame the military for gutless civilian leadership related to the gay rights issue today? In a democracy civilians set policy."

Then Jack asked the teacher if the law was changed and gays could serve like anybody else would that teacher personally start encouraging Chandler students to volunteer, maybe sponsor a junior ROTC on campus. Lots of students, especially the guys, laughed and you could see the faculty was getting really annoyed.

The meeting kind of petered out with the headmaster making some lame remarks about Jack being "well prepared" and having the "right to be wrong," but that nevertheless Jack should think about "balancing his free speech perquisites with sensitivity toward our diverse community."

It seemed a little over the top for a T-shirt.

The T-shirt said:

"USMC—When It Absolutely Positively Has To Be Destroyed Overnight!"

Jack wore it every day after that. A lot of the guys thought it was cool.

Chandler was started in 1967 by a rich couple for their kids. They say that the first classroom was an old yellow school bus that was gutted then filled with desks. It was parked back of Rose Chandler's house in Salem. She kept goats and wrote a book about Rimbaud. The Chandlers were hippies but they were rich. They let the kids at school smoke weed back then. Now you get kicked out. Chandler is still progressive and alternative but they have ordinary rules these days. And the Chandlers are gone. Regular people run it now.

The campus is very swanky. The new Rutherford Theater cost millions. (Jack's grandparents paid for it while Jack's sister Amanda was there.) The new science building just won some kind of architecture prize.

The public high school where I went before transferring, was all about cinder blocks and metal lockers and bells every forty-five minutes and kids dragging their reluctant behinds from class to class and graffiti in the toilet stalls. At Chandler there were no bells. If a discussion ran long we just kept talking. Sometimes classes took two hours, depending on how interested everyone was. And everyone seemed to actually like studying. I loved Chandler.

And if the parents of two lucky students didn't have the $32,000 tuition there was the Rose Chandler Opportunity Scholarship. That's how I got in, along with an African-American, a nice guy who had to commute an hour and a half each way from Roxbury. He was one of the only three non-white students in the school. The other two were some diplomat's kids from India.

I wrote a thirty-one page essay: *Mistress Anne Bradstreet— First Poet of the American Colonies*, for my scholarship application. The essay began: "Seventeenth-century Puritan life was the most self-conscious ever lived. Nothing was so trivial that it couldn't 'speak' a divine message, no disappointment so terrible that it couldn't be a 'correction' from God . . ."

They liked it. I got accepted.

Public school had been driving me crazy. It was Mom's idea that I try for the scholarship. To put it mildly, we're not the usual Chandler types. Dad works at the sewage treatment plant and Mom's at Anna Jacques Hospital as an executive assistant in administration, in other words a secretary. Chandler parents are rich and we're "barely middle class" as Mom says.

Some Chandler parents drive rusty old Volvos that seem to be held together by faded "Arms Are For Hugging" and "Imagine

Peace" bumper stickers. That doesn't fool anyone. Like Dad said, "You have to be wicked rich to be able to afford to look that bad."

Jack lived in Salisbury, Massachusetts. I live in Newburyport. That's ironic because Newburyport is "yuppie-scummed," as Mom says, but Salisbury isn't. Mom says it's one of the "only real towns left around here." Most of Salisbury is pretty ordinary. The people who live there have regular jobs. On the edges of town there are some big historic houses. Jack lived in one of those.

We lived in a saltbox-style two-bedroom Mom says we couldn't buy these days. Her great, great, great grandfather built it. Mom's dad was a carpenter. Mom went to community college in Haverhill and studied business administration. Dad never went to college.

Jack's great, great, great grandfather, on his mother's side (more greats than that, I don't know how many), more or less founded Boston and actually *knew* Anne Bradstreet.

I love her poems, especially the ones about loss. None of Bradstreet's children died in childhood which was lucky back in the 1600s. From Anne's point of view "luck" is the wrong word though. She believed in God's will controlling every last thing, not only controlling everything but even making it happen, what they called predestination. That's why the death of her grandchild came as a terrible shock. She seemed to be wondering why God quit blessing her family after he'd taken such good care of her kids. What was God trying to teach her by killing her grandchild? I think Anne discovered that if you think God's in charge of every little thing it's hard not to hate him.

With troubled heart and trembling hand to write,
The heavens have changed to sorrow my delight.
How oft with disappointment I have met,
When I on fading things my hopes have set.
Experience might 'fore this had made me wise,
To value things according to their price.
Was ever stable joy yet found below?
Or perfect bliss without mixture of woe?
I knew she was but as a withering flower,
That's here today perhaps gone in an hour;
Like as a bubble, or the brittle glass,
Or like a shadow turning as it was . . .

I think she's saying that life should have made her wise enough to know bad things would happen to her. And now she's learned that "stable joy" can't be found "below" on earth. She still trusts God to make things right in heaven but for now figures God is sort of mean, or at least can't be counted on because "perfect bliss" is always mixed with "woe."

Jack's parents bought their brick federal-style four-story when Jack was about six. It sits on a twenty-two acre waterfront estate three miles from Salisbury's non-descript town center and four miles from Salisbury Beach.

Jack's house has twelve bedrooms, fourteen fireplaces and a huge barn behind it that they converted into Mr. Ogden's studio. I only peeked through the door but it's really incredible. The studio was filled with hundreds of paintings, and three huge easels holding canvases at least twelve feet high. I didn't get a good look at the art but it seemed really good and also really unsettling.

Jack's house is only a twenty-five minute walk from mine. We're separated by the Merrimack River where it opens up into Joppa Flats. After we started to go out Jack always walked across the Route 1 Bridge and down to my house.

Jack asked my parents if he could drive me to school. My Dad agreed, since Jack had to pass our house every morning anyway and it saved contributing for car pool.

Every time Jack pulled up I felt a fluttery zap in my stomach. And he always arrived on time. Mornings suddenly became sweet.

One day Jack said: "How about instead of coming over at seven-thirty we meet at six forty-five?"

"How come?" I asked.

"So we can have breakfast together."

I've never been a morning person and could hardly wake up for school let alone breakfast. But the next day I got up so early I saw Dad going to work.

It was after our third breakfast that Jack kissed me. I kissed back. We had just eaten pancakes so our first kiss tasted maple syrupy.

After that, sometimes he'd throw pebbles at my bedroom window till I woke up. He'd drag the picnic table across our back lawn and, by standing on it, was able to reach the sill of my window and climb in. He usually did this at about two in the morning. He'd be gone by about four and always put the picnic table back. We never woke my parents.

8

How exactly was Dad connected to our country? What had he done for anyone? Fuck his pull-up bar! Let the grapevines take it! That's what I was thinking. He was right about me needing to work on my upper body though. I wanted to kick ass on Parris Island. On the way to Jessica's at night I'd stop at the Kelly School and use the swing sets to do pull-ups.

Dad thought the USMC was invented to spite him.

Mom thought anyone who joined who had "better options" must have had psychological problems.

Amanda wasn't home. She had the sense to get the hell out. I was about to follow her.

Jessica was the only person who kept her opinion to herself.

I counted down the days, kept repeating that I'd be on the bus in six short weeks, three weeks, two . . .

I knew the only person I was going to miss was Jessica.

Dad was a hypocrite. All my life he told me he wanted me to be free to "follow my passion." All my life he told me he was glad *he* took the "*unconventional* road," how "*self-expression* is the central fact that gives life meaning." All my life he told me that he had to get away from his parents—"the ethos of the small man"—to save his soul. Then I chose to join the Marines and he went ballistic. He stood there seething with anger at me for making the "wrong" choice and painting pictures of clapboard churches with naked people hovering over them—demonic Chagall meets Duccio on acid!

A few years ago the Met bought two of Dad's works for their permanent collection. We drank champagne.

So *that* was the highpoint of a selfish life? Where were those two paintings? Stored out of sight! Where were Dad's other paintings? In private collections owned by the sort of people he called: "Hollywood assholes," "Japanese fascists," and "Pompous idiots like your Mom's parents."

He was a hypocrite! Dad argued for tradition but then always subverted his subjects, as if painting realistically had to be justified. It was as if he was groveling. "Please Mr. Critic, look how *weird* and *ironic* my paintings are! *See*! I'm modern too even if I *do* paint figuratively when no one else—besides that overrated shithead Hockney—does! Please, oh pretty *please*! Let me in the club!"

He said we're deluding ourselves if we think we can "simply walk away from ten thousand years of figurative expression" and that "traditions evolve for a reason."

Traditions?! A great thing till it came to the traditions of the USMC!

Dad should've had the courage of his convictions. If he wanted to defend realism, why didn't he do it the way Wayne Thiebaud does: without blinking? How can you be "contemporary" anyway? Contemporary is always thirty seconds ago. There's a past and there's a future. There's no present. It can't even be measured.

9

J ack will be in boot camp by the end of the summer, if he really goes through with it. Two scenes stand out. I should have taken each as a warning.

Scene One: Todd was not amused when Jack put the Marines bumper sticker the recruiter gave him on the Mercedes. Todd scraped it off so furiously that he scratched the paint down to the bare metal. While he scraped he yelled: "Why the fuck won't this come off?! He must have worked hard; I mean really sat down and thought about what he can do that will hurt us most! Can't you see that the only reason he's joining is to get at me?"

"I don't think it's always about you," I said.

"It's the way he can aim the lowest! 'See, Dad, I'm aiming low! See, Dad, I'm returning to everything you spent a lifetime trying to grow beyond!'"

"He's not saying that."

"I can't take it from you too! Why are you taking his side?"

Todd tossed the screwdriver away and stormed back to the studio.

Scene Two: The obsession grew. Even so I was shocked when Todd tried to open Jack's files on the computer in Jack's bedroom.

Jack was at the girlfriend's place. I thought Todd was in the studio. He was in Jack's bedroom snooping! After fiddling about for a few minutes Todd charged into my office and ordered me to open the computer files so we could read Jack's essays and whatever else he had written, to "find out who's been influencing him."

I refused. Todd literally dragged me by the arm up to Jack's room.

"Why don't you enroll in Merrimack Community College? They teach computer literacy," I said, as he pulled me along.

"Don't fuck with me! Show me his files, Sarah!"

"Does the word 'privacy' ring a bell?"

"God damn it, Sarah! Do what I say!"

He dragged me into Jack's room. Jack's sports trophies looked forlorn. And his posters of Siena, Miles Davis, and all the rest made me just want to somehow roll the clock back, say to when he was twelve or thirteen.

"Spying on your son is not—"

"Who put him in Chandler?" Todd snapped.

"And what is *that* supposed to mean?"

"It means he's been infected by all your bullshit!"

"Oh shut up, Todd."

"Try explaining this to anyone!"

Todd kept fooling with the keyboard. Of course he hadn't a clue. And I was so angry I walked out. I was furious at him for grabbing my arm. He didn't actually hurt me but there was a lot of rage in that grip.

"Sarah! You get back in here and open his files!" Todd yelled.

That's when I snapped.

"Fine!" I screamed, running back and picking up the monitor. "I'll *open* them!"

I heaved the monitor into the hall where it crashed against the wall, knocked down a painting, then smashed on the stairs. It yanked all the wires out of the computer which crashed off Jack's desk.

Todd backed down fast enough after that! He didn't say much but retreated to the studio.

I've had it!

Jack's done so few things that represent a definite choice. Every other thing Jack did we asked him to do. He played town soccer from the time he was six because Todd wanted him to. He went to St. Martin's though his best friends were in the public school because Todd told him to. He joined the track team when they asked him. Jack has always been quiet about his own interests. And he has always gone along. He only put his foot down about not wanting to do track and now this terrible choice. Ironic: Amanda was the "difficult one" and Jack the "easy one." Now this!

What is it about males and their need to prove themselves physically? I was proud of Jack when he quit the track team and transferred to Chandler. I was proud that he rejected all the non-sense about competition, about "winning." I wonder if Jack brought the Marines up as a joke then decided to join because of Todd's overreaction.

Todd has made such a huge mistake in being so confronta-tional. What has happened to us? Why should I put up with this? There were other possibilities once. In 1975 HLS received seven thousand applications for our class of five hundred and fifty. It was the era of Vietnam and Watergate. Most of us just seemed intent on getting a top job at a top law firm. All my classmates were from places like Yale, Michigan, Columbia, Chicago and Stanford.

We were hot stuff! Except for me, everyone who graduated from the class of '78 has been wildly successful, at least judged by the 25th Anniversary Report.

Women at HLS were still enough of a rarity that some professors hardly spoke to us and almost never called on us. Nevertheless the best advice was to be prepared; if your study was incomplete it was better not to show up; it was a long time before you forgot the humiliation of being exposed as unready in front of your classmates.

Todd seemed to open a larger world. He was my "rebellion." I dropped out, began living with him, moved to New York, trotted along to his openings, watched people look from me to his canvases and back as the light of recognition dawned: Yes, I *am* the spread eagled naked girl, that's me over there too, and there, and there; Todd's model, Todd's lover. Aren't you glad he's a neo-realist and that every pubic hair of mine is as lovingly rendered as the follicles of some prophet's beard in an exquisitely executed Dürer?

How have I come to this gloomy place where my life's work is babysitting a fifty-three-year-old child? I got into HLS for God's sake when women didn't do that! It's as if Jack's Marine escapade has just woken Todd up from a dream, and he's woken up angrier than ever.

Everything has revolved around Todd's "struggle," his refusal to be distracted from his "path." Todd's frame of mind has been defended as if it is a country with borders. Distractions have been eliminated, detractors ignored. In an interview he once said we are a "two-man army," yes one general and one private.

We moved out of our obscenely lovely and affordable rent-controlled New York apartment on Riverside at 110th Street so he could have the "spiritual space" he needed. He had *plenty* of space in his studio and we spent *my* money on the house!

We stopped talking to his parents forever, and to mine for almost ten years, so Todd could transcend the bitterness of trying to live down too common a childhood in the first instance and being intimidated by my mother and all "the Rutherfords" in the second. He indulged Amanda and Jack for the same reason we ended each day with a bottle of wine, as a reward, a distraction, a way to relax, a means to refresh him for the next day's assault on the work.

I have followed him. But I will not follow Todd as he alienates Jack! Todd hectored Jack about Jessica, the Marines, smoking, Jack's nighttime rambles, just everything, in the same way Todd says his father used to hector him. Todd has become a scold! *He* is the fundamentalist preacher now!

I'm the fool who thought that studying law was "square," that being Todd's model was "cool." I was the fool who got on her back, the late-blooming flower girl who gave up the "bourgeois pigs" of the Myopia Hunt Club for Woodstock. Only my "Woodstock" was the Venice Biennale, retrospectives at the Whitney, hanging around Todd's studio.

Even at the office I'm just "Todd Ogden's wife." I used to be pleased that my new identity at least eclipsed the Rutherford nonsense. Then I realized that it had eclipsed me.

Mao had it right: Death to geniuses!

I even have to remind him to lift his weights in winter so he stays strong for his summer passion—that sailboat! And he is strong! When I first saw his tall frame he was wearing a thick home-spun beige sweater. His sand-blond hair was long then, tied back in a ponytail that fell to his lower back. His leather jeans were like some sort of greasy second skin. He wore cowboy boots! He was tan from sailing, tan *and* sweating. The cable-knit sweater was far too warm. No doubt he thought it made him look Hemingwayesque. It did. His dark brown eyes seemed black and mysterious; his waist was narrow, his hips slender, his shoulders wide, and his powerful forearms tan below rolled up sleeves. He talked about sailing because I told him I was crewing for the Kennedy cousins that year. He told me that if he sold a major work he planned to get a bigger boat. Bla-bla-bla!

We did it while the guests were milling around the show munching wedges of Brie. He had handed me a glass of champagne, "the good stuff," he called it, kept in a back office, not "the plonk being served to these assholes." After sex in that cramped little office we went back into the gallery and talked about Todd, a conversation that's been our main topic for thirty years.

My parents hated Todd. I was dropping out of a law school graced by a building named for my great-grandfather. I was "throwing everything away" on a "this man from Maine," the son of some wacky minister, a "terribly obscure" painter, "some hippie" who had gone to the University of Maine for a year or two, then to art school.

I dropped out to coddle Todd, to keep Todd's parents away from him, to change the rotation of the solar system for Todd, to say red is blue and green is gray for Todd. But I will *not* destroy my relationship with Jack for Todd! I will *not* climb into Todd's tower and pull up the ladder!

I tried to remind Todd that this is not the end of the world.

"My grandfather served. And so did about half the men in our family, before the Second World War. Before the war we Rutherfords used to even vote Republican for Christ's sake!"

I accompanied Jack to one "poolee parent's night." Of course Todd wouldn't come. The place was littered with soggy paper plates and casseroles and a cast straight out of southern New Hampshire, women jammed into sweat pants, faces pasty under the neon, white, lower middle-America; splendid and inarticulate rubeness. Then there was the kitsch speech—"America's 911 . . . first to fight . . . two hundred and twenty years of proud service . . . your Marine Corps . . ." bla, bla, bla—by some handsome Marine in dress blues. Jack had the grace to not catch my eye as this man rambled on. The room was awash in flags.

On the way home I said, "Darling, you know I'll support your decision but how do you abide these people?"

10

ow can you do this?" I asked Jack.

I'd gotten up to paint. As I made coffee Jack crept in. I heard the latch of the back door close with a gentle betraying click. I was waiting.

As he walked in he brought a gust of the cool dawn dampness with him, an earthy four A.M. scent of the marsh at low tide. I was already regretting snapping at him as he walked in, yet feeling incapable of getting on top of the situation.

"I just went for a walk Dad," Jack said, yawning.

"You've been smoking, I can smell it. You said you wouldn't smoke. If you go to the Marines a smoker you'll smoke for life, a short life with a cancer finish! Why do you smoke?"

"Smoking relaxes me so I can sleep."

"Use the pull-up bar. You need more exercise. You need to be strong for boot camp!"

"I could kick your ass any day."

Jesus, I thought. *Has it come to this?*

"Okay, forget the bar. Take two Benadryl and two Tylenol. Then you'll sleep."

"I'd pop the piss test."

"The Marines don't care if you take an antihistamine."

"I'm not supposed to take anything."

Jack was standing in the kitchen door watching me. I was clutching my mug of coffee. Usually he would've used my silence as cover to just slide on past and up to bed. Now he seemed to be waiting for me to make the next move. The expression on his face was blank, passive, and impossible to read. I wanted to get him to react, to argue, to fight with me, to get this game over and move on.

"She could come over here you know."

"Jessica would rather I go there."

"It could be anyone, just any girl, and you pick the one girl that doesn't like me."

"I never said she doesn't like you, Dad."

Was he gloating? He sure as hell had me by the balls. Was he sad? His face was so closed it was driving me nuts. Where was my Jack?

Jack: sitting in the back of our rowboat fishing, skin pale, almost transparent, covering the lanky frame shooting up from within. He was so beautiful sitting in that rowboat, alone on the river in front of our house.

Jack: releasing the stripers we caught. He wouldn't use barbed hooks.

Jack: hair ruffled in the tropical wind.

Jack: diving into clear water as the huge cumulous clouds rose in towering white banks over Bermuda.

Jack: watching fish, lost in the turquoise vastness while he swims over the ocean floor.

"Do you think in the Marines they'll let you wander around like this, all hours?" I asked.

"I'm not in the Marines—yet."

"Your bad habits will follow you. You'll mess up being a Marine up like you're messing up this summer!"

"Thanks, Dad. I'm glad you have such confidence in me."

"You wrecked your graduation and now you're wrecking your last days at home!"

"I didn't 'wreck' graduation."

"Yes you did. You went out with Jessica instead of staying home for our family party. It may well be the last chance you had to see Great Grandmother Rutherford."

"You hate her."

"And do you know how embarrassed I was?"

"What?"

"People were shocked. One parent wanted to call a meeting to ask how the school had failed you."

"A bunch of true Americans, huh?"

"Why you?"

"Why not me? Goodnight, Dad."

Jack turned his back and walked out.

"You talk to me!" I shouted.

I ran up the stairs and jumped in front of Jack to block his path.

"You hear me out! Don't you *dare* walk out on *me*!"

Jack sighed and sat down on the top stair. He was looking bored, looking that way on purpose. He had to be feeling *something*. If I could find an excuse to grab his hands I'd know. His hands were always clammy and cold before track meets. It was the way I knew he was nervous, even though he always was able to look so calm.

How had the tables turned? I was the one cowering. Couldn't we somehow just say what was really in our hearts? But I was spouting shit, shit I didn't even feel. What I wanted to scream was, "*Help me Jack*!" What I said was:

"For a start will you or will you not promise me you'll stop smoking?"

"We see death around us but deny it and speak of resurrection," Jack said with a grin.

I couldn't read the smile. What kind of smile was it? Was he trying to make peace? Was he sticking it to me? Was he quoting someone?

"Enough of your bullshit!" I said. "You know what this proves?"

"What?" Jack yawned.

"It proves you're weak! You just can't quit, can you?"

"Quit what? I smoked two cigarettes walking over the bridge. Goodnight Dad."

Jack walked away. I started to follow him. I planned to grab and hug my boy. I didn't. I stood rooted to the lower stairs feeling like I was drowning.

Once I was sure he was asleep I came back in from the studio and peered through Jack's door. I had been sitting alone for almost an hour stewing with the lights off. He lay with a long finely-boned foot sticking out from under the cover. Jack's high cheekbones looked as if they were carved from ivory in the early light. I tiptoed forward and knelt, touched his hand, the one lying outside the cover. It was warm. Was he in good enough shape for boot camp?

Sarah said it was a bad idea me trying to get Jack into shape; let his preparation be his own affair she said. I knew she was right, that Jack had to sink or swim on his own but I wanted to help him develop more upper-body strength, a secret weapon to face the test of mind and body that lay ahead. It was my way of telling him that I'd just been full of my usual shit when I threatened to never speak to him again. Then Jessica wrecked the whole summer by more or less kidnapping him. He was *always* over there! They never once "hung out" at our place. Now there were grapes ripening on the pull-up bar and the big leaves had turned from translucent pale green to a darker shade and were dusty.

As I knelt next to Jack he opened his eyes. He looked wide awake. It hit me that he'd been faking sleep.

"I'm trying to sleep," he said.

"You never use the pull-up bar."

"Sure I do."

"The grape leaves would be disturbed. I check them. The tendrils are firmly wrapped around the bar."

"You 'check' the grape leaves to see if I'm getting ready for the Marines?" Jack asked and stared at me in disbelief.

"Yes."

"Do you know that you've become the world's biggest asshole?"

"I want to send you down there prepared!"

"Now you're 'sending me'?!" Jack stared at me angrily. "This is why I quit track!"

I felt as if the ground was swallowing me.

"I forbid you!"

"I thought you were 'sending' me?"

"Fuck you!"

"How about I go live with Jessica till I go to Parris Island?"

"You're only here a few hours every couple of days as it is! Now you want to move out to her place for your last weeks at home?!"

"Yes."

"No you won't!" I yelled.

Jack sat up and leaned back against a shelf stuffed with Calvin and Hobbes books and Far Side calendars along with his dusty sports trophies. He glared at me then spoke slowly.

"Are you saying I *can't* move in with Jessica?"

"Say I *am* saying that?"

"I'll move out anyway." Jack said quietly.

"Get *out*!" I screamed.

"Fine! I'll pack right now!" yelled Jack.

He swung his legs over the side of the bed so fast his legs clipped me. I sprawled onto his floor.

"*Just what is going on?!*" Sarah shouted, from our bedroom.

"Ask Dad!" shouted Jack.

Moments later Sarah was standing in Jack's doorway.

"What have you done?" asked Sarah.

I said nothing. Jack started violently yanking open drawers so hard they fell out of the chest and hit the floor with a smash. He was grabbing handfuls of T-shirts and underwear.

Sarah stormed upstairs. I followed for a few steps then turned and charged back into Jack's room. He was shoving everything into his old back pack, the one he'd used on our sailing trip.

Sarah yelled after me: "Don't you dare start in at him again!"

"I'm asking Jack not to go!" I called back.

I hoped Jack heard that my voice was breaking. I didn't give a shit if he saw me cry.

"I'm leaving," shouted Jack.

"Don't you *dare* go teenage melodramatic on me!" I screamed.

11

Dad let Jack move in because Dad had served in the Navy and remembered the Marines who were on his ship. Dad said that they were good guys and lots of them didn't come home from Vietnam. If Jack was getting kicked out because he wanted to be a Marine, Dad said that it was okay for him to move in for the few weeks he had left before boot camp. And the fact that Jack and his dad were arguing about me helped, too. If Mr. Ogden didn't like me, then he could go to hell as far as Dad was concerned.

All Dad said to Jack was, "You be careful or I'll cut off your balls. I don't want a grandchild yet!" He laughed, reached up and tousled Jack's hair. Dad hardly ever touched anybody. He liked Jack a lot.

• • •

When Jack left for boot camp it broke my heart. I knew it was coming and the fact that he wanted to become a Marine was one of the reasons I loved him. I admired his determination, the fact he could look at everything being given to him and decide to make a sacrifice and do something completely unselfish. But till the end part of me hoped he wouldn't go.

Sometimes he said he wanted to do something "different." Other times he said he was tired of "all the crap." I think he meant the hanging around and waiting for something, anything to happen. And Jack said: "The Marines tell everyone: 'You're important because we can use you.' I like the Corps for coming right out and saying it."

I didn't want him getting sick of me so I only cried in front of him once and did my other crying alone, not counting the day he left. I couldn't hide my tears when his recruiter finally came to our house after dinner and picked Jack up to take him to the recruiting station in Andover and from there to Logan airport with the other poolees.

Jack held me. He looked nervous and sad and his hands were clammy. He was pale. And I sobbed. I think that was the only moment he really had doubts about going.

He said he'd write. The recruiter told him they allow recruits to bring family pictures and a Bible. Jack didn't have a Bible but he had put together a pocket-sized album of pictures of me and his family.

A week before he left Jack asked me to go into his house and pick up some photographs. We drove over in my mom's car when Jack was sure his parents were out. Jack stayed in the car as I went in through the screen porch back door.

Jack asked me to look for one specific shot. He said he figured it might be in album number fourteen. It was. In the picture Jack and Mr. Ogden were standing by a pink wall and they were both holding snorkels and masks and had their arms around each other. Their hair was wet and they were smiling and happy. I have a copy because I asked Jack to make me one.

Three days before he left Jack said: "Married people see each other naked, even when they're not having sex, just walking to the shower, whatever, and I want to just see you like that."

"But we're not married," I said laughing.

"I want it to be as if there hasn't ever been a time when we weren't together. I want it to be as if we were kids together and nobody was ever here except us."

"You mean like Tom Hanks in 'Castaway?'"

"Yeah, but we get fed, maybe by the gods or something."

"Why would the gods bother to do that?" I asked.

"Because nobody loves each other like I love you and you love me."

And Jack stripped off and started to run around my house naked. And even though Dad was at the plant, and wasn't going to be home for hours and Mom was at work, I still got nervous.

"Put on your clothes!" I yelled.

"Not till you take off yours, and we walk around naked like we've been married for thirty years," he said.

So I did. And it felt *so* weird!

I had been naked in his arms, but stripping was strange. It wasn't like getting undressed up close, like when we made love. Then he was already touching me, not across the room just staring.

I didn't feel sexy, just like a somewhat pudgy girl getting undressed. And Jack knew exactly what I was thinking, because he said: "You have the most beautiful body in the world."

"No I don't."

"Yes, you do. Do you know why?"

"Why?"

"Because it's where you live."

Then I felt better. He was always answering my thoughts.

"You're the only reason I'm sad about going to Parris Island. You are the biggest reason I want to go too, because I think it will make me a better person."

And then we both laughed, because Jack said all that serious stuff and there we were standing across the living room from each other naked and shivering the whole time.

When he said that about married people seeing each other naked I never even thought for one second I didn't want to marry him. It was as if it was planned years ago, and was just waiting to happen.

So was that a proposal? Did I say "yes" by stripping?

We got dressed, and it really did change the way I looked at Jack for those last few days. And Jack's beautiful naked body is fixed in my brain.

I didn't understand how busy they get at boot camp or about how they can't make any phone calls and how slow the mail is. So for the first few weeks I was depressed. I didn't get any letters. And since Jack had left without speaking to his dad I couldn't call the Ogdens to see if they had heard from him. They hadn't spoken to me since Jack's seventeenth birthday party. I knew his dad resented me. Anyway I was checking our mailbox every afternoon.

Jack had been gone two weeks before I got a letter. It was in a small smudged envelope and had been written fast and messy in pencil on stationary with fuzzy black and white photographs the size of stamps of Marines doing training printed up one side. I figured that this must be some sort of standard issue stationary they gave the recruits. And I could tell right away Jack was freaked out. I certainly was. It was as if I opened a door and looked into some strange country.

> Dear Jessica,
>
> This recruit had two DIs in his face screaming till there was spit on this recruit's face because this recruit didn't sound off loud enough on the day we were formed—they weren't interested in hearing this recruit's excuse that was he had a sore throat. "You are the weakest nastiest piece of shit they ever sent here!" "Yes, sir!" "Say something YOU!" "YES, SIR!" This recruit knows what they do and why but it's hard to take. And this recruit hadn't slept in 72 hours and those "haircuts" sting. This recruit can't do anything right, even get dressed fast enough for them. Did you know there is a right way to put socks on? This recruit hates the DIs but our SDI—Master Sgt. Isaac Jackson—is awesome. DI = Drill Instructor, SDI = Senior Drill Instructor. This recruit loves you. Send paper, envelopes and stamps. This recruit lost most of his the first time the DI dumped our footlockers and piled all our trash in the middle of the squad bay.
>
> Love,
> Rec. Ogden

Part II

12

Charleston Airport 0200: not supposed to be keeping journal—hide pages between pictures in little family album they let you bring—waiting for bus—writing on scraps—

Half recruits haven't slept or were drinking last night—ragged—ass! OK—but nervous—

Speech by Marine in waiting area: "You are now an official United States Marine Corps recruit—as such you are punishable under the Uniform Code of Military Justice—UCMJ—set of rules and regulations that all military personnel must abide by—you will be punished—do you understand recruits?"

"Yes, sir!"

"From now on when you speak to a Marine, civilian or sailor the last word out of your mouth will be *sir*—like this: yes sir, no sir, yes ma'am, no ma'am. Do you understand, recruits?"

"Yes, sir!"

"You will be at the position of attention—position of attention is—your heels are together, feet at a 45° angle, legs are straight—not stiff at the knees, fingers curled, thumb along trousers seams, head and eyes straight to the front, and your mouth is shut!"

On bus from the airport to PI—told to keep our heads down—black night—water on both sides of causeway dark as oil—hot damp air—low tide muddy smell, just like Merrimack—arrive darkest night. Only my heart beat—then there's screaming —if you love you will suffer loss—

In-processing—stood on the yellow footprints in the dark packed ass-to-crotch with new arrivals—form up by standing on them—famous yellow footprints stenciled on pavement—step gingerly onto footprints in front of the in-processing building—dark, low, three-story red brick—taking next breath—gritty hardtop—empty road fading away under overhead steam pipes—deprived of all personal space—fearful boys, DIs strutting around—

—Made regulation call home—no answer—left message—to admit vulnerability is to bow to mortality—

Head shaving, not gentle—about 20 seconds after standing in a long line for 20 minutes. Cuts—nicks, sliced off the pimple on my neck.

Sitting at desk in back of classroom head down—writing this on knee when DI is out of the room. He's back—

Filled in paperwork—wrote serial numbers for the cash I brought—$120 in 20s and fill in the questionnaire. DI back—

Another classroom—

Uniform issue—DI walking down top of long table with bins on each side, while we pick up clothes—stripped—

Lost track of time—been here 10 hours, 40, 60?—nothing held back—

Female DI screamed to a recruit arriving on our bus—"Did I give you permission to cry?"

Classroom again—DI out—I can write while it's fresh—speech from the DI when I was on yellow footprints—I can hear it shouted again and again to the next busloads—"The Marine Corps' success depends on teamwork—you will live, eat, sleep, and train as a team. The word 'I' will no longer be a part of your vocabulary. Do you understand?"

"Sir, yes sir!"

"Tens of thousands of Marines began outstanding service to our country on the very footprints where you are standing. Are you ready to carry forward their tradition?"

"Sir, yes sir!"

"Follow me!"

More paperwork, to do with the "disposition" of our bodies if we're killed—after death we can't defend our ideas—we entrust our memory to others and hope they'll defend us—

TD-6—(Training Day 6)—wake up at 0500—chow—clean squad bay—fill canteens—make head call—writing this in the head after lights—write when I can—under blanket in rack—on desk during class when sitting far from DIs—wherever—

Shirts soaked in sweat just from standing there—supposed to drink 12 canteens per day—

Living Chow-to-Chow—

Do drill and hit the rack at 2100—

Writing under covers by light of "moonbeam" (flashlight)—When did we get formed? Was it two days ago? A week? A life-time?—"Met" our DIs like a tree "meeting" a chain saw! Most intense day! DIs marched into squad bay—brief ceremony—DI oath—"These recruits are entrusted to my care—will train them to the best of my ability—develop them into smartly disciplined, physically fit, basically trained Marines . . . "

After oath, the Series Commander left—Senior Drill Instructor Jackson, like a walking black bulldozer—scary, insanely strong, fire hydrant neck—spoke to us for the first time voice one part electric drill, one part threatening whisper—"Training here is tough—Will accept nothing but the best—There is only one way off the Island, the causeway—Do not try to swim off—sharks—tides—we'll send the dogs after you—" then he told his DIs (those junior to him are called "Greenbelts" SDI is a "Blackbelt") to "take charge"—

Then three junior DIs under the SDI's command tore into us like wolverines. Take-charge ritual: we are slaves of DIs—

TD-8
"BACK UP! TAKE YOUR SWEET TIME!"
Seeing who will crack. DIs shout, point, spin—
"Louder."
"*YES SIR!!!*"
"IF I HEAR YOUR VOICE DROP BELOW THAT VOLUME FOR THE REST OF THE TIME YOU ARE ON MY ISLAND I WILL SMOKE YOU UNTIL YOUR HEART POPS."
"AYE, SIR!!!"

TD-9: In head—night now, on the can—Our squad bay (barracks)—long cinderblock room smelling of disinfectant and 80+ hot scared bodies, socks, aftershave, gun oil, whatever the DIs ate last and spit in your face—brown-green concrete floor—white cinder block walls—row of twenty-five metal racks (bunks) on each side of squad bay—One end the "DI House" (DI's office and quarters)—small, spare room. Across from DI House are the showers + heads. Footlockers the size of small trunks at foot of each "rack." Running down both sides of squad bay is a ruler-straight painted black line on which we recruits always get "on line" (stand at attention in row, toes on the line) when ordered. So that's how we're lined up in front of our racks facing each other across the "DI Highway," down the middle of the squad bay. The

DI Highway a big open space about 15 ft. across. We stand in two rows on either side facing each other while DIs stride between us— When on line you pray they won't notice you.

In front of DI house is the "quarterdeck"—about 15-by-15 patch of concrete floor, named for the place on ship where ceremonies are held. Recruits are punished there. Painted on the floor in front of the DI's door are footprints to stand on when banging on a hand print painted on the door post three times—when recruit needs to speak to DI—

On walls and concrete columns that support ceiling: Marine mottoes stenciled like: "CORE VALUES: HONOR COURAGE COMMITMENT." Signs posted throughout squad bay—in showers—in head. Muzzle velocity of M-16A2—procedure for treating sucking chest wound—rules of war—

Over sinks:

"VULNERABLE PARTS OF THE BODY: Temple, eyes, ears, nose, throat, neck, torso, arms, groin, legs."

Over a toilet:

"WEAPONS OF OPPORTUNITY: Rocks are outstanding weapons of opportunity. The E-tool is a very effective weapon."

TD-10: Sun is hot—stench from the row of 10 portapotties—2 to 4 recruits ordered to cram into each for a piss break. We even piss as a team!

After we screw up drill with rifles we drill with canteens, while the rifles are in the stack.

"FUBAR!" DI screams. "You are FUBAR!"

"Yes, sir!"

"Do you know what that is Nelson?"

"Sir, no, sir!"

"Fucked Up Beyond All Recognition! *That is YOU!*"

"Yes sir!"

Each recruit sticks out an arm to the shoulder of the recruit next to him and so on down the line until there's correct spacing all the way—

Then full canteens must be held out at arm's length. The recruit's arms are held out until we are in excruciating pain. Hands tremble; arms begin to sag as the minutes tick away.

"Get that arm up!"

"Aye, sir!"

"The only time you open your mouths is when you are in pain!"

"Aye sir!"

"This arm is made of steel!"

"Aye sir!"

This recruit is crying—SDI Jackson steps up to study his platoon, as if he is contemplating a math problem. He intervenes from time to time to help his DIs, sheep dogs dipping in and out of the flock to keep us in order.

"Ogden, keep that friggin arm UP!"

"Aye, sir!"

TD-11: SDI Jackson—quietly to us at SDI time when we're all sitting there Indian style cross-legged around him at night just before lights. That's when he plays father—

"When I graduated from recruit training it was the proudest

moment of my life. If I tell my wife that, she won't like it that my best day wasn't our wedding but my graduation from boot camp. People stay in the Corps not for the guns we fire or the planes we fly, but it's the person who inspired us. People stay in the Corps because they're inspired by that Marine, they want to be that person. It's the psychological payday. And the day we lose that is the day the Corps is done."

TD-13: SDI Jackson at SDI Time—"I'll tell you what the trouble with America is. This kid, say about seven or eight is trick or treating on Halloween. He's dressed as Robin Hood, carrying this black plastic pot full of candy. And this kid drops some candy out of his pot and I say to him, 'Hey kid you dropped your candy.' And I stop to pick it up for him and drop it back in his pot. And I say, 'It fell out of your pot.' And he looks at me and says, 'It's not a pot. It's a cauldron.' And his mom doesn't say anything at all just looks at me. No thank you from either of them. This is what we're dealing with."

TD-14: Time doesn't exist—only clock is in the squad bay for the Fire Watch. Only know what time of day it is by keeping track of chow—figure second chow is about noon last chow about four or five in the afternoon—rest is a mind-blowing, soul-numbing blur. We take everything we're told on faith. There is no evidence for any belief—We follow examples, not words.

TD-15: In the head again—night—writing. If DI comes into see why I'm on shitter so long I'll flush the writing—Nothing from Dad—all those times he took me to games and track meets, always had the Gatorade and power bars, reminded me to eat carbs—the night before a meet he kept me hydrated and now hearing from everyone but him—And I keep thinking he's the one who will send me the power bars but it won't be him—no letters— not one word.

Everyone here is getting sick—3 recruits are on light duty for pneumonia—I'm coughing up all kinds of crap—"recruit crud"— feet swollen huge blisters—we already have started Marine Corps Martial Arts Program (MCMAP). On my Initial Strength Test I did 121 crunches, 14 pull-ups, and 1.5 miles in 7:31— fastest in the platoon. That was after we had been up for over 48 hours, and it must've been 90° and 100% humidity—could have done better—

All I can think about is telling Dad how well I did in the IST— thought he'd be standing there on the PT field waiting when we came back from the run and congratulate me the way he always did at the track meets—first time I broke down and cried— thinking of Dad not speaking to me—forgot we had the fight—just reverted to the old mental track: I'm running in a race so Dad will be at the finish line. He always was.

Forgot I was a recruit, forgot where I was—

No one noticed my tears with the sweat already pouring—We pretend life has meaning even when we don't believe it and this need to pretend gives hope—

Three recruits were dropped to the PCP—Pork Chop Platoon— because they can't even do *one* pull-up! Turds!

Food is routine—Salisbury steak—beef ravioli, chicken—it's always the same—

When the DIs put us in the pit or on the quarterdeck it doesn't faze me—I won't quit!

Sanchez—Cuban from Miami is my rack mate—across from me Del Rio from Trinidad—look like good guys—once in awhile we whisper something—Sanchez can hardly speak English—We crave food—when we talk about food it's like guys talking about girls—fantasize—baguettes from Annarosa's Bakery in Newburyport for me, KFC for Martinez—BK double cheese for Sanchez—starved! Rather eat than have sex!

TD-16: Feel like I'm coming down with pneumonia, along with the rest. But I'm not going to tell the DI—don't want to get dropped—Maybe the desire for meaning is the voice of God—Whole platoon went to the pit for over an hour because our drill sucks—

DIs say we're the worst platoon they ever trained—Sucking down sand fleas in the hundred degree heat—the recruit next to me threw up—sand and puke mixing—breathing it in—blazing sun—sweat pouring—face buried in sand as the DI screams one inch from my ear "PUSH!"—his spit on my neck sizzling in the sun—"push—up—push—up!"—platoon sounding off—"Marine Corps! Marine Corps!"—all of us working to extend our elbows—muscles weak—collapsing on sand and puke, damp filthy sand filling every orifice—there are no final answers—we find our meaning in the quest for meaning—

Writing in Knowledge class—sitting at back—DI-Instructor

can't see, anyway everyone can take notes—Get so tired my eyes shutting in class—Drill and more drill, slow-motion torture—stand holding rifles four inches away from our bodies—We can't scratch or swat at the sand fleas—have to pretend they don't exist—one landed on my lip so I swallowed him—I couldn't scratch with the DI watching—forty inches side-by-side, feet taking even steps, thirty inches—"striking the ground with your heels so everyone glides"—shoulders back, head straight—

Bayonet drill Knowledge: Get the blade into the enemy—main principle in bayonet fighting—parrying the enemy's attack—smash with butt of rifle—use proper footwork important—the actions taken to enable you to sink the blade—make one straight thrust to disable or kill—

Will Dad break down and write? What a nasty civilian!

Good shit:
SDI Jackson is giving "special attention" to one recruit who can't do his push-ups—
"Do I know your mama?!"
"NO, SIR!"
"Are we friends?!"
"NO, SIR!"
"Get up now! You have no willpower!"
"Aye, sir!"
"You have no will to succeed!"
The recruit struggles to make one more push up and then he

does—SDI Jackson gets down and pushes with the recruit nose-to-nose. SDI Jackson has been up since 0300—He's leading with incredible intensity. He does 10 times more than any of us recruits.

TD-19: 0600: Yelling at the top of our lungs:

THIS IS MY RIFLE. There are many like it but this one is mine. My rifle is my best friend. It is my life. I must master it as I master my life . . .

Good shit:

Hundreds of cheering recruits surge onto the far end of the 3rd Battalion parade deck. They sprint—torrent of recruits in olive green T-shirts—gray sky—running bodies reflected in huge puddles from last night's rain—splashing. They gather in a huge throng of hundreds around Col. Kelley, the base commander. Our SDI has brought us here to watch. Says—"You can be them someday if you don't give up!"

SDI Jackson: "He'll give them a talk before they go to their squad bays to prepare for the graduation ceremony."

They sit on the wet pavement. Col Kelley—tall, thin middle aged man with close-cropped gray hair—stands in the middle of the circle turning from this side to that as he bellows his remarks. He's in running shorts and a sweat-soaked T-shirt—he's led the motivation run.

"Within days, you young men and women will be in your MOS schools then many will be sent into combat in Afghanistan and Iraq—Some here today will not be coming home—You are US Marines, whether you are in uniform or in civilian gear, they ought to be able to tell that you are Marine by the way you hold your-self. Only those who are unconfident of their abilities think they need to act tough. We hold doors open for others. This is the responsibility you have earned. From now on it won't be some-body else's responsibility, it will be yours to uphold our tradition."

"OORAH!" We yell.

Writing in head at night—just told DI Martinez I have the shits—he asked why I'm in here so much—wanted to know if I'm in here jacking off—was about to flush pages but he didn't walk in just yelled through open door—shoved ink stick into skivie shorts. Don't get to know anyone here. Can't talk much except to rack mate, then only a few words unless you want a DI in your face. Got quarterdecked today for falling asleep in Knowledge class—Dreamed spirits of Marines were all over the Island singing cadence along with us, their wounds fresh/bleeding—God was with them shouting at me to wake up. Thought it really was God, sounded real. It was a "greenbelt" junior DI.

He got down and pushed with me screaming the whole time—awesome strength—I wanted to outlast the bastard—but was puddle of sweat and muscle failure before he got done. Made me see I can do more than I ever thought—Once believed we trained hard for track—that was nothing—more intensity on the quarter-deck in ten minutes of being smoked than any training session—Wondering what Jessica would think of me with the DI just about sucking on my ear screaming spit till it ran down my face—abuse—one long howling yell in a gravel voice that sounded like broken glass scraped over sandpaper—Oorah!

Cough is worse, so is everyone's. Letter from Jessica—she sent a picture, so far away, not just miles but a life she never imagined— Every waking thought: how do I obey the next order and do it the way they want me to, fast—How do I sound off loud enough even though my voice is shot? They say it will come back later in training stronger—bet no former Marine ever sang opera!—voices so changed, ruined. There are absolute truths once we begin to live within the framework—overall meaning, if there is one, is unknowable—We act as if there are facts when we know there are none, know that we can't know—

Good shit:

SDI time, SDI Jackson: "My MOS was 0311—infantry. The Second Marine Division was quite the command. If you could march, shoot, and were strong you could do well. So I had something tangible to aim for. But I busted out my knee. I ended up getting knee surgery.

"The reconstruction of my knee failed so they sent me to Bethesda for a ten-day eval. And those ten days became four years and six operations. Somewhere in there I became a sergeant and I stayed in shape by doing pull-ups and sit-ups. Every time I got close to being fully rehabilitated they put me on limited duty. My knees were just out and out weak.

"After four years of no progress I got an evaluation for discharge from the medical board. I wasn't happy about that. See I had struggled to get there, worked like you never worked in your life.

"I got my company gunnery sergeant to say some good things about me. The med board said if I could run a good PFT the next day they'd change my evaluation. I ran a two-ninety. I ran three miles in eighteen minutes and my knees were dead. Then I went back to the board with my score so they sent me to the command and told to get me a new MOS besides ground-pounding. So I got sent to the XO and I recognized him. He was a colonel that I had been working out with in the gym. 'Are you a medical hold Marine?' he asked. 'Yes sir.' 'Well what do you want to do?' 'Whatever the USMC will let me do to stay a Marine.' 'How do you feel about corrections?' 'What's that?' 'Prison guard.'

"It's supposed to be an eight-month tour at CCU. I spent two years there. It's not really a prison. It's basically a boot camp for Marines who commit crimes but that the Corps believes can still be good Marines, if they can straighten out. And I was an instructor.

"I had to do everything they did, just like a DI. Well I pushed them a little too hard. I got in some trouble and got eleven non-punitive letters of caution. A few complained because I got too close to the 'awardees,' which is what they called our prisoners. I'd shove them around if they gave me attitude. And one time, while my awardees were doing training with logs, one got dropped on somebody's foot. So of course that was my fault too."

Mail Call—Letters!—None from Dad—Fuck him!

Chow—got to eat an almost full tray before the Guide was done—meal over "Get Out!" Losing more weight I don't have to give, getting weaker, not stronger—they don't care about your body here, just your soul, Marines are a religion. We are warrior monks!

First Aid Knowledge Class: Restore breathing—stop bleeding—treat for shock—protect the wound—

Good shit:

A recruit took something with his hand out of a serving dish, rather than using the tongs—

DI # 1: "Do you know how nasty that is?"

Another DI grabs the recruit's fork—

DI # 2: "You eat with your hands now!"

DI # 1: "Every day it's you!"

The recruit stands, holding his tray, not certain if he may sit or not. His fork is gone maybe he won't be able to eat at all.

DI # 2: "Boot laces not tucked in!"

"Aye, sir!"

DI # 1: "It's always you!"

"Aye, sir!"

The recruit begins to eat tentatively with his hands—

DI # 1: "Are you are a filthy disgusting nasty person?"

"No, sir!"

DI # 2: "That's how you perform, as friggin *individual*!"

"No, sir!"

DI # 1: "You *are nasty*!"

"No, sir!"

The recruit is eating fast and looking down at what food is left—

DI # 2 zeros in and throws recruit's food—"Somebody give you permission to look at your food?"

"No, sir!"

Another recruit has his pockets emptied by two DIs.

SDI Jackson: "Yesterday he brought bread with him back to the squad bay and got caught."

DIs throw everything from the bread thief's pockets on the ground. They make the recruits sitting on either side of him empty their pockets too.

"You stealing food again?"

"No sir!"

To recruits sitting next to the accused: "Did he give you something to carry for him?"

"No sir!"

"Get out!" yells SDI Jackson.

Chow is over. Most recruits not finished eating—

"Get out now!"

Starving!

Marching back to the house—

"Is that heal to toe?"

Back in the squad bay—Drilling with rifles.

"One and two!"

Four recruits are being sent to get the clean pillowcases and sheets—The rest drill with our rifles on deck. Meanwhile the light-duty (injured) recruits sit and study Knowledge.

"Right shoulder! Out! Present! Rifle!"

"Aye, sir!"

"Across the chest!"

"Aye, sir!"

"What are we doing? *Across the chest*!"

"Aye, sir!"

"Your arm is parallel *across the friggin chest*!"

A recruit reaches out to another to raise his elbow before the DI can see the recruit has screwed up—putting his arm in the wrong position. The DI notices the recruit is helping the other and screams at the recruit who needed the help—

"Yeah, you lost Marty, you LOST! Get your thumb where it's supposed to be!"

"Aye sir!"

"*Rifle across the chest*!"

"Hey, Maas, you steal some more chow?" screams one of the Greenbelts to the bread thief.

"No sir!"

"We can't trust you!"

"No sir!"

"I want to see veins coming out of your neck!"

"AYE, SIR!"

"You didn't shave did you!"

"Sir, this recruit did shave, sir!"

"You calling me a liar YOU?"

"No, sir!"

"But you are a thief!"

"No, sir!"

"Take your trash off!"

The recruit who took the bread is sent to the quarterdeck.

Four other recruits are waiting to be punished on the quarterdeck, sent up by the DI who is doing rifle drill—

"You don't want to drill? Come up here and play on the quarterdeck!"

They start to push—"Stand—run—push—mountain climbers—faster!—faster!"

Recruits being punished are at the end of a day that began at 0400 they've run, PT'd, marched, drilled all day, now they're on the quarterdeck red faced, sweating, gasping for breath—

"Are we going back to drill? Listen to the goddamn DI!"

"Aye, sir!"

"Push—up—down—hold it—run—mountain climbers—push!"

"Aye, sir!"

The recruit who stole the food has been on the quarterdeck the whole time. He's nearing collapse. The DI on his case is screaming each push-up into this recruit, willing him to continue. The recruit collapses. The DI shouts into his ear for a solid three minutes. One last wobbly push-up. The floor is covered in sweat, piss, tears. The recruit is sobbing out his "Aye, sir!" voice reduced to a shrieking whistle.

"I've got news for you, YOU: there are no individuals in the Marine Corps! Somebody said stop?"

"No sir!"

"You stick your butt in the air and give up?"

"No sir!"

"Your idea of reality isn't real!"

"Yes, sir!"

"Faster! Faster! Faster!"

"Aye, sir!"

"That's how we do push-ups, right?"

"Aye, sir!"

"Shake your head Godfrey! Now open your mouth!"

"Sir!"

"We gonna drill or die?"

"Drill, sir!"

The DI sends the sweating recruits back to drill along with the recruit who stole the food. He is so exhausted he can barely pick up his rifle. We help him.

TD-21 Good shit:

SDI Time—Recruits sitting at the far end of the squad bay—cross-legged circle on the floor—around SDI Jackson.

"I got this letter from one of the recruits I trained two cycles ago," says SDI Jackson. "He just got his Purple Heart. Good to go?"

"Aye, sir!"

"I'm gonna read you some of his letter. It'll give you a head's up better than I can say it."

"Aye, sir!"

"Cause this Marine knows how to write all this trash down. Good to go?"

"Aye, sir!"

"He's enlisted just like you and me but he writes like some kind of friggin officer."

"Aye, sir!"

"So here's what this Marine wrote to me. I'll put it on the board for you to study. Good to go?"

"Aye, sir!"

SDI Jackson reads it out:

"'I'm in the hospital in Germany. An IED hit us three weeks ago pretty bad. Then we had a hell of a firefight. I was lying here thinking about some things; mainly how you kicked my ass, a piece of which got shot off, no kidding, Ha, Ha! When the shit came down I wasn't thinking, just reacting and when it was done I was alive and I took one in the chest. When I woke up they told me I did okay and so did all my Marines. And I started to think about who taught me to function in a world of shit. Then I started to think about what it means to be a Marine. You asked me a simple question: 'Do you have what it takes son?' When it started raining shit I didn't shit the bed. I guess I just answered that question. Thank you sir for teaching me what I needed to know.'"

SDI Jackson folds the letter. He shifts a big wad of chew slowly from one cheek to the other and spits into a Dr Pepper can.

"Good to go?" SDI Jackson asks quietly.

The squad bay rings out with the most deafening "*Aye, sir!*" ever.

"The day's almost done, another day almost done gentlemen, one day at a time—that's the way it goes. Letters!"

SDI Jackson pulls out a thick stack of letters and calls names. As he calls each name he tosses the letter, not to the recruit who answered but in the opposite direction so that each letter must be passed from recruit to recruit until it gets to the recruit it's for. Even the mail takes team work. Several recruits get no mail. I get a letter from Jessica and one from Mom but none from Dad.

Dad, you motherfucker!

SDI Jackson goes into chainsaw overdrive—

"GET ON LINE!"

Recruits leap to their feet clutching unread mail—A few seconds and we're all on line—SDI Jackson stalks to the DI house and kicks open the door and then kicks it shut. A moment later the door is smashed open again and the junior DIs surge out snarling and screaming.

I will be a Marine.

13

Dearest Jack,

I received your second longer letter. What a culture shock this must be for you. "TD-1" this "TD-2" that! And "SDI" and "DIs" and "head"? You must be learning a lot of new and perhaps bewildering military terminology. I sympathize! A legal education was just like learning a second language. What we were going through seemed very like some sort of language assault course, our own "boot camp." There is a disconcertingly odd written style for argument in cases that is deliberately contrived to make the legal writer seem almost inhuman. It took some getting used to.

Todd is calming down. I am sure he'll write to you soon and make one of his florid apologies. In any case you must know that he is proud of you. You have shown remarkable pluck. Stay well and write soon.

Much love,
Mother

Little Brother:

I haven't told anybody here about what you're doing. I don't know much about anyone in the office and they don't really know much about me but I have this feeling that you being in the Marines might not go over too well. Did I tell you that Matt and I broke up? Never mind two pricks in a row—literally and figuratively!

Write to me!

I love you,

Amanda

Dear Jack,

I'm so empty. My big worry is—will you change? That's my only fear. I love you the way you are. But if you come back thinking differently, say you think you made a mistake hooking up with me and are different now, don't love me anymore, say so. I don't want you to feel stuck with somebody from another life.

Love,

Jessica

Dear Jessica,

It's Sunday so this recruit gets a few minutes to write. Boot Camp is not going to do anything to change this recruit's love for you! This recruit will be able to make our rack fast and tight, and do more push-ups than you, and if you want to fight him with a bayonet this recruit will probably win, but other than that all he wants to do is hold you.

TD-36 is over! They can't ever make us do that again—unless this recruit gets injured and recycled to MRP (Medical Recovery Platoon) and has to start training over—NO! Lost 9 pounds so far—try eating rice off a plastic knife when the DIs are pissed and punishing us by taking away the forks! So HUNGRY!

Church today—stained glass of a flamethrower, Marines guarding heaven, as described in the Marine Hymn—"If the Army and the Navy ever look on Heaven's Scenes; they will find the streets are guarded by United States Marines!"

Later: There is time now—briefly—to write more than before. Nothing prepared this recruit for the "welcome" from our four DIs. As Bertie Wooster would say they're "like wolves who just spotted their Russian peasant!" In your face screaming—"You are the sorriest piece of shit!" "You look like 10 pounds of shit in a 5 pound bag!" And they yell—and we yell (sound off) back, "Sir, yes, sir!" Just like *Full Metal Jacket*. The DIs are animals, but SDI Jackson is scariest of all.

Love,
Jack

Dear Jack,

I'm so glad you still love me. And whatever else is changing, that is staying the same.

If ever two were one, then surely we.
If ever a man were loved by a wife, then thee . . .

Bradstreet's poems are *hot* when she writes about her husband. The Puritans got a bum rap about sex. I think that the Victorians get confused with the Puritans. "My love is such that rivers cannot quench . . ." doesn't sound too uptight to me. Speaking of quenching, I wish you were here!

Love,

Jessica

Dear Jessica,

We're run ragged every day by the DIs and they not only do everything we do, but do it longer, harder, better. It's about how far above and beyond you can go—not just "do your job," not just "meet the minimum." And they teach by example. SDI Jackson takes leadership to a whole new level.

Being scared shitless doesn't mean that you can't do something. "Who's afraid of heights?" one rec. puts his hand up; and they put him on the platform and PUSHED his ass off first! Okay that was this recruit!

Fear is the only reason we can't do something. Keeping this recruit's inner eye on two prizes—respect from SDI Jackson and a good "quenching" from you! This recruit keeps getting back to his feet.

Love,

Jack

Dear Nutboy!

Daddy is going to be in some retrospective of American neo-realists at the Tate—London. The GREAT MAN continues to triumph; so don't take his "You've ruined my life" shit too seriously!

I never realized how many Marines there are. Jesus, every time I turn around I seem to be reading a Marine-related story. Even here at the *Times* whenever there is a story about somebody who was in the Marines we ID her or him as such in the first paragraph very much as we ID an Oscar nominee, you know, "Former Marine Senator so and so . . ." And by the way every time I see a letter from a Marine I send it up the line with a star for Jason, not that he does what I say, but at least your big sister is taking care of your "band of brothers" as best she can!

Thanks for the *very short* letters! How about more than 3 lines next time? And stop calling yourself "this recruit." I bet Jessica is getting more mail from you! By the way I bought a book called *Making the Corps* by

Thomas E. Ricks. He gives a good account of daily life at boot camp though I hear he works for the *Washington Post*. I had no idea what you all go through. I'm proud of you.

You should write to us. I'll try to get Jason to publish it. Most of what we publish comes in as emails. But if you stick in a letter to the editor in the next letter you write me I'll slip it to Jason.

Thanks for telling me that you picked a "non-dangerous" job. "Supply Administration" sounds comforting. It's bad enough you going in with the Bush fiasco underway, let alone looking for trouble. So I'm RELIEVED you'll be safe. Keep it that way Nutboy. No heroics.

I love you,
Amanda

Dear Jack,

It got cold and the little children are all bundled up when they play across the street. Their arms stick straight out because they have so many sweaters on under their snowsuits. They look like hot dogs plumping up on a grill.

I'm enjoying my year off before college, but mostly I'm thinking I should have just gone to U-Mass, instead of taking the year to work and save money for Colby.

There's a big hole in my heart but you know that.

I put a Marines sticker on the car. Dad said it's okay with him even though he went Navy! I got it at the Andover recruiting station from your recruiter Patrick. I asked him if it's okay to put it on the car. He said it was fine because even though you're "still only a recruit" he said you are one of the best recruits he ever sent to PI and he's sure you'll make it. So am I.

I love you,

Jessica

Dear Jessica,

We have a DI who saw combat in Iraq and just got home. Sacrifice is the difference. We sacrifice for love and we love because of sacrifice. This recruit will probably get sent to war—but with this recruit's MOS—supply admin—nothing much will happen. But life will not be long enough however long this recruit lives to be with you. Forever is too short a time to love you. We are here a blink of an eye—even less if measured by geological time. In that little moment we call a life we look up and around and we feel and see. We see the world and the universe and it doesn't see us. So which is really bigger? Which lives longer—the blind universe or we humans alive for only a heartbeat but in that moment aware of infinity?

So Jessica—in this heartbeat this recruit loves you!

Jack

Dear Jack,

"This girlfriend" understands what you said about us being bigger than everything because we see it and think about it but the earth and the stars don't. In school everything we studied in science seemed designed to make us feel small, like we're just specks of dust on a golf ball in outer space. But I think loving you is bigger than the universe is.

I was walking on the Newburyport boardwalk last night. The boats have all been taken out of the river now so it looks so empty. I walked halfway across the RT 1 Bridge and I stopped and watched the moonrise. It was bright white. I stood watching the moon till it got high enough to cast a path of silver on the water. I was thinking about what you said about us seeing everything. It's as if our feelings wrap up all experience into kind of a story that writes itself.

My love for you marched down the path of silver moonlit water and found you looking at the same moon at that very instant. And when the trucks made the bridge tremble under my feet, in my story the earth was shaking because of how powerful my love for you was walking down that moonlight path, as if each stride made the earth tremble.

Love,
Jessica

Dear Jessica,

In the Bhagavad Gita, Krishna stops his chariot on the battlefield where the armies of the Pandavas and Kauravas are preparing to fight each other. Arjuna looks at the two armies. His eyes fill with tears. He's confused about his duty and refuses to fight. The rest of the text gives Krishna's teaching about duty, discipline, God, self. Krishna teaches Arjuna to be strong and take a stand, how to see with the clear eyes of a yogi. To see the world clearly, Arjuna has to discard sentimentality that clouds his vision. In that condition pity is not a weakness but an achievement to be earned. He learns that love and combat are sometimes both right.

This may seem a little weird but we learn about love here. In the world, at least our nasty civilian world, you get laughed at if you talk about loving somebody enough to die for them. You know that's how this recruit feels about you. But what this recruit didn't know is that the reason Marines die for each other is for love too. The point is that survival is the most basic human right. We have the right to defend ourselves. Who will do the defending? It can't be some ass hanging around the mall, let alone some soft little Harvard wimp who thinks that all life (and school) is about is striving to position himself for that high-paying job he "deserves."

When the shit hits Marines have to be ready. And being ready isn't some kind of idea. SDI Jackson explained it at SDI time tonight. Our tradition is not giving up or giving in. It's all important from the way we pivot to the way we qual at 500 yards on the rifle range. Our tradition says even if it's peacetime and you're a Marine waiting around, and even if you never go to war you'll still hand down what you know to the Marine who follows you onto the yellow footprints. And you'll hand it over in good enough shape so if he's called on he'll be ready and has a chance to survive combat.

SDI Jackson says we're always prepared because a Marine we never met 10 years ago or 50 years ago did his job. SDI Jackson said the perfect Marine is a Marine stranded on a desert island that still raises and lowers the colors. And even if he's there alone for 10 years on the day he's rescued he has his dress blues pressed out—this presumes he was stranded with an iron!—and his M-16 is clean and he'll be hydrated and pissing clear.

"So if you want to feel good about yourself you'll have to stop talking and do it," SDI Jackson said. "And the way to do it right isn't to wish but learn. Because you know jack-shit but the Corps knows everything."

Then he told us some more stuff about himself.

"I remember I walked into the commanding officer's office and he said; 'Jackson, I've been looking at your record. You need to go to be a DI.' 'You're kidding. I'm not going down there. Those guys are crazy,' I answered.

"Of all the things I've done in the USMC DI School was the hardest." He said. "They put you through everything a recruit will go through and more. Every day I got up wondering how I could ever get through it. My knees were both shot and I'm older than the other guys and I'm wondering if I'll drop out. Will I make it?"

SDI Jackson is awesome!

When Hsuan-tsang traveled through the villages of seventh century India he discovered that to see the evidence of the Buddha and hear his teaching didn't mean that he needed to read books. What it took was the guts to travel in the steps of Buddha. We started with 87 or 88 recruits and now we're down to 81. All the turds are gone and everyone left deserves the title so we want every recruit—even ones we don't like—to graduate. They've earned it. We have traveled the path.

My (I'm a little less crazed now so can drop the "this recruit" stuff—at least to you) rack mate has a stress fracture—he got stress fractures in high school too so he knows what it is—and he doesn't want to get dropped this far along in training. We put the heavy shit from his pack in our packs and on long humps we put two recruits next to him to hold him up when the DI is upfront and can't see. We will all graduate together if there is any way it can happen.

Gotta go—

Later—I'm finishing this letter the next day.

I look at the lights on the water when I'm on fire

watch (part of a four man team that's making sure all the rifles are secured and that no one has run away or tried to kill themselves—which does happen down here). I get it about the moonlight path between us, only we've had a lot of overcast skies at night so I never did see that full moon but the light on the water reminds me of our river. I like that idea about the moonlight path.

I read that if a beam of light is shot into space it can go more or less forever until it's blocked. If light can do that so can a feeling so strong it melts two people together. The light travels on. If you could catch up to it you would see it all over again. That's how our love is, it's something you could fly to and pass and feel washing over and through you. It doesn't fade, because it doesn't depend on matter and energy. It doesn't need time or space. It doesn't need a place to exist. And if someone smashes and buries the laser that fired the beam of light it doesn't change the light. That light still keeps on going forever. It can't be taken back or undone.

When you fell asleep in my arms I kept awake so I could look at your face. When I'm an old man I'll remember the way your eyelids fluttered while you slept and how I always wondered if you were dreaming about me. If I get one wish it will be to meet you in that dream someplace.

I love you,

Jack

Dear Amanda,

Graduation in 2 weeks! I'm glad you're coming down with Mom. I figured something out. I can be happy with a simple life.

When some person or a whole class of people divorce themselves from the cycle of love and sacrifice we resent them and history speaks of them as selfish trash! Dietrich Bonhoeffer rejected natural life as an end in itself and life as a means to an end. He taught that war involves subterfuges that peace might prevail. He stood up to Hitler and died. Are we sorry he took a stand?

This recruit has a rack—M-16—pack—canteen—chow three times today—a place to PT—Knowledge to learn—a DI to smoke him—and this recruit is content. What was all that other bullshit I used to think I needed? The warrior tradition I've joined has been going for thousands of years all over the world. But like fourteenth-century Buddhist teaching the affective response to *mujo* is: "If man were to never fade away like the dews of Adashino, never to vanish like the smoke over Toribe-yama, but lingered on forever in this world, how things would lose their power to move us!" There's something worse than anything: the power to no longer be moved.

If it wasn't for Jessica there's no reason to get out of here except to put what we know into practice. Simple is good. Weird to say so but I'll miss PI in a sort of backward perverse way!

Mom keeps making excuses for Dad in her letters. But I know he won't be here for grad. He never wrote once. I wrote to them both. Mom answered, Dad never did.

Love,

Jack

Dear Jack,

I don't know if I'd compare what you're doing to fighting Hitler, let alone Bonhoeffer's martyrdom! Hey, smarty-pants, I studied him too at Chandler in that Gandhi, Bonhoeffer, and MLK "Responses to Aggression" humanities class, but we'll argue later. Maybe you're just making a case for opposing aggression, then you have a point re passivity being no answer as in "Let someone else do it." However, this current war—at least Iraq, though I tend to think Afghanistan was somewhat more justified—is another matter!

I've been doing a lot of reading about the Marines and doing a lot of thinking about our family, my job, and your "job." I'm wondering why I've been too embarrassed to tell anyone at work that you're in the Marine Corps. I'm ashamed of myself.

Okay enough serious crap!

In my office we have "the board" where we put up letters we can't publish but amuse us. Current examples:

"If we have separation of church and State, why is the capital of Minnesota 'St. Pauls'?"

"Has anyone noticed that a car with 'gull wing' doors is impossible to get into or out of in a crowded supermarket parking lot?"

"Apparently I sent the attached letter to the editor last night after way too much to drink. Sorry. It is incoherent. You don't have to publish it. It won't happen again."

Manhattan is too expensive for most of us. I'm the only person in Letters living in Manhattan. Everyone else is in Brooklyn or Queens, mostly Astoria. Mom has been helping with the rent.

I met Veronica Blackwood (staff Editor-Op-Ed/Regionals) today. We met by chance in the cafeteria. She used to be at the WSJ. She was saying she did ROTC in college and was in the Reserves for 10 years. She also told me that there is one reporter here, Chris Chivers who is a former Marine. But we were talking about how almost nobody here under 55 (post draft) served in the military and how people are so surprised when they find out Veronica was in the reserves. So I blurted out that my brother is at boot camp!

It felt good to finally come clean. And you know what? She couldn't have been nicer. Anyway, Veronica and I were talking about how no one here has anybody in the military. We were sitting under these cold fluorescent lights in the cafeteria, really ugly, sort of big aluminum chandeliers with these terrible lights on them that make everybody look dead, I mean even worse than usual—why is everybody here, other than our few token blacks, so short, old, or terminally WASPY?

I'm getting a little tired of how ideological the paper is. I've decided that if someone can be identified as either of the left or right, it's an indictment of her intelligence. Ideological consistency, let alone "purity," is a sign of small-mindedness, maybe even stupidity. I think political ideology is right up there with religion as a bogus form of self-protective madness. The need for certainties—political or religious—is a real problem. And that is what I'm getting most tired of about most of the letters to the paper. Our readers almost *never* deviate from their ideological scripts. I mean why should you know where everybody stands on *every issue* just by reading one line of a letter? For that matter the paper is SO predictable. Just for once I'd like to read an editorial that surprises me.

I'm working up the courage to put a Marines sticker up on "the board"!

Love you little brother,

Amanda

Dear Jessica,

I'll probably see you at grad before you get this. In the world where you are "free" you actually do less. In the world we have all these choices but what do we choose? We choose to watch the same dumb shit every one else is watching. And we choose to play the same stupid computer games. We think the words "I want" are sacred. But we experience more here where all our freedoms (and "I wants") are taken away than I experienced in any year of "choosing." We learn more in one day than we ever did at Chandler in a month.

The point is I'm not just rejecting Mom and Dad and our background. I'm joining another kind of elite, only this elite bridges class and is about more than greed. We're equal here because we suffer together. Buddhist thought always valorizes the goal of achieving a state of mental and emotional self-control in the face of trials, say boot camp. This is the goal of Gotama the Buddha sitting in meditation under the bodhi tree, unmoved as Mara repeatedly tempts him and more important—unmoved by all the frightening things thrown at him!

A heart-mind
dyed in blossoms
still remains
in the body I thought
had shed the world.

All our "trash" is packed and the squad bay stripped of everything but our sea bags, hanging bags and the uniforms we'll be wearing at grad. Now for the first time, just as I'm about to leave, I understand that this squad bay and Parris Island is the only place besides your arms that I'm comfortable. I feel frightened and sad to be leaving.

Love,
Jack

Subj: Jack's "graduation"
Date: 11/21/2003 7:53:51 AM Eastern Standard Time
From: SarahRutherford@aol.com
To: AmandaOgden@NYTimes.com
Amanda: My flight arrives in Savannah at 11:20 a.m. I will pick up the rental car. Meet me by the Avis desk when you get in at 12:03.

According to Map Quest the drive is about 50 minutes from the airport to Parris Island. (I printed out a map and the directions all by myself on the computer!) Jack said if all else fails he'll meet us in front of the Iwo Jima Memorial (I thought that was in Washington D.C.?!) at 1:30 p.m.

Todd is still refusing to come with me. He's very stubborn and quite ridiculous. All he'll say is "He made his bed now he'll have to lie on it." I said to him: "The only person who is being hurt is you. Jack has done what he set out to do and you're cutting off your nose to spite your face."

I gather that Jack's girlfriend made her own arrangements. We haven't seen her since Jack left. I do hope Jack spends some time with us and doesn't just disappear with that girl! We'll see Jack for five or six hours on Family Day and then again after graduation the next day. I think if Jessica is tagging along the whole time it's going to be rather awkward. What on earth can we talk about?

Jack called on Sunday. It's the first time I've heard his voice in three months! No indication of how he really is. He sounded older and very hoarse. I gather he gets a few days off after boot camp but he says that he is going to spend it at Jessica's place. This is getting so silly!

See you soon,
Mother

14

hen we were on the long causeway that leads onto Parris Island I was struck that, for a place which loomed so large in my imagination, ever since my brother went there, the geography was so simple. Gray choppy water, marsh, patches of close-cropped lawn, cypress trees bearded with Spanish moss. A picnic area flashed by as our car, windows down, filled with the tangy scent of sap. The whole place was nothing more than a sandy bump just a few feet above the high tide.

After passing several one-story brick buildings and driving under clusters of white pipes we were directed into a large parking lot just beyond the hard-topped parade area and the Iwo Jima memorial, rather some kind of replica of it.

Suddenly there was Jack in uniform striding toward us through a crowd of families with a scattering of Marines milling around. Mom and I both started to cry when we saw him. His close-cropped haircut left pale skin exposed above a tan-line where his "cover" (what they call a hat) had protected his scalp for three months of sun-baked marching. His short haircut made his angular face appear practically hawk-like. His expression was hard to read.

He was so thin! He wasn't smiling, just looking at us as if we were insects. I threw myself into Jack's arms. It was like embracing a post, hard, unbending. Jack put one arm around me stiffly and stood rigid. Mom tried to hug him too then sort of bounced off and stood back and looked up at him, her eyes welling tears.

"Congratulations. You're a Marine!" I said.

"Yes," said Jack in a husky voice.

"I'm so proud of you!" I said.

"Thanks."

"Dad didn't come," said Jack without looking at us.

"He sends his love," said Mom.

"Nice try," said Jack. "Did you read the paperwork I sent?"

"Yes," Mother answered.

"So you know I have six hours of liberty, but can't leave the Island. Tomorrow make sure you're back early for grad because the stands fill up fast. Eight platoons graduating. After grad I can leave the depot."

"But my dear I wanted to take you to lunch," said Mother.

"We can eat at the commissary food court. I'm *so* damned hungry!" said Jack. It was the first real animation in his voice.

"I'm sure we can do better than that."

"Mother, that's why I asked if you read the paperwork. We can't leave the depot today."

"Oh, but surely they won't mind us just slipping out for a decent lunch? Anyway who's to know?"

"You don't get it do you?" Jack snapped.

"Whatever you say dear," said Mother with a nervous laugh.

As we were walking back to the car Jack said nothing. He

looked over our heads at other Marines and nodded, called out a name or two, saluted officers, received greetings from other uniformed young men and women and barked out an authoritative, "Stay motivated recruit!" to two scared-looking boys we passed. One was on crutches. The other walked slowly, somewhat doubled over. They both wore camouflage.

"MRP recruits," muttered Jack

"What darling?" asked Mother.

"Medical recovery platoon, got injured. Fate worse than death. They'll have to pick up with a strange platoon later. And if they don't get better they'll be dropped."

In our letters to and from boot camp we seemed to have been developing a cheerful, even, close relationship. But somehow this was not translating into anything natural or comfortable in the flesh. Maybe it was just Mom he was reacting to, or Dad not being there. The closest I got to understanding why Jack seemed so put out was when he said, "It seems really weird to see you here. You just don't belong."

Jack kept trying to walk in step with us as he glanced at our feet. Finally he asked Mom and me to walk in step. We all laughed but I could see that he was sincerely disturbed by us walking any old way we wanted.

"When is your girlfriend coming?" I asked.

"Jessica will be here tomorrow. I'll be leaving with her right after grad."

"Perhaps she'd like to have dinner with us," said Mother.

"That's okay, we're going out."

"Do you have a rental car?" I asked.

"You can't rent cars till you're twenty-five. Del Rio's lending me his."

"Who is he?" asked Mother.

"He's in the rack next to mine, lives in Beaufort just a few minutes from here. He's got his mom driving his car to grad so he can lend it to me."

As Jack tried to play tour guide he got lost several times. After about the fifth wrong turn he explained that he had never seen PI from the inside of a car. There were whole parts of the Island he'd never visited. And Jack had never been allowed to look away from whatever path he was on. Other than the roads he marched on, Jack really didn't know the Island. After a while we just parked and walked.

Jack showed us what he said were the actual set of yellow footprints he'd stood on the night he arrived on the Island, the ones at the front by the curb.

By the end of the afternoon Jack finally started to talk in sentences of more than a few words. Mom talked a lot, but never mentioned Dad. And she asked few questions about boot camp life, as if least said soonest mended. She was rambling on and got progressively more nervous. I watched other families with their new Marines. We didn't seem to be the only people feeling dazed.

When I happened to walk on painted piece of concrete floor right in front of the drill instructor's office door in the squad bay Jack urgently whispered, "Amanda! You *can't* step there!" Then he looked bewildered for a moment, laughed, and said, "Oh, I guess *you're* allowed. I guess they can't smoke sisters. Boy, if I ever did that I'd be pitted for hours!"

At the end of the visit we left Jack where we had met him, standing next to the Iwo Jima Memorial. He wasn't alone. As we walked away several Marines came over to Jack and they all began to talk and laugh. Jack seemed relieved when we left.

We drove to our hotel in silence. Mother remained uncharacteristically quiet until she had a few drinks. Then all she would talk about was how angry she was with Dad for not backing down and coming to see Jack, that and how terrible Jack looked: "A real concentration camp victim!" "So horribly thin!" "What on earth did they do to him?" "He's just acting like some sort of robot!"

I wanted to argue but didn't, at first. I felt as if I was with someone who had just visited the Sistine Chapel and all they could do was talk about what a waste of paint it was. What kept going through my mind was how small and useless I felt on the Island with all those Marines. Then I did sort of flip out and Mom and I got into an argument about how everyone we know is just so disconnected from the idea of serving anyone but themselves.

• • •

The next morning Mom and I drove back to the Island in silence, parked and took our places in the stands. We hardly saw Jack that day.

I met Jessica after graduation when she ran over to Jack after the ceremony. Mom had scanned the crowd but hadn't spotted her. And if Jessica recognized us she hadn't said anything. And of course Jack wasn't around to introduce her to me. We only saw him as his platoon marched across the parade ground. And at first he was hard to spot, till suddenly I realized that he was the only Marine in dress blues and *leading* his platoon while carrying their flag or "guidon" as they call it.

As soon as I saw Jessica throw herself into Jack's arms I figured that this was the girlfriend. She got to Jack before we did. She was *very pretty* and *very quiet* and Jack hurried away with her as soon as the ceremony—marching, yelling orders, music from a Marine band and speeches—was over. Some Marine told us that it was a big honor that he was the "guide" for his platoon.

The big surprise was the overwhelming feeling of pride I had. When I saw him march past with his platoon I was on my feet screaming. I felt as if I'd explode. I can't explain it, but it was a bigger emotional moment than my own graduation from NYU, by far. Mother didn't yell but she did clap furiously. They looked so young and so beautiful.

Part III

15

THE BOOT— A Newspaper Serving the Marines and Sailors of MCRD Parris Island South Carolina— August 26, 2004

Some Marines wait an entire career for the opportunity to prove their mettle in the crucible of combat. But after only one week of deployment in his first tour of duty Pfc. Jack Ogden (Salisbury, MA) proved again that every Marine is indeed a rifleman and that no MOS in the Marine Corps prevents a Marine from having the quality of his courage and training tested. Pfc. Ogden's MOS was 3051, warehouse supply administration. He was killed in action on January 23, 2004, less than 23 weeks after first stepping on to the yellow footprints. He was flown to Kuwait only two weeks after completion of his MOS training at Camp Jackson, then deployed into Iraq three days later. He was killed after one week of serving in Iraq.

Pfc. Ogden was posthumously awarded a Silver Star and Purple Heart on July 4, 2004. Pfc. Ogden's battalion was responsible for supplying all of the forces involved with 1 MEF. Pfc Ogden was tasked with being part of a convoy that was to establish Support Area "Bedrock."

The convoy had been moving smoothly when they began receiving incoming mortar and medium machine gun and rocket propelled grenade and small arms fire from what appeared to be a coordinated ambush. With the convoy en route to resupply Marines with critical war fighting sustainment items such as ammunition, fuel and chow, the attack could have drastically hampered any success of that mission. To help counter that assault Marines immediately left their vehicles and took up positions around the convoy.

According to the citation Pfc. Ogden's calm, measured reactions allowed him to engage the enemy. Though "only" a supply administration specialist, Pfc. Ogden took over a machine gun position after the machine gunner suffered a fatal wound. Pfc. Ogden then manned this machine gun, though not specifically trained on that weapon other than a brief introduction at MCT to machine gun operation. Single-handedly Pfc. Ogden took a M240G machine gun and positioned it on top of one of the convoy's seven ton trucks so that he might have a better vantage point to direct fire at the enemy who were hiding behind a low berm. In so doing he exposed himself to great danger but also provided covering fire for the convoy.

Major James Yardley who was pinned down with the rest of the members of the convoy some 200 yards further up the road said: "Pfc Ogden's action single-handedly pinned down the enemy so that we were able to escape what otherwise might have been a fatal encounter for the whole platoon since we were trapped between buildings on one side and a deep canal on the other side of the road. The covering fire from the top of one of our seven tons enabled us to move the platoon down the road and reposition ourselves in such a way that it allowed us to survive the attack. Pfc Ogden's quick thinking most definitely saved many Marines' lives."

Pfc. Ogden received three wounds during the action; the last of which proved to be fatal. Nevertheless he maintained position as the corpsman made his way to him to give him medical attention. Even after the corpsman arrived on the scene Pfc. Ogden continued firing.

Captain Smith W. Taub Jr. said: "He was not just there to accomplish his mission, he was there to support every Marine near him. That is the kind of person he was. He took care of his Marines. I feel proud to have been his brother Marine."

CITATION

The President of the United States takes pleasure in presenting the Silver Star medal to Private First-Class Jack Ogden, United States Marine Corps

Citation:

For meritorious achievement in connection with combat operations as Private First-Class Combat Service Support Battalion 121st Force Service Support Group 1 Marine Expeditionary Force January 23, 2004, in support of Operation Enduring and Iraqi Freedom. Private First-Class Ogden brought his expertise and training to a combat operations situation. He was instrumental in defending the 1st Force Service Support Group. On January 23, 2004, while Combat Service Support Battalion 12 advanced Pfc. Ogden was tasked with riding in a truck with a tactical convoy consisting of 18 vehicles along Route 7 in order to establish the much-needed support area. As the convoy traveled it came under mortar, medium machine gun and small arms fire from a coordinated ambush. Private First-Class Ogden's calm, measured reactions allowed him to engage the enemy, maintain communications with supporting establishments, and enabled him to play an instrumental role in saving the convoy from danger. In so doing Private First-Class Ogden's total effectiveness, and loyal devotion to duty reflected great credit upon himself as he upheld the highest traditions of the Marine Corps and United States Naval Services and exhibited distinguished conspicuous gallantry at great personal risk giving his life for his country.

For the President, James T. Conway Lieutenant General, US Marine Corps Commanding General, 1st Marine Expeditionary Force.

16

Dear Baby Jack, I'm writing this for you while everything is fresh even though I know you won't read it for a long time. Right now you are just one week old. I could tell you later but then it might be too smoothed over, and I want you to know everything. I want there to be a record in case something ever happened to me.

You comfort me. So does Anne Bradstreet. When you find someone who feels the same it doesn't matter if she felt that way hundreds of years ago.

> Commend me to the man more loved than life,
> Show him the sorrows of his widowed wife;
> My dumpish thoughts, my groans, my brackish tears
> My sobs, my longing hopes, my doubting fears,
> And if he love, how can he there abide?

She's angry too. Her husband went away. Jack chose to leave and got killed. He *chose* this! "And if he love, how can he there abide?" Neither of us has an answer. Anne was talking about her husband who went to Ipswich. But your daddy is dead.

Nobody told me when he died. Nobody knew you were in me. I was just "the girlfriend." They keep a list of who should know, like wives, like parents, but I wasn't on any list.

I found out because Jack's death was reported in the *Newburyport Daily News* and Mom saw it and walked into my room where I was resting. When you're pregnant you get *so* tired and I had just come back from Shaw's bagging groceries, and plunked down. I wasn't showing but was crazy tired and throwing up. Mrs. Ogden never called, Amanda Ogden didn't and of course that prick, your other grandfather didn't.

I was furious with Jack. I still am, so angry and so in love, and so sad. And he isn't here to yell at!

I was going to abort you. If your daddy hadn't died I would have. So you can thank him for your life—twice. I didn't want to kill more of Jack.

I didn't know you. I admit it's a lousy excuse. A mother should know to defend her baby before they meet. We hadn't met, it was nothing personal. So whatever you do to me I'm forgiving you up front, even teen bullshit, even drugs, whatever, if you'll forgive me for wanting you dead. And that is sort of crazy because here is the thing: That night he didn't use a rubber, I knew he wasn't, he knew and it was sort of exciting, like, okay we love each other *that* much. And I knew it was dumb. Someplace in my brain I was thinking: I just finished my period yesterday so chances are it'll be okay. I wanted the romantic moment and the safety net of thinking it couldn't happen at the same time. Dumb!

I was so mad at Jack for leaving me and going to some war where the only reason he was killed was because of all his bullshit: "When Hsuan-tsang traveled through the villages of seventh century India he discovered that to see the Buddha and hear his teaching all it took was the guts to travel in his steps."

That sort of bullshit got him killed!

He had this crazy idea that he loved the USMC, and he made it all sound so wonderful, what's really messed up is that he got me pregnant and then left for his new religion. They say they leave no man behind. Well he left you and me! His only excuse is that he never knew I was pregnant. It's a good excuse.

Someday you'll know you can hate the person you love most. Do you know what it's like having somebody you love go to a war? They might volunteer but you're drafted. I'd thought that Jack in boot camp was the worst. It was nothing. The Drill Instructors were on his side. However hard they busted his ass, they weren't trying to kill him.

Right after boot camp Jack went to MCT (Marine Combat Training). He wrote one letter from there.

> Dear Jessica,
>
> I hate almost every second of MCT. We're at Camp Lejeune, North Carolina. MCT is to teach all Marines except Infantry—who have their own school—basic combat skills—from how to fire a machine gun, to the placement of shaped charge explosives—grenade throwing—so on. Bitter cold snap—ground frozen makes living in the field into winter camping in a

fighting hole—Other services may have "fox holes" but, as our instructor said to us, "Foxes use holes to hide in. Marines use them to fight from. They are 'fighting holes' to us, not 'fox-holes!' WE *don't* hide!"

Several Marines are hospitalized with pneumonia—stress level is high—we're in live-fire and other dangerous exercises while our fingers are too numb to feel the trigger—This two week taste of life as a Marine "ground-pounder" (infantryman) instills the greatest respect for the Infantry—Humping an eighty-pound mortar plate over rough terrain in freezing rain is fucked—so is sleeping half-standing in a muddy fighting hole night after night—

Threw grenades (fun), fired SAWs and 240Gs (Squad Automatic Weapons and 240 Gulf machine guns) and fully automatic grenade launchers (more fun)— FEX (field exercise) and we spent the majority of those days sitting in frozen fighting holes, vigilantly looking out for the "enemy" (other platoons) who never showed up—big waste of time! There are no shortcuts. We love the voice we miss—your voice is the place I live. Being separated a door to ourselves closes, a room crumbles away.

Love, Jack

When I found out I was pregnant Jack was back at Camp Lejeune doing his MOS school. After MCT he stayed down there studying supply administration for four more weeks. Actually he came home for two weeks after MCT but went right back down for his MOS.

It was right after boot camp grad and the night we did it in Savannah that I think I got pregnant. About six or seven weeks later I took a home test after I was late and a day later he was calling me to say he was deploying!

I figured I'd wait till he got home to tell him, or at least till he had been over there a while. Then I thought about aborting you and maybe never telling him or anyone. Anyway, I just couldn't figure out how to say goodbye to Jack and I hadn't seen a doctor yet to know for sure before he left.

By the way, we always practiced safe sex except for that one time. And that's why I think it was the night of Jack's graduation from boot camp it happened. We were in Savannah like I said. We had waited three months! Someday you'll know what this means. Someday you'll know sex is a sort of insanity, that you can know all the facts and in one moment it all goes away and what's left is two people feeling as if they're the only people on the planet and that they're about to burn everything else up so who cares?

Anyway to back up a little, I stayed at a motel on the highway outside Beaufort. I took a shuttle service, then a bus and then got to the stands early and sat way up at the top so I could see everything. About half an hour later lots of other people began arriving and I recognized Mrs. Ogden, your other grandmother, sitting next to Jack's sister. But I chickened out and didn't go over. See, your father had a big fight with his dad about joining the Marines. And while he was away at boot camp the Ogdens never called me, like I didn't exist. It was weird to see her there and I just didn't want to talk.

Weird to think that *at that very moment* the egg that was about to be you was getting ready to meet one of Jack's sperm swimming around. He was probably sure that graduation was the big moment when actually the most important thing he'd do that day, or in his life, would happen about eight hours later when his one lucky sperm, the only one that could make you, met that one lucky egg. And sure you looked so small I would have needed a microscope to see you but then, from the moon you can't see anyone on earth and six galaxies away they don't even know we exist.

Always remember this: Some stuff is not as important as people say it is. Because the things we *aren't* in charge of, like falling in love and getting pregnant make all the things we choose sort of fade away and life takes over, and we see we aren't in charge of much. The only choice we really have is to love or not to love.

For a long time nothing happened while lots of families arrived and packed the stands. Then I heard the platoons singing what they call "cadence." It gave me goose bumps. All those boy's voices were so strong and so beautiful. And when you hear people singing out loud and joyful, like they really mean it, that is really something! They were marching from their squad bays to the parade deck where they lined up, platoon-by-platoon for the ceremony. There were eight or nine platoons with about eighty recruits in each. You should have heard all those feet smacking down together! They call it "Marine thunder!" You should have seen them all moving like one long snake, I mean with not one hair or foot or hand out of place, as if they were all part of one big creature.

Then came the parade and the upbeat bullshit speech like something Disney might have come up with for a new USMC ride.

But the first man marching up front, top of the row of Jack's platoon was a tall Marine, your father, leading the rest.

I cried.

None of the Marines looked our way no matter how much we screamed their names. Eyes front, they stood at attention. They were *our* Marines, and all the people, white, black, yellow or brown were *my* family. I knew that we all felt the same thing, pride that one of ours was becoming something it is so hard to be—a US Marine. I think we all felt the fear too. All of a sudden the war in Iraq terrified me! All of a sudden it dawned on me that every road leading from that parade deck was leading to trouble.

A few minutes later we cheered and almost broke our necks rushing off those packed bleachers. People were hugging their Marines, and searching for their Marines, and finding their Marines and throwing themselves into their arms. And everyone said how much their sons and boyfriends and brothers had changed, how they couldn't even recognize them.

Then I met Jack's sister, and said hi to his mom. It was *very* uncomfortable. Jack had spent the last part of the summer not speaking to his dad, but no one mentioned it. Then we packed up and hauled Jack's sea bag and his canvas hanging-bag to the car Del Rio lent Jack for the night.

Jack's last words on Parris Island were, "Stay motivated!" He yelled that out the car window to some recruits as we pulled out of the parking lot.

The first thing Jack did in the hotel was change into the jeans and shirt I brought him, that and ate the three baguettes he'd asked me to bring from Anna Rosa's Bakery. Bill and Jane heard I was coming down so they wouldn't let me pay for the bread, said to give it to Jack with their congratulations and gratitude for his service.

When he stripped off his socks his feet looked like two huge filthy blisters and stank like cheese. One big toe was a swollen, twisted lump. Jack didn't seem to care about pain.

"A lot of the guys' feet are in the same shape. It's no big deal," he said.

"They let you march on *these*?!" I said.

"I hid the problem. I might have been recycled."

• • •

While Jack was home he went to lunch with his mom but never visited his house or called his dad. And his dad never got in touch with him. Either one could have walked over the bridge and in a few minutes been at the other fool's door.

Jack came back from that lunch really pissed off because he said your other grandmother spent the whole time telling him that now he had graduated it was time he grew up and got out. She told him she had already asked lawyers in her family about it, and they could fix it all up and get him out. So he walked out of Michael's Harborside Restaurant and refused to speak to her when she called later. He said that what made him maddest was that she talked that way while he was wearing his uniform. "She has no respect for the Marine Corps!" Jack yelled. And after that I shut up about wanting him to find some way to make up with his family.

Jack's MOS school only lasted four weeks and then he was sent right over there. I mean *literally right over three days after school ended*! I was shocked. And it was too late for me to rush down. I think Jack was shocked too, though he tried to play it cool. I thought it would be a lot longer before he went.

I think if Mr. Ogden had known about what was going to happen he would have made up with Jack. I can't say for sure because men are really stubborn, but I sure know I would have rushed down even if I had to drive three days straight and only got to give him a goodbye kiss. It would have been better than nothing. And you remember this—the macho guy kind of stubbornness leads to all kinds of trouble. Don't you *dare* pull any crap like that on me—*ever*!

Jack called from Cherry Point. It was the last time I heard his voice.

"Stay in touch while you're over there," I said.

"Remember, no news is good news."

"When can I tell my mom?" I asked.

"Wait till it's one hundred percent sure I'm going."

"What is it now?"

"It's about ninety-nine percent."

He'd been issued his gear he said. He had new cammies, sand-colored for desert. He had desert boots and, a bulletproof flack jacket.

I could tell Jack was excited but he was trying to keep his voice sad for my sake. Still I could hear a tone that told me the idiot really wanted to shout: "ISN'T WAR *SOOOO* COOL?!"

"Wear your flack jacket," I said.

Jack laughed.

"I will when I need to."

"I love you Jack."

"I love you Jessica."

I wanted to dive through the phone and grab Jack and drag him home and scream: "This isn't a game!"

"So when do you think you'll be going?" I asked calm as I could.

What lame bullshit! If we had an honest conversation it might have gone like this:

Me: "What did I do to make things turn out this way?"

Jack: "I thought you were proud of me."

Me: "Did I mention I'm pregnant? I hope you're proud of *that*!"

• • •

I was glued to the TV watching the war 24/7, trying to see his face, hating it when there was any other news, especially hating anything to do with celebrities having a good time, all that meaningless *People* magazine and *Entertainment Tonight* crap. Didn't they know we were at war? It didn't feel fair, that Jack was at war when everyone else seemed to be having a party. I'd yell about it to my parents.

"We're paying for sucking on that big oil tit with our eyes closed," Dad said.

When I heard about any Marine killed, a sick feeling suffocated me. There'd be a few seconds, an hour, maybe a day, before I knew it wasn't Jack, but every announcement, "Today a Marine was killed . . ." grabbed my heart and squeezed. I worried that Jack might hesitate, especially if he was up close and could see their faces.

On the news it said four Marines were killed because they stopped to help a man change a tire. He blew himself up and killed them. I was scared because your daddy was so kind. When he'd play soccer for Chandler he protected the smaller guys, and wouldn't tackle a small opponent hard if he could help it. I mean he got the ball away, but not by hurting anyone even though he was always the biggest guy on the field. I hoped he'd kill those people before they killed him. At least that way he'd be alive. You think that's harsh? I didn't know them. I did know Jack.

One day I jumped into our rusting pickup and turned on the radio. "Today an American soldier was killed and five wounded . . ." I stopped the truck and sat in the driveway. My hands were shaking too hard to drive. They said a soldier, not a Marine, but nobody bothers to keep the two straight. They don't know shit. None of them ever served. The kind of people who work for CNN or FOX NEWS or the *Boston Globe* just *talk* about other people's wars.

Jack was only at war two weeks but it seemed like a year—like ten years! One night I thought they called me to tell me Jack was dead. I woke up crying. The phone wasn't even ringing. It was just a bad dream.

A few days later Mom sat next to me on the bed. This time it wasn't a dream. I was asleep and still had on my Shaw's apron from work. She put her arm around me so when I woke up she was already holding me tight which was good because it kept me from exploding. All of a sudden I was screaming *no* before I even knew I'd heard her say Jack is dead. I screamed that it must be a mistake, and screamed *please* again and again as if Mom could make it stop. Then I got this picture in my brain of you inside me hearing the screams and feeling the panic pouring through my blood into you and waking you from your dreams. I remembered something I read about babies hearing their mother's voices and getting to recognize them before they're born. Okay, you were still only a speck of life so probably couldn't hear anything but it was the first time I thought about you as my baby and not my problem. But the second I knew Jack was dead I knew I was going to let you live. And this was before I told Mom or Dad or anybody about you. Anyway, so that's when I stopped screaming. I didn't want to scare you.

We lay there, all three of us, you, me, and Mom. I quieted down enough for Mom to go to the kitchen and get the paper and read the notice about how "a local boy" was killed in Iraq three days before. But in the paper it didn't say how. We sat together holding hands till after dark when Dad came back from the treatment plant. Then he cried too.

Then I told them about you.

If Jack hadn't died I think Dad would have absolutely busted my chops. But I think they were so sorry for me that I got forgiven right off. No one even brought up the idea that I would do anything but have you, just like no one ever said you should be adopted.

Mom started making plans. Dad said he'd be proud to help raise a Marine's child. But they still looked so old and tired, as if between Jack and you and me we'd figured a way to age them about twenty years in ten seconds.

Dad didn't know what to do because like he said, "Usually I'd call up his dad." And even if Mr. Ogden was a prick for Jack's sake my dad wanted do the right thing. And Dad's idea was that he wanted to tell your bad grandpa how sorry he was and buy him a beer and then tell him that he had a grandchild on the way.

Mom made an appointment with the doctor because she said she wanted you to get great prenatal care from the get-go. And you did. I took all the vitamins, and watched my weight, and did the ultrasounds, and kept the appointments, and ate the protein, and took the folic acid, and drank the milk and took a long walk every day. And on those walks I'd look across the bay at Jack's house and wonder if Mr. or Mrs. Ogden ever happened to pick up a pair of binoculars and look over the water and wonder who was walking there on Water Street with that big round belly.

Like I said, Dad planned to tell Mr. Ogden about you over a beer at the American Legion post. Dad said that there was a picture of Jack from the paper blown up poster-size and framed with a candle burning in front of it and men were paying their respects and the flag was flying at half mast and men at the bar were lifting their glasses and toasting Jack, and planning to get together an honor guard to march at his funeral. But when Dad called, Mr. Ogden wouldn't talk to him. In fact he told Dad to fuck off and slammed down the phone. Dad tried again and called back a few hours later but your other grandmother was so wrecked all she did was sob. So Dad never said anything about you. She hung up on him too.

Before I tell you more about Jack's family the main thing I want you to know is that your dad was a hero whoever his shitty parents are and however ungrateful this shitty country is. And I'm still angry and would slap Jack if he came through the door. But that doesn't change what he did which was to be a hero.

The war wasn't his fault. And there will never be a perfect

world. Everything is somewhat messed up, even good stuff. So there would be no heroes if everyone waited for a perfect war just like there would be no babies if everyone waited for that perfect moment to have a child. All we can do is take a stand and do the best wherever we are.

And the copies of his Silver Star and Purple Heart and all his other medals over your crib in the special box I ordered from the Marine Corps Association, prove he chose to do his best when he was asked to by his country.

When you fall asleep on my chest listening to you breathe is like hearing sweet words whispered about how love is so strong it hurts. And when tears trickle down the side of my face and puddle in my ears it isn't only because I miss Jack, or because I'm so mad at him, it's because I'm glad you're lying on me. And I breathe in the clean warm smell of the top of your head and I feel your pulse through the soft spot with my lips. That's when your daddy feels close.

17

ear Baby Jack, this part is too hard to write all over again. So I'm just putting this copy of my diary pages in the baby book. You were born about eight months after your daddy's funeral. Today you're almost five months old. I wrote these diary pages about a year ago. I can't reread them.

Jack lay so still that he made the pews in the church, even the floor and ceiling, look as if they were rushing off some place. Somebody asleep isn't really still. Even if you try and lie absolutely still you move, even if you hold your breath there's blood pumping, the skin has a sort of tension like a drop of water that holds its shape. Jack was *so* still!

First we were outside St. Simeon's Episcopal Church—stone—a couple of hundred years old—high roof—bell tower—brick wall topped with granite slabs. Most of the week there's a few old people coming in and out because they do some kind of thing, feed them or something. Today it was thousands of people—all ages.

Outside the church they have this big blue sign painted by their Sunday school kids of a globe with kids' handprints around and it says: "Hands Joined For Peace Around The World." The hands are different colors, white, brown, black, red and yellow.

I'm stuck in front of that sign for what seems like an hour. I'm in line for more than six hours inching toward the church. The handprints were made by kids dipping their hands in paint. Some even have fingerprints. What's it like to wait to see the dead father of your baby as if you're just anybody? It's fucked!

Crying—thinking crazy thoughts, anything to distract me, making up a sort of insane desperate story about this kid who gets grabbed by some pervert and the only way they find him is because there are these fingerprints on the child's handprint on the peace sign and a smart cop notices and traces the kid or something.

Mom and Dad try and comfort me. I get furious because people are talking in the line, talking about regular shit, even laughing and Jack is dead! I yell, tell them to show respect and one says something back. I lift my hand to slap him but Dad grabs my arm and Mom says to calm down. No one near us says shit after that or looks at me but I can hear them whispering about the "crazy girl."

The whole town waits. The line is from the post office all the way to the church. Channel 7 sends a truck.

By the door to the church state police in white

gloves keep guard. Inside: Marines in dress blues. We step through the door and see more Marines—wall of chests flashing with medals, rows and rows.

Marines everywhere—six up front, three on each side of the coffin, four men, two women. Four white, one black, one brown. Priest standing to one side—looks uncomfortable, as if there's a rip in the sky and another world just crashed on her. This priest is squatty middle-aged, a pale white woman with short gray hair.

Religious people have this sort of layer between them and the rest of us. They talk different, act different. Either they're nuts or think they're better than the rest of us. They talk in soft squishy voices that I guess they think makes them sound holy or something—really just makes them sound soft, as if they're out of focus or made of foam rubber.

But not today! Today she doesn't look like she's made of foam rubber but of burnt sugar, ready to crack!

Today she has no idea how to look because the Marines make her and everyone else appear half dead. It's like the rest of us just crawled out of someplace and just learned to walk on our hind legs. The Marines seem to have evolved thousands of years ahead of the rest of us. We all look like we're lit with a flashlight while they're lit by the sun.

We're in line moving so slow I study the cracks in the paving stones all up the aisle of the church. Then there are the old men from the Legion Post on each side of the coffin. They're wearing caps with the names of wars and medals pinned on them. I see them when I glance up.

Mrs. Ogden, and Jack's sister Amanda are there. Mrs. Ogden looks taller than I remember her. She's holding herself so stiffly it's as if her back's made of glass. Amanda is glazed over with tears and staring blindly. I try and say something and she turns and looks at me but there's nothing at all on her face except sort of squashed shrinking hopelessness. Mrs. Ogden notices me and turns away.

At first I don't see Mr. Ogden, then I do when we get about five or six people back from the front where the line turns right and files past the coffin. Mr. Ogden is crumpled down to one side, lost in a bunch of flowers piled high there, sort of kneeling, scrunched away from everybody in the line. People glance down at him then look up, fast, like they just saw their mother or father naked.

A Marine stands next to Mr. Ogden and keeps his hand on his shoulder. I want to stop crying long enough to say goodbye to Jack.

Mom and Dad don't say anything as the line turns. Finally we're in front of Jack. They hold me, one on each side. And we get weird looks because, like, what's this? Everyone is sad, but nobody is crying really hard except Jack's family. So who are these weird people who sob for a stranger? And who's that girl who can't even stand up?

He's lying there looking like his boot camp graduation picture but smaller and so still, and his lips are pressed together and I know what they do to dead people, how his lips that kissed me are glued together, and all I want to do is rescue my Jack, carry him away someplace where he can be alone with me, and wash off the make up, and unglue his lips, and take out whatever they put in him, and lie down with him and let my heat pour into him a little at a time till he's only sleeping and not so still, till he rolls over and throws an arm over me and says, Hi-ya babe!

Then Mr. Ogden screams.

At first I think he's screaming at me.

I'm not feeling anything about the screaming, just sort of noticing it.

Mr. Ogden turns and rips down the American flag one of the Marines is holding.

Mr. Ogden steps on it and spits on it and screams, "You killed my son!" at the Marine. "You killed my son! You killed my son!"

Marines pick up the flag.

There's a blur of Chandler kids.

Girls cry.

Boys shrink away.

The old guys from the Legion post look so shocked.

And the light sparkles on the medals on Jack's chest.

Then Mom and Dad are hustling me out.

• • •

I haven't taken any of your daddy's letters over to the Ogdens. They've never called since they hung up on Dad. And they still don't know about you. And since I graduated from Chandler we don't meet anyone they know so maybe they never will know about you. I never take you over the bridge in the stroller. And anyway if they saw me with you they'd just figure I was baby sitting.

18

I've been married longer than women used to live. Jack has been dead for a year and I feel no better. When is enough, enough? I need to be somebody other than Todd's wife right now, other than a grieving mother, other than a Rutherford, other than me.

I think Todd will die. He cries in the night. I'm done crying. If I had my way I'd set up a stall by the Scotland Road exit of I-95 and beg the passing commuters to fuck me till I'm obliterated, or at least till memory is wiped clean. Memories collide: Mothers were far away from daughters. I smeared myself on grateful boys at every opportunity in fields and attics, even, once in a tree house filled with mildewed dolls.

They lay under me, their backs pressed into a bed of hard boards of the attic floor. They undid my top button and lay back. Halter top pushed up and jeans down; all I had to do was roll away, roll off, rock back onto my knees and pull up twisted panties. He, whoever he was, could fend for himself, find his own way home as his juice trickled into my jeans.

Then a few minutes later I was twenty-two and there was Todd.

I walked to his studio every morning at eleven. I'd even bring him breakfast, a donut anyway. He'd drink coffee then I'd strip and he'd begin to draw. Then we'd have sex. Then he'd let me run off to HLS.

Then a few minutes later there was Amanda and then a few seconds after that Jack arrived.

I never imagined the havoc, the wreckage, the blood, and the burst vessels in straining eyes. Bloody hands pulled me, stitched, wiped probed for placenta with no more reverence than fisherman gutting trout. I was reduced to a passageway.

I tamed Amanda and Jack, taught them to take the bottle from Todd's hand so I could sleep a little just before dawn to dream. Sometimes I dreamt of the one that got away, the one I had scraped, flushed. Todd never knew.

I sweep Rubin's curly black mane aside and brush my lips over his pale neck. He doesn't seem to notice. I kiss him again, this time softly. Rubin's eyes open wide. The boss is *not* supposed to kiss her young assistant. And I'm fifty-four with a dead son. Rubin is twenty-one. A crisis to him is a problem with his new cell phone.

I kiss this little boy with a pale weedy body. Todd could break him with one punch; hoist him up the mast dangling from a rope the way he did with that shark Amanda caught off Nantucket. I feel the hard, warm surface of Rubin's teeth with the tip of my tongue. Rubin closes his eyes like a suckling puppy. He trembles and I bet he can't be more than two or three fumbling fucks in some stuffy little Brandeis dorm past virginity.

A rush of sweet warm coffee-breath fills my mouth. And, at last, I'm able to complete what I imagined as I breathed in Rubin's scent of damp hair and warm skin, poor boy, always late, always damp and fragrant from a hurried shower. I suck Rubin's breath deep and hold it. For a moment I forget Jack.

The night before I kissed Rubin I stepped out of our house to fetch an armload of firewood. There was a ring around the moon that meant snow. I stood with my arms full of cold wood; the pungent tang of tannin from the split oak logs filled my nostrils. I thought about Jack. I hoped he was below the frost line. Then I hoped he wasn't. I gazed through my bright kitchen window, my breath streaming up toward the hard winter moon in a long white trail and admitted to myself that in spite of Jack's death if I was a stranger I'd covet our house, the art on the pastel walls, the floor-to-ceiling books, the ocean view and long driveway under thick trees. I'd have wanted to be the lucky woman who lived in this ideal home, married to the beautiful famous man who, at that moment, was gliding around our well-appointed kitchen—my man in paint-spattered LL Bean, lambskin moccasins, black jeans, gray cashmere sweater.

I was *skewered* by the repetition of Jack's name, doubly damned. His death ended my patience for what might someday be. The paint on Todd's slippers was a year old. He hadn't touched a brush, or me, since the CACO officer drove under the maples that line our drive.

The day we heard Jack was dead the trees were bare, glittering from a freak ice storm, cracking under the weight. He pulled up and came to the door, him and a chaplain and another young Marine. They looked terrified. Then the world ended.

We are meant to die *slowly*! We know time is passing. Who

would say, "I've had enough of sun-warmed tomatoes exploding in my mouth, enough of the feel of freshly cut lawn under bare feet, let it end quickly?"

I regret the Monarch butterflies, took them for granted as they wafted through my garden, flitted past as if they had all the time in the world. They slowly made their way on gossamer wings such vast distances across a continent just a few wing beats ahead of the killing frost which follows. They died piled high under the trees that were supposed to shelter them. Jack is dead.

I never belonged to these pale people. In a world of color my clan perfected gray. In a world of sensuality we were so proudly frumpy. The more ludicrous our Rutherford pretensions, the more backward we became. We lived in old ruins of homes in tribute to ancestors. We would not change a stick or stone and lived in places we inherited as if they were borrowed from angry landlords who might come back at any moment to reclaim them, scream at us if we painted the kitchen a new color.

We wanted everything in the past tense, as if the fact our family had done so much for so long somehow made our present noble. But what we never seemed to understand was that for the early generations there must have been *something* in the present tense. There must have been a moment when we weren't "the Rutherfords," just people striving like everyone else. When was our name cast in bronze? When did the past eclipse the present?

Mother always wore the same straw excrescence of a "hat." "Why, Mother," I asked, "have you never bought a new gardening hat?" "We already have hats," she always answered. She had three hats inherited from her maiden aunts. Their old hats were in the

Maine place too, and several in Boston in the front hall closet of the Charles Street townhouse. We already *have* hats!

Everything had been done and done better by some ancestor. There was an aunt in Marblehead in the 1880s who also "took lovers." "So what are you trying to prove, Sarah? Who is this Todd creature anyway? Your great-grandmother ran off with Singer Sargent in 1907 on one of his rambles around Europe and came back pregnant. At least he was a *real* painter!"

I took Jack and Amanda and visited our fallen ancestor in the Museum of Fine Arts where she hangs, a small part of a hastily painted minor Sargent sketch, a group portrait of picnicking friends in his entourage lounging in the Swiss Alps near Sion above the Simplon Pass.

Everything was done before. There were no surprises, no shocks. "You are doing nothing original Sarah."

Amanda and Jack loved me, came home to me every night for many peaceful years, home to our kitchen where I helped them with homework and packed them off to happy hours of bedtime stories.

Jack is dead. Todd killed him. He pushed him away, that's why Jack rebelled. I owe Todd nothing.

I shove Rubin's chair across the room until it crashes against my office couch. We tumble onto the yielding leather. This soft boy falls under me, his legs thrust to the side, his feet on the floor. He told me once that I look like Sigourney Weaver. I press down on him, stretched full length.

He's breathing fast, almost gasping, with crimson splashes on his cheeks.

It was my fate to present a world of order, even faith to my children. I can only say what I know, that I loved Jack and was begging the god I never believed in to watch over him. The god who is not there and never was failed me.

I said goodbye to Jack at that curbside at the Savannah airport. I flew home after the boot camp graduation alone and crying. Amanda flew to New York. He was not coming home. He wanted to stay another day with Jessica in Savannah he said.

I took Jack to lunch when he came back so horribly briefly. He was staying at Jessica's. Todd still refused to see him or speak to him. I suggested to Jack he'd had his little adventure and that it was time to get his life back on track. He threw down his fork and stormed out with every waitress hungrily watching the tall young man in a perfectly pressed olive-green uniform.

Rubin slips off his jeans. His underpants are plain ice-white. Todd wears no underpants. I haven't touched such a round white belly since Jack was on his changing table. Todd's stomach is washboard flat and ribbed; at least it was a year ago when we last had sex on the very afternoon the CACO officer drove up to kill us. I had no underwear on under my robe when he knocked and could still taste Todd as the news washed over me and I sank beneath it.

Hauling the sails up and down on that boat kept Todd obscenely fit. The tan-line from the sailboat summers never faded. Rubin is white as a fish belly, really quite disgusting. I touch him lightly with my fingertips; a surgeon checking where he'll make the cut? Rubin's hollow chest is resilient, yet soft as the small of a baby's back. His penis radiates warmth, smaller than Todd's and without that old satyr's veins. Of course he's circumcised. I've long since grown accustomed to Todd's generous foreskin as if his was the only penis in the world. Todd's pubic hair is dark and wiry. Rubin's is soft, reddish brown, not much more than a pubescent shadow, downy. In the flat hallows on either side of his pubic bone Rubin's skin is tinted a tender violet wherein the veins run close to the surface. Shrink him to about a two feet tall and give Rubin little wings and he could hover over some reclining baroque Venus.

I slide down to lie between his legs half on the couch, half-kneeling on the floor. I do not want to undress in my office. The door is locked but the light is bright and we've not grown old together. Rubin's eyes won't forgive my stretch marks, flaccid breasts, dimpled bottom.

Grief has washed me clean. I feel no guilt.

Mother said Jack's killing reminded her very much of my great, great uncle Nathaniel Rutherford's death in Belleau Wood. He was killed on the first day he got to the front. I slapped her. Jack's death will *not* be folded into our family history as just another example of what it "reminds" the Rutherfords of! For once we will live in the present!

As I use Rubin's body I hear Jack's voice:

"Mother, the river *is*! Conscious life, every whisper, every half thought, every spoken word, every remembered deed it's all here: the slow burning realization that there is no such thing as *was* or *will be* only *is*. We in the river hear each voice separately each mind open, every thought laid bare standing in perpetual judgment of every other thought. There are no secrets. In one instant we know. We are the creator in that distant future: every voice and conscious mind traveling back to the beginning making itself from nothing."

19

New York is the only place I can be right now. Getting to work, riding the subway, being in the city, just being in the office forces my brain to function. And then reading the hundreds of letters, the ocean of words from people, clamoring to be validated by the *mighty paper of record* . . . it numbs my brain.

Jason doesn't seem to mind my weird moods—yet. He's being sweetly patient. Though of course he doesn't know that one morning I deleted all those letters—never even read them. I just couldn't stand one more word from anyone that had no personal stake in Jack's war. That was about six months ago. Now I feel better in some ways, worse in others.

I wandered all over today. I started on the tenth floor a few doors down from our office in the dingy hall outside Andrew Rosen's office. I stared absently at the pictures of our editors— Howell Raines, ed 1993-01, Jack Rosenthal, ed, 1986-93, Max Frankel, ed, 1977-86, John Oakes, ed, 1961-78, Charles Merz, ed, 1938-61, walked past Gail Collins' office—I slipped a flyer under her door—around the library—I left a bunch on a table—to the elevators past the old mail shoots, checked the other side of the elevators—offices of Bob Herbert (room 1035), left a flyer under his door, and William Safire (room 1040), left one there too—stepped into the women's room to cry and leave a stack—took the elevators—left some in the elevator on the way down to the third floor.

To the right the News Department—to the left the Business Section, walked into News, passed the security desk—left some on the table along with the union notices—into the news room—lots of chest-high cubicles, passed Metro Reports, through the National Copy desks and the National Backfield, News/Makeup desks, clocks on every column, down to the Foreign News desks, under the wall with clocks set to times all over the world with names of cities posted underneath—New York, Rio, Paris, Johannesburg, Jerusalem, Moscow, New Delhi, Jakarta, Beijing, Tokyo. *New York Times* newsworthy cities. Under the Moscow clock there's a piece of paper taped with the word "Baghdad," in magic marker.

It's as if no one ever figured Iraq deserved its own clock. How long has this sign been taped here? Did someone put it up during Gulf War I? Or was it put up for Jack's war?

I didn't know Moscow and Baghdad are in the same time zone.

I continue wandering. Every journalist's cubicle has a few personal pictures stuck on the divider walls, family pictures mostly.

I'm conducting my own survey while on my surreptitious flyer distribution mission. I want to see if there are any pictures of men and women in uniform. Does *anyone* at the *Times* have someone in this war? I'm also dropping flyers in the empty cubicles.

Out of flyers—I made about two hundred on our copy machine before any one else came in.

Back up in room 1055: I'm at my desk gripping the scrap of newsprint with Jack's name on it. It is a year old and starting to yellow. It fits into the little clear plastic window where I keep my driver's license inside my wallet. He made it into the paper in a license-sized box on page sixteen. There were three other Marines, one soldier and one National Guardsman sharing Jack's box. Their names were in smaller type than other news, just their names, rank and service branch.

It lists Jack's home as Salisbury MA. There's nothing about the circumstances of his death, nothing about his life, and nothing about him winning the state 400-meters, no mention that he loved P. G. Wodehouse, that he quoted Buddhist philosophers. Nothing about the movies he liked or that he was in love or that he'd read three biographies of Dietrich Bonhoeffer and underlined them. And of course there was no mention of his heroism, a word that seems to embarrass people here.

I went into the archive. In the past—at least pre-Vietnam—it was common for our paper to generously cover military heroism stories—even give them front page attention. These days' reporters at the *Times* write about casualties and how our troops are victims; about how badly wounded they are, about mothers in trailer parks crying, soldiers with no legs learning to walk, victims again. But they never do stories about the heroism of our warriors. Maybe they worry that stories about bravery, nobility and willing sacrifice might be mistaken for support for a war they disapprove of, or worse, for a president none of us voted for. Maybe it's just some post-modern thing—heroism just isn't cool any more but being a manipulated victim is. But I have a feeling if the publisher had a son or daughter in uniform there would be stories about the heroic acts of our men and women regardless of politics.

I subscribed to *Leatherneck* after one of the Marines I met at Jack's funeral sent me the copy that had Jack's story in it. Every month they have stories about heroes. That's what my flyer is, a few of those many stories no one here cares about. That is what I left in the women's rooms and elevators and along with the union hand outs and for Gail Collins and at the entrance to the News Room.

SOME STORIES THE *TIMES* FORGOT TO REPORT—

- Brad Kasal led a handful of Marines into an insurgent-held house to rescue three trapped and wounded comrades. During the course of the rescue, Kasal was shot seven times, and used his body to shield an injured comrade, absorbing forty pieces of shrapnel. He survived, as did all but one of the other Marines.

- Twenty-three-year-old Todd Bolding was handing out soccer balls and school supplies to a group of Iraqi children, when the children came under attack by a rocket-propelled grenade. Bolding did not retreat to safety, but rushed to the children, struggling to treat their wounds, when the attackers struck again. Bolding was fatally wounded.

- Jason Hendrix spent his own savings to buy other soldiers night-vision goggles, flashlights, and facemasks. He donated his rations regularly to hungry Iraqi children, and gave his Christmas leave to a friend to go home and see his new baby. In February 2004, Jason's squad deliberately attracted fire in an attempt to draw enemy fire away from advancing troops. When the vehicles in his squad burst into flames, Jason ran back to the various vehicles repeatedly in an attempt to save his comrades. He managed to save six soldiers from fiery deaths before an explosion killed him.

• Pfc. Jack Ogden was tasked with being part of a convoy that was to establish Support Area "Bedrock." The convoy began receiving incoming mortar and medium machine gun and rocket propelled grenade and small arms fire. Pfc. Ogden manned a machine gun, though not specifically trained on that weapon. In so doing he exposed himself to great danger but also provided covering fire which saved the convoy. Pfc. Ogden received three wounds during the action. Nevertheless he maintained position. Even after the corpsman arrived on the scene Pfc. Ogden continued firing. He succumbed before he could be evacuated.

After work I huddle in my studio apartment, wishing that the Columbia student renting next door didn't have any friends. I've told her to not talk so loud on her phone. And what does she run the water for at two in the morning? Is she making tea, doing dishes? How strange to know exactly what her apartment is like, a mirror image of my own 1930s oblong thirteen by twenty foot room; ten foot ceiling, a small bathroom with subway tile, the kitchenette filled with appliances too big for the space, dishes stored in the defunct dishwasher, a door too narrow for the convertible couch to get through, so I had to have men come to take it apart and reassemble it in the apartment. I keep the AC unit on for white noise so I can sleep.

Sometimes at lunch I stand next to the little recruiting office on the island in the middle of Times Square. It's less than half a block from work but might as well be a world away. It's hard to imagine that these young and painfully anonymous Marines, sailors, airmen, and coastguardsmen breathe the same air that we masters of the universe on the tenth floor of the *Times* breathe. I watch the young Marine recruiters step out to smoke. The recruiting office looks so insignificant compared to the huge billboards, and the towering buildings.

You don't expect your family to fall apart. You don't expect the world to end. Jack lay in his dress blue uniform. There were six ribbons on his chest and his shooting medal, the crossed-rifles of an "expert." I was glad I'd read enough about the USMC so I understood a little of what his medals meant.

He looked as if he was carved out of yellow wax. I couldn't see any wounds.

Dad had on a rumpled dirty suit and looked as if he hadn't bathed for days. He fell down next to Jack, and lay on the ground sobbing. Mom cried the whole time without making a sound.

The Rutherford clan was dressed in black suits and gray skirts and stood to one side of the church frozen, a tableau of dreary pale women and self-satisfied men. None of them cried. The Chandler students stood transfixed.

I cried, at first, but watching Dad disintegrate was so scary it sobered me up. Jack's girlfriend sobbed until her face was sparkling with tears. When I saw her in line it was too late. I felt sick that she had stood in line like everyone else for all those hours and hours. It was just another wrong and terrible thing on a wrong and terrible day. But since Jack was killed I hadn't thought about her till that moment. We didn't speak at the viewing, we haven't since. I can't face it.

The cataclysm: Dad yelling "You killed my son!" at the Marines and spitting on the flag.

They looked like somebody slapped them. It was the only time those Marines seemed to lose their cool. They froze up, like a freeze frame in a movie, just stopped in whatever positions they were in.

A second later Dad was slumped down again, till a Marine got him a chair. By then Jessica and her parents were on the way out. Next day they didn't come to the funeral.

Only family and Marines were there. The viewing the day before had lasted from ten in the morning till midnight. My legs ached so badly from standing rigid next to the casket I could hardly walk. I was glad. It felt right for my body to hurt.

When my dad dies I'll bet there won't be ten people at the wake. Jack had the whole town.

After the funeral Mom's parents left. There was no get together.

Dad's parents didn't come. I don't even know if they're alive. He might as well have been born out of a seashell for all I know. I've never seen his parents.

At the grave there were lots of Marines. It's a blur, as if my brain just shut down. I only remember colors, sort of, like one of the mistier Monets. In a swirl of blue, black and shiny brass they came up to say something and Dad turned away. Mom shook their hands, Dad wouldn't. They handed Mom the flag. I don't know where she put it. Things dissolved, went from impressionist to abstract, then to nothingness.

Later Mom called Dr. Schwartz. Dad is still taking some sort of pills to calm him. He won't look at me. He acts as if everyone in our family is dead, as if we've all disappeared. I don't know what is worse for Mom, Jack killed or the way Dad has turned into emptiness.

When I came home to New York I was so disoriented I got off the train in Hartford and had to catch the next train to Penn Station. When I got off the subway at 103rd Street I walked the wrong way on Broadway and was outside Tomo the sushi place past 110th, before I realized and turned and walked back.

• • •

I still don't sleep much most nights. Then I'll sleep for a whole day and night.

• • •

Today I started deleting more email letters.

• • •

I talk to the Romanian waitress at the Metro Diner. Her two sons are in Iraq with the Rangers. We hugged and cried when I told her about Jack.

• • •

You'd think the Marines would be angry that their guys get killed. But they seem to accept it. Today I asked one outside the Times Square recruiting station why he isn't angry with our president.

"We don't make policy ma'am. We just carry it out," he said.

"No matter what?" I asked.

"We're told not to obey unlawful commands but otherwise, we've taken the oath. We're there to carry out the President's orders."

I just looked at him, like, *what*?!

• • •

I kept something a mother wrote to us at the paper about her son killed in Iraq: "I don't know if my son was a 'hero.' He did what he was asked to do, and he did it without hesitation. Maybe that's heroic. It certainly was bravery, and honor and duty."

Jason wouldn't print it. I could have scratched his eyes out.

How do I remember Jack? Gentle. Most people seem to want something just out of reach. Jack was content to be in the moment. He said that at least in the Marine Corps there would be a reason to do what he had to do, instead of just playing "dumb games."

Dad was angry when I chose NYU after I was admitted to Harvard. But my rebellion didn't kill him. Jack's has. Dad came to my graduation and we never stopped speaking. Before the first semester was done Dad told me he was proud of me and approved of the fact that I was an art history major. When I got the job at the *Times* Dad sent me a bottle of champagne.

With Jack Dad never got the chance to say he was sorry.

A few days after he wouldn't print that mother's letter I asked Jason why there are so few articles about the heroism of our troops as opposed to articles about the prisoner abuse scandal. "Well," he said, "the prison scandal is news. Where people perform valiantly under conditions of combat isn't news."

Later I remembered what I wanted to say but didn't. What I wanted to tell Jason was that I think the point is that the military, and how we feel about it and how we report it, should be above politics. I think that mother had it right in her letter. Heroism is doing your job when you're asked to at great risk.

Jack's country said it needed him and he stepped up and it feels like an honor to be his sister—a crushing, terrible soul-ripping honor but a privilege nevertheless.

I'm glad the war is still going. It's weird but as long as the war is going somehow it makes it seem as if Jack is part of something in the present, not forgotten, not dead and that maybe he didn't die in vain, that maybe things will work out.

Six months after he died they awarded Jack the Silver Star. The event was held at Camp Lejeune. None of us could face going.

He was a great little brother. Everyone always says someone is sweet after they die but he really was. He was kind. I miss him so much.

How long will it be before I can say or write the words "I miss him" without crying?

I go home as little as possible. I know this is wrong. I know they need me. But when I'm home it's as if I don't exist. Dad has faded away to nothing more than someone waiting and watching. Mom is a ghost.

Every time I step back onto the sidewalk my feet melt into the flow of traffic and sooner or later I look up and realize I have just walked ten, twenty, even thirty or forty blocks or across the park and me and eight million other people are just swirling around and I can just be.

20

There is no distance between experience and being. I don't even pretend that I am more than grief. That is what I am. I *am* grief. I would leave Todd except I don't have the energy. Every conversation fades till all I hear are Jack's words I repeat again and again:

"Mom, I can't say for sure why."

"But Jack, you could take more time. Why now? Why this summer? There are people who already are doing something. It doesn't have to be you."

"Mom, why should it always be someone else?"

The folded flag is a wall between my son and memory. How can this have happened to me?

Rubin is clean as white apple blossom on fresh mowed lawn. And I'm monogamous—was until the day before yesterday not to mention menopausal to my hot-flash gills. Rubin looks surprised to see me but unlocks his apartment door. I glance at the cluttered floor. He follows my look and smiles ruefully. Books, clothes, DVDs, video games, old copies of the *Boston Globe* are scattered in an even layer.

"I wasn't planning to have visitors," says Rubin, glancing at the mess.

"It's kind of spur-of-the-moment," I answered.

A small kitchen is visible through an open door to my right. Dishes, mainly Winter & Pierce coffee mugs emblazoned with our owl-perched-on-a-book logo, sit to one side of a drab yellow sink. So the little prick steals dishes from the office. No wonder no one can ever find a clean coffee mug. Pictures of Rubin's sister's wedding are stuck to the refrigerator with magnets shaped like red peppers.

I methodically prepare to betray Todd again while thinking about how badly Rubin compares to him. Everything about Rubin is tepid. This will be our second tryst, the first outside the office. The second time with Todd we fought our way through zippers, unself-conscious as puppies snarling over a torn slipper. There was no thinking, just *doing* on a sleeping bag in the basement of his father's church.

From the outside the church looked just like any other eighteenth-century white clapboard Congregational meeting house set on the village green; postcard New England. But it had been invaded by a very hot revival after Todd's father snapped—Todd was eleven when it happened—and went from mainline Union Theological Seminary-trained minister to a full blown maniac after he became convinced that he had been healed of prostate cancer. The "healing" came by way of the prayers of Jack's mother and a handkerchief she'd laid on his rectum that she ordered while watching Oral Roberts. It was a "prayer cloth" he sent to donors, a cloth he claimed he'd taken to the Garden Tomb in Israel that would confer a special blessing on his so-called faith partners. It worked, or something did. Todd's mother had been trying in vain for years to bring Todd's dad along to her "true faith," and he instantly converted to his newfound, fevered Pentecostalism. From then on he conducted healing services almost every Sunday, and the church grew.

It was the last time we were there. Todd never saw his parents again. He wanted to show me where he grew up, let me "taste the insanity" as he put it. I think it was his way of telling me he was serious about us, so serious he'd risk showing me Exhibit A of his dysfunctional childhood—Ma Ogden gushing tongues and Pa Ogden proclaiming prophecy, in all their born-again madness.

Todd seemed to take special pleasure in having sex in that church basement, as if he was exorcising some sort of ghost from his childhood. He ejaculated like a fifteen year old doing it for the first time, before he made it past the elastic of my panties.

My face was jammed between Todd's warm cheek and the dirty laundry spilling from his backpack. We lay side-by-side listening to the sound of hymns being sung upstairs in the sanctuary while Todd whispered bitter memories.

I wrote it all in my diary a few minutes later—

Todd: flow of consciousness post-intercourse, Saco ME, basement First Congregationalist Church, October 22, 1971—

"Wednesday night prayer-'n-praise I hear the Lord 'speak.' The voice of Lord Jesus Christ is as clear as if he's standing right behind me on the platform. I drop my drumsticks and start to cry in the middle of the chorus of, 'We Adore You.' We've been singing 'We Adore You' for about two hours, moaning, swaying and clapping. There is a 'mighty outpouring' that night. Everyone's glistening with sweat, so worked up in the Spirit no one notices I'm crying, except Mom. She thinks I'm being moved by the music and doesn't know I'm coming down with a prophecy. Everyone else keeps right on singing. We have cherry Jell-O with marsh-mallow bits at the fellowship potluck after prayer-'n-praise. That's when Dad has it laid on his heart the Lord will use me so mightily that the 'mantel of prophecy' is about to pass from him to me. The folks gather round clutching mounded plates, fists full of cornbread while Dad proclaims that I'll be sent forth to witness to the lost before the imminent return of Christ, to prepare his chosen to receive their king as a voice crying in the wilderness. I'm thirteen and lie face down, 'slain in the Spirit' unable to move, pressed and smoth-ered by the Holy Ghost while the smell of extra sweet coleslaw makes me feel sick. It was a great 'sign and wonder' and, as Mom said again and again, year after year, as she tried to pry me loose from my art and my 'back-sliding' ways, 'no one who saw God work in your life that night can doubt his mighty hand is on you! Praise Jesus! Oh when will you heed his call and come back to the Lord, Todd, when?'"

• • •

Rubin leads me by the hand a few steps to the edge of his narrow bed. The white eiderdown is pulled back. Once we're on the bed Rubin starts to push against me with surprising force. I catch myself wondering why *Todd* is behaving so strangely then remember—this isn't Todd! And at that moment, in which my disorientation is complete and *déjà vu*, call it monogamous muscle memory, is overturning reason, at *that very moment* Rubin moans, "*Oh*!" and arches his back, opens his legs and pulls me to him while I'm thinking of how little his penis feels in me and of Todd's face when he sleeps in moonlight, a thought that crashes this party from God knows where.

My so-called orgasm is dreary as the winter afternoon, something that doesn't even measure up to the most half-hearted result of any pre-Jack's-death early-morning tumble with Todd.

I feel so horribly eternal, trapped. I would kill myself but that would end Jack's story. All that would be remembered is that his mother killed herself. I will not usurp his tragedy and fold it into the Rutherford legacy. I will crouch on the edge of memory and stay out of the light.

21

He left a message on the answering machine the night he arrived at boot camp. I listened, and then erased it out of spite before Sarah got home from work. It was something like: "Dad, I'm here. Don't send packages. We aren't allowed to say more. But this recruit is on Parris Island Marine Depot." Those were his last words to me. He didn't say Mom and Dad, I'm here. He said *Dad*, I'm here.

I had another chance. I could have picked up the phone when Jack called the Sunday before graduation. Then a few weeks later I knew it was Jack calling from Jessica's to set up lunch with Sarah. *He was less than half a mile away!* Then I knew it was Jack when he called from Germany on his way to Kuwait. Twice I had my hand on the receiver. Twice I gripped it. Twice I was too full of pride.

Jack phoned once from Kuwait. I was in the studio. He talked to Sarah briefly. She buzzed me on the intercom to beg me to pick up, but I didn't. Later she told me he asked for hand sanitizer, soccer balls and pens. The pens and balls were for children he said. They wanted candy too. He asked Sarah how I was and she lied and said I asked her to send my love.

I arranged Jack's personal effects on the dining room table, his dog tags, a comb, his book of family pictures, and the copy of *Innocents Abroad* Sarah gave him for his twelfth birthday. I found several hairs of his on the comb. I cried all night.

There's a little dried blood on the book. I press the bloodstain against my lips while looking at Jack's boot camp graduation portrait, the one where he is staring at the camera trying to look tough. I have no answer for the challenge in his eyes.

Jack was always jotting things in books. In the flyleaf of *Innocents Abroad* he wrote: "Peter Viereck—last lecture at Mount Holyoke: 'I can think of nothing more gallant, even though again and again we fail at attempting to get at the facts; than attempting to tell things as they really are. For at least reality, though never fully attained, can be defined. Reality is that which, when you don't believe in it, doesn't go away.'"

I asked Sarah to let me read Jack's letters. For most of the year since he died I couldn't look at them. Jack's first letter was not a real letter. The second was no more personal. Both are just printed forms.

My hands shook too hard to hold the paper so I propped them side-by-side on my drafting bench. I sat in front of them for most of a day. The first form letter has thirteen words in Jack's scrawl. The second has twenty-one or twenty-four if you count the zip code and other abbreviations.

COMMANDING OFFICER
RECRUIT TRAINING REGIMENT
MCRD

PO BOX 16001
PARRIS ISLAND SC 29905-6001

I HAVE ARRIVED SAFELY AT PARRIS ISLAND,
SOUTH CAROLINA
MY NEW ADDRESS IS:
RCT _Jack Ogden_
PLT _1095 1st BN B co_
PO BOX 11004
MCRD PARRIS ISLAND SC 29905-1004
FROM JUNE 1ST UNTIL NOVEMBER 1ST IS
HURRICANE SEASON. IF MCRD IS THREATENED
BY A HURRICANE, YOU CAN CALL 1 800 343
0639 ENTER THE NUMBER SEQUENCE 1-3-1
FOR UP TO DATE INFORMATION. INFORMA-
TION ON FAMILY DAY AND GRADUATION
EVENTS CAN BE OBTAINED AT THE SAME
NUMBER BY ENTERING THE SEQUENCE 1-3-2
FURTHER INFORMATION CAN BE OBTAINED
AT (www.parrisisland.com)

(Mom, give this information to Dad please?
Thanks!)

Dear _Mom + Dad_ Date: _03 08 24_

I have arrived at Parris Island and have been
assigned to Platoon _1095_ which is composed of _87_

recruits from various parts of the country. Our Senior Drill Instructor's name is _SDI Jackson_ he is the one who is responsible for our training here. We will live and train together for the next three months until our graduation date on _Nov 20_. There are 4 Drill Instructors assigned to my platoon and I am told there will be at least one with the platoon each day we are here. I will send you their names later. Because of the balanced diet we will be on, it is recommended that you not send packages containing food items to me. I am enclosing my address again to be sure you have all the information needed to write to me. Be sure you address all mail to me just as I have it below:

RCT Ogden Platoon 1095 Bravo Co, 1st RTBN MCRD PARRIS ISLAND, SOUTH CAROLINA 22905-1004

• • •

Today I saw my mother for the first time in twenty-eight years. I'd forgotten the drive only takes two hours. I had forgotten we're on the same planet.

Mom's hair was white. Her breath still smelled like hot oil when she lifted up her hands to my face, parchment-wrinkled now, spotted and thin-skinned. Mom's voice was strong as ever as she brandished her worn-out _King James Bible_, waved it like a club with which to drive the Devil from her son. She told me Dad died seven years ago of cancer.

"If you cast yourself on the blood, claim the precious *blood* he will in no wise cast you out, for there is more joy in heaven over one repentant sinner than over ninety-nine of the saved!" said Mom.

"Jack died," I cried.

Mom stroked my hair. We held each other and began to rock back and forth. She shed no tears.

"She's no good for you, Todd! Those Boston women deny the risen Christ! Thank *God* from the bottom of your heart that he's been merciful! I *knew* he'd bring you back to me some day!"

"I've lost Jack!"

"He worketh all things to the good of those that love him, praise be his precious name!"

Mom began to sing "Just As I Am." She sang it for what seemed like an hour in her high reedy voice as the sun set.

Twilight falls. We are hunched over in the darkening living room clutching each other. I glance through a blur of tears at the big picture of Jesus over Mom's dining table, this reproduction of a bad painting, circa-1920s, of Jesus as a young girl. He is praying in the Garden of Gethsemane, hands clasped in front of him, large liquid brown eyes imploring heaven to spare him his cup of sacrifice. And the beam of light that illumines his upturned, tear-stained face is even brighter than I remember it.

"Pray for me, Mom."

As a child I spent many nights trying to see the angels Mom said were hovering in the light just beyond the edge of the gaudy white and gold frame. Mom said those angels made a "mighty column" that "stretched from Jesus up to the Father beyond outer space." Mom said the angels were "all crying too" and begging the

Father to let them save Jesus who, at that very moment, was waiting for Judas to lead the soldiers into the garden.

I gaze at Jesus' slender womanly hands and picture the rusty nails that will soon be pounded through them. And I wonder what the Lord will be thinking as the hammer blows are driven by my wickedness. I see Jack dead, Sarah undoing the top four buttons of her flower print dress, the belted one with shoulder pads, the silk one with the tiny violets on black cut in that 1940s style that gives her such a wonderfully narrow waist. Another image unbidden: Sarah's high cheekbones gaunt and beautiful, her legs gloriously long below the hem of her short, green maternity dress, she wears brown stockings, support hose, sensible as any mother-to-be with swollen ankles, she strips in front of the studio heater, the livid stretch marks creep up Sarah's stomach. I draw her at every stage, from every angle; her ripening body fills pages of countless sketch-pads. Every inch of her swelling belly, breasts and hips is lovingly recorded in passionate charcoal destined for the dust cloud that blossomed over lower Manhattan. Jack stretched her out so far she looked as if she was having twins.

I promised Mom I'd visit again and knew I never would.

• • •

I read Jack's letters again, one in particular.

> Dear Mom and Dad,
> Had our boot camp pictures taken today. You'll be getting copies after grad. None of us are Marines yet so

we don't have our dress blues. They had the white cover and dress blue blouse ready for each recruit—it was slit down the back so it could be slapped on to us fast, assembly-line style with the buttons already done up, the picture shot and the line moved on. Only corpses have jackets put on them slit up the back to make for easy dressing the dead!

Love, Rec. Ogden

He sent one letter from the war, written in installments over several days. It arrived two weeks after he was killed.

1/18/04

Dear Mom, Dad and Amanda (Mom, please fax a copy to Amanda)—Hello from fabulous Kuwait! I'm doing fine—slept on the C-17 out here from Germany. Much better than a commercial airline—all the room to stretch out under a bulldozer!

Arrived at the Bridge Park or Davisville by CH-46. Davisville is the home of a Naval Mobile Construction Battalion (Seabee) command. The place is a big empty quadrangle of dirt about 800 meters long and 250 meters wide. The Seabee operation is contained within a berm—dirt piled in a wall 5-8 meters high.

Sand—from Plum Island-type (white and fine the way it is on Sandy Point and across the water on Crane's Beach), to powder-fine—so insidious no orifice is protected! I'll email everybody as soon as I can get access. Still getting squared away. Haven't gotten to a phone yet.

1/21/04

An-Nasiriyah today—filthy—Marine unit HQ in the center of town on the south side of the Euphrates River. The battle here was bad at the start of the war. A Marine M1A1 Abrams tank fell into the river killing the crew. Since then lots of IED trouble—Worse now than ever they say. We're planning a mission back to Kuwait to collect gear and replenish supplies.

1/22/04

The trip is in the back of an open-air HWMMV in a heavy dust storm—about 11 hours inclusive of vehicle breakdowns—67-vehicle convoy—impressive! My phone credit card stolen or lost—Cancel it if you can Mom. I'll try to email before you get this so you'll probably already know. Chow with Arabic written on the boxes, bad food from those war profiteers and assholes at Brown and Root. The meat definitely doesn't taste like beef—camel? PX truck arrives once every 3 days—the line is at least 2 hours long. Loaded up on Twix, no baguettes!

The public at home thinks everyone here hates us because all you hear is about the IEDs. But kids wave and a lot of the people seem to have pride in their country—most are friendly. I had several shake my hand and tell me they need us here. Made me feel good.

Shooting practice—zeroed my sights fired 16

rounds into the target, grouped the last five shots the size of a golf ball. Still could qual "expert!" Awesome!

Cpl. Clay (awesome Marine) in big fight with his mom because he lent his phone card to somebody never got it back—$4,300 phone bill to his mom. She told him he'll have to pay the bill, and then she emailed him: "I don't want the last words I speak to you to be about a phone bill. I'll pay it. What if you got killed?"

Sgt. Mills got a letter saying his wife has breast cancer. She's only 26. How can that happen at only 26? She didn't tell him because she didn't want to worry him before he deployed, only emailed now because he's on his way home and she had a breast removed. He's been here for 7 months. How come the same guys have to do it all? This was his 3rd tour! Where is everyone else?

Mostly sitting around and shit happens like the phone card and cancer. A chaplain baptized some soldiers at a Sunday service. I never saw that before, did it in a wood trough lined with plastic under netting. Don't worry about me. But worry about your friggin phone bill if somebody got that card!

Love, Jack

I made xeroxes. I'm afraid I'll wear the letters out, so I just read the copies.

When he played on Plum Island his blonde hair was a halo of translucent gold backlit by the setting sun. His books are still in his room. The three he had in Iraq were returned by the officer who accompanied Jack's body from Dover AFB to Boston and then to here; *Innocents Abroad, Jeeves in the Offing* and *The Odyssey.* Everything was in a paper bag—his dog tags, clasp knife, the books. The officer handed it all over in the office of the funeral home on High Street in Newburyport before the body was moved to the church for the viewing. Sarah was crying too hard to take them. I was still keeping it together. I didn't lose control until the viewing.

He had pictures too, three of Jessica, one of Sarah and one of Amanda at her graduation, and a picture of me. Laminated. It was inside his Kevlar helmet. It was of us in Bermuda. In the photograph he's smiling and I have a hand on his shoulder. And he also had a laminated reproduction of a Duccio Madonna, same one he copied as a little boy.

He grew four inches that summer. We drove to New York twice that fall, once to see Patrick Stewart in *The Tempest* and once to spend a weekend visiting the Metropolitan Museum of Art. We stayed at the Hotel Edison on West 47th Street. Jack loved the coffee shop—"the Polish Tearoom."

Once when he was five we walked all the way from 110th and Riverside to 47th. We ate breakfast at the Polish Tearoom that spotless April Sunday morning. By the time we were down to about 86th Street Jack complained he was tired. I said, "Only one more block and we'll take the bus." We walked another block and by then he forgot that he was tired and he walked ten more blocks till he remembered to complain again. He walked the whole way and it took two hours. Jack especially liked the long rows of fruit piled up on the block-long stall outside Fairway market. We tried to count all the green apples but eventually gave up: Talking about how much fruit was in any one pile, how many apples and mangoes, strawberries or peaches were under each stack hidden from view—was it hundreds or thousands, was it solid fruit or was there a box under there?

We'd brought *The Wind in the Willows*. After we ate we took the subway from 50th Street up to 72nd, then I walked the long east and west blocks with Jack riding on my shoulders. I cut through the park to the jogging path and followed it around the reservoir till we got to the bridge that leads to the Met.

We lounged on a bench across from the granite pumping station at the southern end of the reservoir. I read out loud. Jack stretched on the sunny bench and laid his head on my lap. He fell asleep and later said he had dreamed that Ratty—his favorite character in the book—was on the reservoir in his little boat.

I watched Jack sleep for more than an hour. When the sun moved overhead I held the book open to shade him.

The CACO officer said that Marines often keep a "precious picture or two tucked into the webbing inside their helmets."

That was where he had my picture.

• • •

We get a phone bill for $2,673. Sarah pays it after she tried to call Sprint but burst into tears when they argue with her. She says, "My son was killed in Iraq, he couldn't be using this card. It can't be him making these calls from Kuwait." The operator turns out to be an Indian or some such person in God knows what time zone and he doesn't know what she's talking about and asks her to please spell the word Iraq. Sarah starts spelling the word but can't finish. That's when she bursts into tears and throws the phone. It takes her half a day to cancel the card while being shunted from one computer message to another till finally she gets another live operator and shrieks at him that she'll sue him personally.

When did he slip away from me? Why didn't he give me a chance to talk him out of it?

Is Mom right? Did that bastard God kill Jack to bring me "back to himself" as Mom claims? It wouldn't surprise me. He killed his "only beloved son" as a sacrifice for the sins of his creatures because they broke arbitrary rules he made up out of thin air.

I should have choked Mom when she said, "Jack died for a purpose."

I'm trying to forget the bible verses she welded into my brain: *"Then one of the twelve, called Judas Iscariot went to the chief priests and said, 'What are you willing to give me if I deliver him to you?' And they counted out to him thirty pieces of silver."*

• • •

I am alone in a dark room; I am Judas with the body of the Son of God. His skin is pale, almost blue. His feet are yellow. His eyes are half open. I'm touching him. His body is cold. The cold is seeping into me. We are both still as statues. I'm alive only in the sense that I am aware of the cold and he is not aware. My last words to him were: "This is the stupidest thing you've ever done. Don't bother coming home!" I yelled that after him as he walked up our drive.

Who is this laying so still in dress blues? I do not know him.

He looks so small. He is an effigy, a mockery. The uniform cuts him off from me. I am screaming at the Marine before I am aware. I am powerless to raise him up. I am alone in this darkened room, naked with the naked body of my son. I lost Jack twice. I lost his life. I lost his love. Now the third death: I can't feel Jack. I can't picture him. He sent home the Parris Island boot camp portrait. He stares from the frame, a stranger, a painted flag on a wall behind him, just another faceless Marine portrait like one clutched by some grieving mother in a trailer park. I thought we'd reconcile someday. I thought he would explain. We will never have that talk. I will never know why.

Jack as he fell asleep in my arms; the smell of sweet flesh, warm against mine, the way his cheek pressed into the hollow between my neck and shoulder. I try to remember the sound of his breathing, soft, soft breath of a baby destined to be shot, the breath of the stranger at whom I screamed: "Don't bother coming home!"

What music played? There must have been a sound track. Was it a dirge sung by Sister Gertrude Morgan to the beat of her tambourine? Did he lift up his eyes? Did he smile? Is he riding in one of Sister Gertrude's airplanes along with her Jesus? Or did the angels from the Met's Angel Tree carry him home with their silk robes forever swirling? Did he scream, Daddy help me!? Was he afraid as they worked over him, fumbled for a vein to get an IV started? When they did chest compressions did they break his breastbone? Did he know his life's blood was running into the sand?

I see him firing that machine gun, a tall figure against the pale yellow sky of a cursed land. I rearrange the universe one molecule at a time and beg it to let me be the one who takes those bullets.

Marines wrote and called. They wanted to console us. Sarah talked to them once. I never talked to them.

• • •

I read his letters again—so prosaic—six of them, none longer than a paragraph or two except the one I cling to, the one where he seems whole, like my Jack.

Amanda says she got four. She says she'll send me copies now that I've begged to read them.

Letters all about this training day, or that and what they did in the "swim test," how he can float with sixty pounds of equipment, about "A-Line" and going to the rifle range and learning to shoot by "snapping in," about too little food, not enough time to eat and about how hungry he is, about wanting power bars and cough drops and drill and more drill and what this or that DI said.

Where are the reasons? Where is some word of real explanation?

Sarah says she sent power bars. Sarah says she signed her letters to him from both of us. He wrote my favorite letter two weeks before graduation.

I read this letter again and again.

> Dear Mom and Dad,
> It's the small things. The small things add up to the big things—the perfectly made rack, the perfectly squared away locker, the perfectly clean squad bay, the perfectly clean rifle locked to this recruit's rack, the perfectly executed drill movement, the loudest sounding

off we can muster with cracked voices. This adds up to the perfect day. A perfect day when this recruit isn't yelled at and a perfect week is a week we aren't pitted. To make this happen every other recruit has to have a perfect day too. And for that to happen we have to watch out for every recruit. That's the point—no compromise with bullshit.

Love, Jack

I am repentance that can find no forgiveness! My grief is not located in time or place. It is the ocean I swim in, my personal lake of fire. I open my mind to Jack. He says:

"Memories jostling down the river, a mighty damn burst, and then we're hurled down. The floodwater sweeps away everything and we ride forever miles of churning water beneath us. Minds of the living mingle with the dead."

22

Dad has this idea that he has to retrace Jack's steps. A year later and Dad is no better. In fact he's worse Mom says. After he piled everything of Jack's on the kitchen table Mom decided Dad was going crazy, and needed to be hospitalized. He refused. She's afraid.

I can't say I'm sorry for him. I'm not sorry about anything, sorry or glad. I'm past sorry or glad.

Mom called me at the office. "Something terrible happened," she said. Mom asked me to come home. I can't face them.

I think Dad is one of those people who never settled down after the 1960s. From what I've read it seems everything got so loud, and if you weren't getting blasted you just didn't notice anything. Maybe that's what the sixties drug "culture" was about: reality wasn't loud enough. When Jack and I were born it had to be more—louder. We couldn't just *be*. We had to fulfill our parent's need to "experience parenthood," as if we were just another drug. We weren't kids. We were the "family experience," the next entertainment.

Dad has been plunged into reality for the first time since he was my age and he just can't handle it. I don't think my parents are made of very dependable material.

The 1960s were supposed to be this laid-back time when everyone was so "authentic," but it produced these hard-driving ambitious assholes. From Woodstock to SUVs the size of houses! Who are these people? It figures he'd visit his mother again!

23

To the Commandant of United States Marine Corps

Dear Sir,

One year ago my son Jack Ogden was killed while serving in the USMC. When my son volunteered after high school I was angry with him. I was shocked when Jack came home one day saying he had stopped to see a recruiter. At first I thought he was joking. Then I took it for some kind of teen rebellion. We stopped speaking. We never spoke again before he was killed.

You are probably about to put this letter down and despise this "father" who would stop speaking to his son. Each and every action I took is now a cut in my heart. I would trade all the experiences of this life for the chance to go back to the day my son left for boot camp if I could say goodbye. I am asking that you please have mercy on me and allow me to visit Parris Island. I realize that this request is unusual. But I'm asking you to help the father of a Marine. Please let me stand on the ground he stood on. Sir, help me find my son.

Yours sincerely,
Todd Ogden

24

aby Jack, when you were born Mom was with me. I guess maybe the doctor thought that since I was just a teen I didn't deserve to be taken seriously. He talked to me as if I was a child. And he handed you to Mom. But Mom put you in my arms. I didn't want to let go of you. It was as if Jack was using my arms to hold you.

I was thinking about how Jack took me to that room in a motel in Portsmouth as a surprise when he was home from MCT. He put red roses on the bedside table and had strewn red rose petals over the bed. He lit the room with candles. I guess this was as close to a honeymoon as we ever got. You were there too, not that I knew that yet.

Your daddy and I talked for a long while before we made love and for even longer after. And he told me he loved me again and again and held me. I fell asleep hearing him say my name. And now I wish I had stayed awake. I didn't know time was running out. I would have liked to hear more of his voice.

With you in my arms the day you were born it's as if I got a second chance to be with him. I could smell red roses.

25

Dear Mr. Ogden,

Thank you for your letter. Please allow me to extend my condolences for your loss on behalf of the Commandant. You may visit the recruit training depot on Parris Island as per your request. This will give you a chance to observe the recruit training cycle.

The Commandant contacted Gen. Kennedy, at Marine Corps Recruit Depot Parris Island. Major Dan Clima of the public affairs office will act as your liaison. Please contact him at his office. He is expecting your call.

Major Dan Clima, Director, Public Affairs
Marine Corps Recruit Depot/Eastern Recruiting Region
Public Affairs Office
PO Box 5059
Parris Island, SC 29905-0059

It is my sincerest wish that you find solace. Your son was an exemplary Marine.

Semper Fi

Major C. B. Legato

Office of the Commandant, United States Marine Corps

Part IV

26

January 20, 2005, 2043 Parris Island—Dad is on my island a few days short of the one year anniversary of my death. There's still some light in the sky, just a slash of pale blue and pink on the horizon. Dad is sitting in the car waiting for Major Dan Clima. Some stars are showing. Three minutes ago Dad drove up to the gate. He had been trying to imagine this moment during the trip from Logan to Savannah and the one-hour drive from the airport to the holy gate—the moment he will stand where I stood.

When Dad identifies himself the guard checks his driver's license against a list on a clipboard.

"Sir, please wait here for Major Clima," says the guard.

The Marine points to where Dad can pull his car in across from the guardhouse. The guard calls Major Clima. The two guards at the gate are the first Marines Dad has seen since my funeral. They wear cammies and carry M-16s. Their sleeves are rolled to mid bicep. Their cammies are pressed and starched, so stiff that they could stand up alone. The one who spoke to Dad is polite. His nametape says "Reyes." He speaks with a heavy Hispanic accent. His face is round and shiny and the color of mahogany. He is a lance corporal. He loves his mother, the Virgin Mary, the United States of America, and his little sister in that order.

Dad never saw me in uniform except for my dress blues. Dad feels a sharp stab in his heart, a literal stabbing pain. He's wishing he'd seen me in a uniform alive, standing tall, serious and stern like this young Marine. Dad's picturing me here at the holy gate wondering if I ever did guard duty. He knows nothing about Parris Island. Recruits never are given jobs like that. Dad thinks that somehow you become a Marine just by signing up.

Reyes doesn't ask this stranger why there are tears on his cheeks. Dad loves me, Mom, Amanda in that order. Everything he was has been stripped away. He is naked before God.

And God isn't even paying attention. Dad lost me and now he's lost Mom. I asked God whatever happened to my last letter to Dad.

"He never got it, and never will," said God.

2125 Parris Island officer guest quarters—Osprey Inn—Room 17—a plain suite, kitchenette, pale gray linoleum floor, bedroom, shower smelling of cleaning materials and mildew. The mildew isn't the fault of the Marines who field day here. It's under the linoleum, the price of doing business in the humid coastal south.

The suite reminds Dad of Amanda's studio apartment in New York, only the windows in this guest quarters have a view of the parking lot and the water beyond and her room faces a dark inner courtyard. Since she's on the fifth floor of a sixteen-floor building there's hardly any daylight.

Major Clima told Dad that officers visiting PI stay here. Seven male Marines and one female have gone forth from this room to die. One was killed in Beirut, one in the first Iraq War. The others died in my war. All but one loved their mothers. Three of them had young children. One died slow and spent his time praying for his son. God paid no attention.

I know how they felt after they died. They felt relieved.

The relief comes when you realize that the only real question just got answered:

You are still conscious!

Take every prize you ever won, the first kiss, the first time a girl lets you touch her breast, the moment just after a roller coaster takes that plunge—take all that and multiply it by ten, then subtract everything that ever worried or scared you, *that's* how it is when you know that *you're still you!*

Then of course the memories start and you begin to hear the conversation in the river. That's when you realize that you're going to remember *everything*.

That's when you almost wish you had gone out like a light.

This is how Dad's arrival unfolded: Major Dan Clima of the public affairs office pulls up in a little white car. He's wearing cammies like the guards. They salute him. He returns the salute. He's short and stocky and seems slightly uncomfortable around enlisted Marines, a little overly hearty. He's in his early forties. For him being a Marine is just a job. Some officers are like parents about Santa Claus, it's something for the kids but the grown-ups know better. They play the game and take care of us enlisted fools who really believe everything our DIs told us. Not all officers of course. Most believe, just like us enlisted, they believe just like Jesus believed in his own divinity. Those are the officers that walk on water, the ones we die for.

The major loves his wife and two children in that order. But everything is pale for him. He mostly thinks about what he'll do after retirement.

Like the young guard the sleeves of the major's cammie blouse are rolled to mid-bicep. But his biceps don't bulge with muscle the way the young Marine's do or mine used to. I looked squared away in uniform, except in my coffin. When your skin is plastic and your ass packed with tampons it's hard to look good.

Dad and the major shake hands. He knows why Dad's here but he's uncertain how to proceed, slightly embarrassed, thinks the commandant is setting a bad precedent. Lots of Marines are dead and what would happen if all their fathers showed up? Then again the commandant didn't tell the major the full circumstances. The commandant is an honorable man; a true believer and he kept Dad's secret shame between them. The commandant just said Dad was the father of a KIA and to let him look around. The commandant protected Dad's secret for my sake. I am his brother Marine.

The major seems to be somewhat lost for words. He doesn't mention me. He should have told Dad that he was sorry for his loss. All he says is that Dad's been listed on the pass as a reporter.

Dad is relieved. He made his confession to the commandant. Dad doesn't want to confess to anyone else. So the fact the major is somewhat rude works out well for everyone.

"Easiest category to put you in," the major says. "I'll be telling the Marines you visit that you're here to observe. Is that okay?"

"Yes," Dad answers.

Major Clima hands Dad a red visitor card.

"Place it on the left hand side of the dash."

I swim in Dad's car across a causeway. Last time I rode onto the island I was a terrified recruit in a bus, literally in the dark and ordered to keep my head down. At the time I didn't know why. Now I do. The DIs don't waste one minute in starting to cut you off from the world, a failed place full of selfish soft Americans, too fat and undisciplined to defend themselves. If the DIs are going to convert you to the truth in three short months they need your undivided attention from the get go. They need to turn night into day, make every breath a lesson, every heartbeat an opportunity from the first moment you're in their clutches.

Like God, the DIs see men's souls and change them. Actually God doesn't give a shit one way or another about changing men's souls but the DIs do. The DIs save more souls than all the priests and pastors put together. They feed more hungry than Mother Teresa ever did. They lead each recruit to the altar as Abraham did with Isaac. They prepare to sacrifice him or her. And at the last moment they spare them. But they were ready to do it!

Dad is driving behind the major. The causeway isn't much wider than a two-lane road—miles of water on both sides—gray and flat stretching out to wetlands full of tall reeds. Sometimes desperate recruits try to swim for it. They drown or are caught hiding in the tall grass. Mostly they give up and swim back to the depot. Then they wait for months while the Corps messes with their paperwork and then are sent home in disgrace. The Corps never sends you straight home unless you try suicide. Then they want you off their island fast. So anyone sick of boot camp knows the fastest way off the island is to graduate or kill yourself.

From the gate to the Osprey Inn Dad is surrounded by water most of the way. He doesn't notice. His heart is broken. Memories are rattling in his mind.

Dad is thinking:

I hover over mother and child. Sarah's eyes are exhausted, dazed. Someone is fixing the hospital roof. The smell of the hot tar mingles with the scent of Jack's newborn mat of jet-black hair. Sarah's face is puffy and exhausted. They're stitching her. My neck is scarlet, chafed from wearing the surgical mask too tight. I've spent a lifetime feeling as if I am looking in on, not participating in life, whatever that is. Jack, I am alive only in the sense that I know I am dead.

• • •

We drive for less than two minutes before we're on PI and then for only three more till we're at Dad's quarters. PI is a small place. We pass several low brick buildings. One is my old squad bay. It's filled with recruits and DIs I never met. But I know them. Each DI is every DI and each recruit is every recruit and each training day is the same for every recruit who passes through the holy fire. The DIs have screamed every line a million times. Every recruit has been told he is the worst recruit every DI has ever seen. Every DI is the best actor in the world.

We drive under the big steam pipes. We pass open fields, pull-up bars and ropes, trees, live oaks covered with moss, a few palms and the Iwo Jima Memorial next to the bleachers.

The recruits are asleep. DIs sit in the DI houses awake, so tired they feel every cell in their bodies cursing them. Their wives put babies to bed who hardly know their fathers. DIs kiss sleeping children in the dark when they come home and when they go out. They fall asleep on the way home and crash cars. They pull over and cry alone in shitty parking lots. Their wives sometimes leave them.

God loves Marine drill instructors best of all, not that he'll ever lift a finger for them.

They run, walk and march four miles for every mile run, marched or walked by their recruits. They lead step-for-step from the front. The platoon marches forward and they pace around them, watching, instructing and loving the recruits, though we never knew that the deepest love came packaged as a kick in the ass.

I linger for a moment in my old squad bay; listen to the breathing, the coughing, the recruits who shout "Yes sir!" in their sleep and do a port arms with their pillows.

Some cry.

Some chew their pillows as they dream of food.

The squad bay is dark and full of stale air. It's been sucked into sick lungs, farted, sighed, screamed and sobbed, then breathed again and again by the living and the dead.

The polished concrete floor glistens from the light over the quarterdeck. A lone recruit gets up to go to the head and steps lightly trying to make himself as invisible as possible, as invisible as a big black kid from a small town near Mobile, Alabama, can be creeping to the foot of his rack and from there picking his way past the end of all the other racks, never stepping over the line into the DI highway, trying not to brush up against the M-16s locked to each rack by a cable and padlock, till he reaches the quarterdeck and then the head doors.

As he crosses the patch of light on the dreaded quarterdeck he's hoping that the DI house door is closed, hoping to escape those X-ray eyes. A recruit is guilty until proven guiltier. The recruits on fire watch take note but do no more than flash the red light of their moonbeams in his direction as he pauses momentarily shivering in his skivvie shorts and T-shirt.

He loves his mother, sister, little brother, the USMC, and God in that order.

Usually I'd stick around to see if he, like me, in my bad old days, is getting up to write something, maybe a letter, while pretending to go to the head. Tonight curiosity will have to wait. I want to concentrate on Dad.

At this moment Dad loves me, me, and me in that order.

I swim down the DI highway and bless each sleeping recruit with this prayer:

"Graduate with your platoon, recruit, don't shit the bed and always come home safe to the one who loves you most."

Before Major Clima drops Dad at his quarters the major points out the red brick squad bays in the distance. They look like schools to Dad. They're dark except for a few lit windows.

"Lights out in the squad bays is usually at twenty hundred," says Major Clima. "Sometimes a little later if the DIs are doing some extra activity with the recruits. Those lights you see on are in the DIs' offices, what they call the 'DI House.' That's where they stay and all those other windows are the squad bays where the recruits sleep, what you'd call a barracks."

Dad is thinking:

When Jack was here, he would've been asleep by now.

Goodnight Jack.

I'm thinking:

Goodnight Dad.

27

January 21, 2005, 0350—Room 17 Osprey Inn—Dad woke two minutes ago. He's naked, crying and sitting across from the kitchenette at the card table in the corner. The only light is coming from the open door to the shower. Dad left it on so he could find the head in the night. He hasn't bothered to turn on other lights.

Dad is thinking:

Jack, how long will it be before Sarah will touch me?

Jack, have I lost her too?

Jack, what have I done?

Everything has stopped.

I'm hollowed out.

My bones are melting.

Where is mercy?

When is enough, enough?

Jack, will Sarah forgive me?

Will she ever touch me again?

She says she wants to divorce me.

I begged her for one more chance.

Will anything become clear?

The motto painted on the sign at the holy gate is "Parris Island—Where It All Begins." This means, where the journey to become a Marine begins. But what about Dad, what begins for him? Maybe this is where it ends for my father. Maybe this is where Dad gives up.

Dad is thinking:

Jack, I owe you honesty.

Jack, a few weeks ago I grabbed your mother and banged her head against the wall. She screamed at me after I was nitpicking her again about why she didn't work harder at persuading you not to enlist. Something snapped. She shrieked at me and I wanted to stop that shrieking.

Jack, I make no excuse. I banged her head against the wall, just short of knocking her out. She ran upstairs. She locked me out of the bedroom. I waited all night in the studio crying. I drove her down to Mass General next morning. She looked dead, so tired, so washed out. She wanted to get checked out, or at least make a point, or gather evidence for a divorce.

When she looks at me it's as if I'm a stranger. There's nothing in her eyes. Sarah didn't want to go to the emergency room at Ann Jacques. She knows too many people there. She says she wants to divorce me, Jack.

She says she told me—after the time I slapped her when we were young—that there are no second chances about abuse. I begged her for one more chance. I never fucked up again till this time. I'm begging again now. I don't feel like a monster. I wanted to cancel coming here. She said not to. She was so relieved to get me out of the house.

She will not touch me. I don't mean just sexually. We don't have sex anyway, haven't since you died. I mean she won't touch me *at all*, steps aside, and won't even brush past me. She wouldn't shake my hand when I left. I tried to shake her hand, or kiss it, or anything, after she wouldn't even look at me when I got down on my knees and begged for forgiveness.

Jack, what should I do?

We were young and made love in her parents' house in Boston. There was a cedar cupboard filled with ratty mink coats that must have been a hundred years old. We took all those minks out and burrowed under them. Sarah naked, just twenty-two, sneezing from the dust, laughing, framed by mink. Mothball smell and her sweet secretion scent mix. We fucked till we were both too sore to walk. We—

Dad! Shut the fuck up!

Jack, I am a wife abuser!

28

January 21, 0945 Public Affairs Office—Major Dan Clima, in his office—the major introduces Dad to the three enlisted Marines who work for him. He gives no reason for Dad being there—they're young and polite and working on articles for our newspaper *The Boot*.

Two are fatherless.

One is motherless.

They each love the remaining parent, their girlfriend, God and the USMC in that order.

None of them feel like a real Marine because they sit in this office all day while others are at war.

They would give anything to be in combat.

One of them wrote the article about my death for *The Boot*.

They get a lot of visitors and no one seems to think Dad's presence is unusual. They assume Dad is just another reporter. There are two teams of journalists already on the island today, one from NBC's *Dateline*, and a documentary crew from Japan.

The major's office is cluttered with memorabilia from nineteen years of service—a Marine recruiting poster—the one where the DI is screaming up at a young recruit signed by that famous DI—the major with other Marines, a graduation photograph from the University of Michigan, a picture of the major in the desert next to a dusty helicopter with a little brass label on the frame: "Gulf War I." That was his big moment.

The major has pale blue eyes. He gives Dad the usual spiel. In his mouth the truth sounds insincere and colorless.

"Someone needs to keep the standard high . . . Marines, unlike the Army, keep the standards high . . . Young men and women of all races and all types pulling together for our country . . . One aim . . . They'll never again hear the word 'I' the same way . . . They learn that the word 'I' leads to defeat and the word 'we' leads to victory . . . We are a family . . ."

As we get ready to leave his office the major pushes a paper across his desk.

"I Googled you, sir, and printed up this interview. I took art history in college. Would you mind autographing it?"

The page the major printed:

Dad, frozen in another life, another universe, smiling from the world before I died; a world before Mom told him she wanted a divorce, a world before some Hajji shot me, before Dad banged Mom's head on the wall and life turned to shit.

There's a photograph of one of the pictures in the *Sarah by the Window* series. Mom is so beautiful and so pregnant. That picture vaporized in an inferno of jet-fuel. The article is titled, "Who Is Todd Ogden?" *Art in America*: September, 2001.

Doc—our corpsman—was fighting for my life. I'd been bull-shitting with him a little, saying I wouldn't die, that if I did it was because he was killing me. I even called our sergeant an asshole because I could get away with it and because he looked so scared when he checked out my wounds. So I kept bullshitting to pass the time. I really didn't figure I'd die. I only realized I was dead when I swam into Doc's thoughts. As Doc tried to stop the bleeding he was thinking about his girlfriend, remembering the curve of her ass. It made me laugh. He was crying for me and this vision of her just popped into his mind. He meant no disrespect.

I was the first Marine to die in his arms, my blood warm on his hands soaking his flack jacket. I bled out fast. He loved me—for that moment at least—the USMC, his girlfriend and his mother and his father, in that order.

Sometimes Doc swims with me. He was killed the next day. At least I died in combat.

A certain Sergeant Anthony—he always was a turd's turd who should've been dropped from boot camp by TD-10 but wasn't—installed a bolt backward in the flight control linkage. It shimmied loose. The mechanical flight-control quit working in the tail rotor and the body of the Bell 402 started to spin uncontrollably in the opposite direction to the main rotor.

They went down—the pilot, Doc, three Marines and a Hajji interpreter.

Doc spent his last ten seconds wondering if I'd be there waiting or if it would be his grandmother or Jesus or maybe Satan—because of all the fucking around he did on Okinawa with underage whores.

He wasn't afraid, just curious.

He shit his pants nevertheless when they hit the ground. But it wasn't fear. And he'd done his job, not shit the bed like that a-hole who installed the bolt. Anyway everyone craps in the supreme moment, along with every man, woman or child who ever blew out their brains.

29

January 21, 2005, 1330—The major takes Dad on a tour of the Island. First stop: Drill Instructor School—Stan O'Malley First Sergeant, Chief Instructor.

The DI School is next to 4th Battalion where the female DIs train the female recruits. We couldn't look at the females when I was a recruit, no eye fucking, as the DIs called it. The other services train men and women together. Only the USMC has the sense to say no to all that happy horseshit.

O'Malley's face could be on a poster of a WW I Marine; "tough" hardly covers it. He's not tall—wiry—bone, gristle, face with less flesh than most skulls, hard hands, nose broken, head shaved, steel blue eyes. Voice: classic DI buzz saw.

The major introduces Dad as the "father of a Marine." O'Malley asks Dad no questions.

This is the first time the major has mentioned me albeit in an oblique manner.

Dad and the Marines walk around the small spare DI School. Dozens of photographs of Marine Corps Medal of Honor recipients line the white painted cinderblock hallway. The words

"Honor," "Courage," and "Commitment" hang from the hall ceiling on red and yellow boards. Doors lead to cinder block classrooms on either side.

The DIs-in-training are out on the parade deck marching around with their swords learning how to execute sword-drill moves. I enjoy swimming with future DIs as they get their asses kicked!

O'Malley loves his Marines, his three young sons, his mother, the flag of the Untied States of America and his third wife in that order.

O'Malley believes in the mission of the Corps. His faith is pure.

They chose the right man to make the Marines who make Marines.

God says O'Malley is "without guile."

O'Malley keeps the American flag in front of his two bedroom military housing unit lit and changes the floodlight bulb every thirty days in case it might burn out and leave his flag in the dark.

God loves Stan O'Malley First Sergeant, Chief Instructor most of all the people alive on earth.

O'Malley reminds God of King David. At least that's what God says; then again he says a lot. But God claims he loves O'Malley even more than he loved King David. Anyway, that's what God tells us Marines. Maybe he tells the Navy and Army guys something else.

God says that if only King David had gone to Marine boot camp he never would have sent Uriah the Hittite into battle to die so that King David could fuck poor old Uriah's wife. O'Malley would never have done that.

When O'Malley killed men with his sniper's rifle—eighteen confirmed—they felt lucky they had such an honorable executioner. He never gloated or took pleasure in their deaths.

Most of the men O'Malley killed didn't feel a thing—that's the advantage of a clean head shot—except the general weirdness of dying and of course the Hajjis got that sinking feeling all religious fanatics get as soon as it hits them that they've more or less wasted their lives trying to please God and he not only doesn't give a shit but doesn't even like them.

It's a really nasty surprise to wake up and find you're in paradise with a bunch of infidels and they got here without even trying. The born-again Christians get the same sinking feeling. Eternal life turns out to be such a disappointment for true believers.

Sometimes the dead are so bummed they even argue theology with God. A few days ago a newly arrived Southern Baptist preacher was so shocked by God's profanity that he told God that he thought *God* needed to repent and accept the Lord Jesus Christ as his personal savior. "What are you talking about?" God yelled, "I'm an atheist for Christ's sake!"

None of the religious books prepare anybody. My Buddhist books sure didn't. The Bible doesn't. The Koran doesn't. And most art doesn't help either.

And all I ever heard God say about religion specifically was when he called Jerusalem "the stupidest place on earth," and then muttered, "three great mono-theistic religions my ass!"

God said, "Georges Rouault's *Miserere et Guerre* prints show anguish is the only road to salvation." God says Fra Angelico is the only painter who got the afterlife right. The left-hand panel of

Angelico's triptych of the Last Judgment, where he painted the angels and the dead dancing through a field of flowers "for love," on their way to the gates of paradise, is pretty close to the way it is. It's more like that than all this streets of gold crap, only to us the dancing feels like swimming, and there are no gates, though there are Marines all over the place so the "Marine Hymn" about Marines guarding the gates of heaven is more or less accurate.

O'Malley didn't brood over killing people any more than God does. Like God, there is no part of O'Malley's brain that harbored self-doubt when he killed. He believes in the greatness of America and that enemies of the USA are the enemies of God.

"Of course I don't give a shit about America but O'Malley's brain radiates a clear light," God said.

O'Malley has it wrong about the enemies of America being the enemies of God. To have enemies you need to have friends. And what O'Malley and almost everyone else just do not understand is that God has no friends, and therefore no enemies.

God doesn't give a rat's ass one way or another, at least not about the things that people think are a big deal, destiny, the rise and fall of nations and all. To God countries, nations, peoples and tribes come and go, are no more important than leaves swirling on a driveway. He does have likes and dislikes, though, but it's nothing to do with any rules. With God it's all personal. Take Gauguin. God is very angry about how he treated Van Gogh. He says Gauguin "drove Van Gogh to suicide" and he says Gauguin is overrated. "Muddy" is how God describes his paintings.

You'd think that the usual suspects and evil doers would top God's shit list, Hitler, Genghis Khan, Mao, Stalin, Lenin,

Napoleon, Caligula, bin Laden, whomever. But God tends to make excuses for them. He likes drama and big things happening "keeping it interesting" as he says.

God says: "A million martyr's voices rising up crying 'Lord Have Mercy!' Talk about an off-stage chorus giving me chills!"

All he'll say about Jesus—usually in a southern DI sandpaper drawl he likes to imitate—is: "I'll tell you what; it was FUBAR to send him to the Middle East! We should've waited and sent him to Finland, maybe Denmark. They're reasonable people." Other times he'll say, "'Second Coming' my ass, not after how it went down the first time around. *You* try and talk him into it!"

God's favorite composers are Vivaldi, Bach, Verdi, Duke Ellington and some ninth-century Hindu I never heard of.

God's favorite movie director is Bob Altman. He quotes him all the time. "I don't direct, I watch," God says whenever I ask if he's really in charge. God says, "Bob and I see it the same way. Like he says, you can pick the best six things in anything I made and none of them were planned. It's the mistakes I'm interested in. That's where you hit the truth button. What I really want to see from an actor is something I've never seen before."

And so it goes. He rants and raves but really doesn't do much more than occasionally strike down people who bother him by talking or rustling candy wrappers in operas, concerts and plays.

The list of the people he doesn't like is just too long to go into.

30

D ad, the major, and O'Malley sit in a conference room at an oval table that seats twelve—O'Malley is across from Dad.

O'Malley is about to speak and many Marines swim into the room. O'Malley is our favorite. We like to hear him talk. And we often swim over him out on the parade deck when he's teaching Marines how to teach drill to future recruits. He pulls a huge crowd, sometimes it seems as if just about every dead Marine is there.

And it doesn't hurt any that God likes to hang around him too, sort of classes up the parade deck. It's kind of funny when you think about all those pilgrims going to all those so-called holy places all over the world when the only places on earth God seems to like to hang out (besides Mount Athos in Greece with those Orthodox monks) are Parris Island and MCRD San Diego.

We come to the position of attention when O'Malley speaks, or at least to our bodiless version of it.

"That was the motivation for me," O'Malley is saying to Dad, "I was an infantryman and sniper. I came back here to relearn what I forgot. The DIs train the recruits the same way they were trained. They want to leave their mark. You can tell who a recruit's DI is. Great Marines had great DIs. I came through when I was seventeen. My DIs never wasted any minute. I had no intention of staying in. But I never forget my SDI's name. What's the most important job in the Corps? It's to train Marines! Who does that? We the enlisted men! You don't see officers marching with recruits. It's the working man runs the show. That's why the tradition stays. The DI-school Marines' heart carries them further.

" 'Aye, First Sergeant!' that's what I hear all day at DI School, shouted by men some of them older than me that's been in the Corps maybe ten, maybe fifteen years. But they all got one thing in common, they want to be DIs.

"To get them back into that discipline they had when they were fresh, they have to humble themselves. They get broken down again. Weeks six and seven see a difference; they go back to being Marines again, as a team again. To set an example's the key to being a leader. To set an example, is why we're so hard on them. Setting an example is the key to being a Marine and it's the key to teaching old Marines how to be DIs."

"Oorah!" yells God.

O'Malley continues.

"In the Army training stops for Christmas. What example does *that* set? It says there are more important things than being a warrior. Not here! We train three hundred and sixty-five days a year. Where is a Marine DI on Christmas morning? I'll tell you what; he's on the quarterdeck at 0400 getting eighty recruits on line. He's on their case and in their face and if they're lucky he'll give them an extra thirty seconds in chow to eat a bite of turkey.

That's it. He'll pit the whole friggin' platoon on Christmas Day if they need it.

"If the Marine next to me shits the bed then we both go down, sir. My wife says, 'When will I get to know you? I know your sergeant knows you.' But what keeps us going is that we have to be perfect every day. We have to be perfect in front of the recruits. You just can't let your Marines down. You just can't do that."

"*Oorah!*" we shout.

"*Good to go!*" God roars.

31

The day after I was KIA Mom packed a box of candy, books (mostly P. G. Wodehouse), baby wipes, and hand cleanser to send me. She wouldn't learn I was dead for another day. I was swimming in her. The moment I was dead I went back to my mother. We all do, at least for a few moments. She asked the lady at the Newburyport Post Office if they were getting a lot of boxes sent to APO addresses to Iraq.

The lady shook her head no and said, "Are you kidding?"

• • •

The day Mom took me to lunch she lied for Dad.

"He says he's proud of you, he says he's sorry he didn't come to the graduation," Mom said.

"Where is he now?" I asked.

"In the studio."

Mom was still crying when she walked into the studio and told Dad how I walked out on her when she suggested I try and get out of the Marine Corps.

The whole scene was playing and replaying in Mom's brain. It was one of the first thoughts I swam into and I heard and saw it all.

"Call your son! He is going over there! Do something!" Mom yelled at Dad.

"He couldn't be. They don't send people that fast," Dad answered.

"Call him!"

"No! I will not be emotionally blackmailed! He owes us an apology. When he admits his mistake we'll talk."

"Todd you're a fool."

"Get out of my studio! Get out now!"

"You fucking prick! You asshole!"

"If you say another fucking word I'll ram this easel down your throat!"

"Do it! I dare you! Do it!"

Dad backed down but he wanted to hit her. Eleven months later he did.

• • •

While Dad smashed Mom's head on the wall she felt nothing. She would've picked up the carving knife and plunged it between his shoulder blades if it wasn't for Amanda. The knife was on the countertop, soft French carbon steel, the kind you can really sharpen.

Mom didn't want to destroy Amanda's life. Losing her son was enough. That's why Mom didn't stab Dad. She figured Amanda deserved a chance to get on with her life.

I was proud of Mom.

Mom wasn't thinking complete thoughts. Emotion was eclipsing the conversations within her brain.

Mom was thinking:

I'll divorce the prick and watch my lifetime investment in this asshole swirl in the toilet bowl and disappear along with my best years . . .

I'll go back to HLS and finish what I started before the madness of Todd infected me . . .

I'll finish what I started though I loathe them all . . .

Jack!

32

Jessica is talking to our baby. He smiles and reaches for her face when she bends close. I think that for a four-and-a-half-month-old Jack seems really alert. I swim in him a lot and I'm not sure what he should be thinking by now, but he seems very intelligent or at least zeroes in on stuff, colors, Jessica's face, the feel of poop in his diapers, hunger, milky satisfaction, music, whatever, very keenly. I'm pretty damned proud of my son. I asked God and he said he's normal so not to worry.

" 'Normal,' above average? Normal how?" I asked.

"Relax! He's no dumber than you were. Okay?" God said.

Jessica loves our baby, me, her Mom and Dad in that order. Jessica doesn't believe in God but is mad at him anyway.

Swimming in Jessica and our baby reminds me of those times as a child when I'd be falling asleep in the living room, hovering just on the edge of consciousness, and hearing beloved voices as if from a great distance. It was so comforting to be there, about to drift to sleep and yet surrounded by those who love you. It was so much better than going to sleep alone. I'd want to stay downstairs when Dad would come over to pick me up and take me to my room.

Jessica talks to me. This was what she was saying while breast-feeding our baby at the same time Dad was with O'Malley:

"Jack, you wouldn't believe how stacked I got when the milk first came in! You would've loved my boobs those days, except maybe the milk leaking would've freaked you out. You can get a pump and pump out and the hospital buys it. I do this every couple of days because I'm pretty well broke. Sometimes I still have big wet patches on my Marines T-shirt. And it really shows! Red's a bad color to wear when you're leaking milk! You know what's strange is that we learned all that shit in school in so-called health class about sex and condoms, but nobody ever taught us about *having* babies. They teach you about how to *not* get pregnant but not how nice it is to feed a baby. And they never told me my breasts would be so full I'd leak. And they didn't say anything about how when you feed your baby it feels sexual.

"I lay awake and terrible pictures invade my brain. Then I try and remember you standing naked in front of Mom's chair. And the horrible pictures of your body are chased out. You stand there naked and alive and smiling. That picture is stronger. And it's a great thing to have locked in my brain. It's the only image that's powerful enough to chase the other ones away when they get really bad and especially when they wake me up, and I'm already crying.

"In my dreams I try so hard to let you know that even though I can't help you I still hope my voice was the last thing you heard so I keep trying to say, 'I love you!' as the blood comes out and you look at me.

"When I wake up that's when you stand there naked, and I look at your wide shoulders, and you turn around. And from the back your shoulders are even wider looking, and your neck has such strong muscles. Then your face leans over me smiling and you say, 'Take a good look, because you'll need to remember this while I'm gone!' And you meant gone for the three months to Parris Island. But it turned out it was forever."

"Is she great or what?" God says.

The right to privacy is *not* something God respects!

"If you like her so much then why did you let me get killed?" I ask.

"Everyone dies," God answers.

"Not when they're nineteen!"

"What's a few years give or take?"

"You know what I mean."

"You saved your son. She was going to kill him."

"So does that make me Jesus?"

"Whatever you say, Pfc. Ogden."

33

Amanda went to Harlem tonight to listen to the old guys play jazz. My sister was commemorating the anniversary of my death.

She was looking for Odell Williams. Odell is one of the old jazz guys Amanda met at Smoke, a jazz club four blocks from her apartment.

Before I died she went there sometimes, and talked to the barmaid-Columbia-sociology-grad who presides over a loyal group of regulars. Sometimes Amanda stuck around for the first set.

When Amanda met Odell he said he was an Army vet. This was back when I was still in boot camp. Amanda noticed the Korean War veteran pin he wore and mentioned me. Odell—a big man with a friendly fleshy craggy face—told my sister that he organized a jam session every Sunday at American Legion post in Harlem.

On any given Sunday evening he said he'd be there and to "come on up."

Standing room only, about eighty people packed into a space the size of an average living room. Odell was playing his Hammond B-3 organ and launched into his signature tune—"Harlem

Shuffle," feet flying on the pedals pounding out the chest-thumping base notes while his big hands caressed the tune out of the battered instrument.

Wall-to-wall handsome black women, most middle aged, some older, a few younger, tricked out in fur coats and fancy hats, a few nerdy white kids from Columbia in jeans, and lots of old black guys wearing American Legion baseball caps, three-piece suits and silk ties, a few wearing time-warp fedoras.

The place was hopping. God likes jazz so he swam with me for a few minutes. He even played the drums using a French exchange student who was jamming for a set.

After the set Odell walked Amanda's way hugging and greeting everyone. Then it was Amanda's turn.

"Hey! Where you been, baby? How's your brother?"

"He got killed," Amanda said and started to cry.

"Oh baby, baby that's such a shame! Oh sister!"

Odell folded her in his arms.

Odell turned to a Sax player who looked as if he was about ninety.

"Her brother was killed over there!" Odell shouted.

One of the old black guys in a Legion baseball cap stepped over and asked if Amanda was okay. Odell explained.

The old guy was the commander of the post. He took the mike off the stand.

"Hush, I said HUSH!" he said in a deep voice. "We have some real sad news."

Almost everyone got quiet; people talking at the bar were told to shut up by some of the guys up front.

"We have a sister with us tonight who lost her brother in Iraq. He was a Marine. For God and country, sister, for God and country! Bless you!"

"Semper Fi!" an old Marine shouted.

The white kids looked everywhere but at Amanda. They were there for the jazz and till that moment didn't even know they were in an American Legion post. They didn't know what the American Legion is.

Odell kicked into "Misty" and a couple of the old guys bought Amanda drinks. The drummer snapped into high gear, kids lined up to jam. The love jar was passed and Amanda dropped in a ten on a heap of crumpled ones. And somebody's hand was on Amanda's shoulder or somebody's arm was around her till later when she caught a cab home. She didn't feel better but as close to peaceful as she had been for a long time.

34

Dad's at weapons and field training range shed. Eighty-two recruits are being trained with the M-16. Familiar phrases deadened by the heavy humid air drift out of the three-sided open shed. For January it's hot. The sweating recruits sit on benches and watch their instructor at the blackboard.

Eighty-two recruits praying they don't fail the rifle test.

Eighty-two recruits who know it comes down to this.

The instructor has one recruit at the front with him demonstrating how to hold the M-16.

The recruit loves his mother, his Ford Mustang, that he'll fix up someday, and his girlfriend in that order.

The instructor loves his dog, his girlfriend, his dad, and teaching shooting in that order.

"Any bone support? Using muscle only, what's happening?" asks the instructor.

"Sir, he's shaking sir!" shout the recruits in unison.

The instructor adjusts the rifle and places the recruit's hands on it correctly.

"See how he's holding the weapon now?"

"Yes, sir!"

"See why it's so important we keep on bone support?"

"Yes, sir!

Recruits shooting five hundred yards lying in a row in front of the tower—the mobile white hut observation and command post, about the size of a small garden shed on wheels and two stories off the ground, sits on stilts and has steps to the back door. Instructions are bellowed over a fuzzy loudspeaker. The range stretches into the hazy distance to the grassy slopes of the berm that holds the targets. The targets pop up from behind this mound and look so far away Dad can't figure how anyone could ever hit them. In a concrete slit trench inside the berm sweating dead-tired recruits are "pulling pits," in other words hauling the targets up and down so they pop up to be shot at then get pulled down to have the hits marked.

For every two recruits shooting there's a coach. Supervising is the range instructor in the tower. He sees the major and Dad walking over and steps out of the tower. He salutes the major and introduces himself—Master Sergeant Timothy Nugent—to Dad.

The master sergeant loves his wife, his daughter, the Marines, and beer in that order.

Figuring that Dad's a journalist he begins to spout facts without being asked:

"On the range is the first time in the training cycle they're challenged to do something alone. Instant feedback—target goes down and you put a spotter on it or not."

Behind Dad recruits are being punished in a sand pit. The major tells Dad that the recruits probably fell asleep during one of the classes on using the rifle.

I used to doze through that endless bone support lecturing, too. Shots crack.

I swim over the line watching recruits squeezing off shots. Intensity and concentration is complete.

Dad asks the major about the crossed rifle medal he's wearing and what it means.

"I qualified 'expert' with the rifle. I'm forty-three, a major and about to retire and I'm still proud of this damn thing!" says the major with a laugh.

For a moment he feels like a Marine again.

"We have to re-qual and I'm always relieved that I get the 'expert' score. I'd get all sorts of shit if I came back to my office with a pizza box, that's what we call the lower shooting qual medal."

Dad doesn't tell the major that he noticed his expert medal because it is the same as the one I had on my chest in my coffin.

Dad feels a welling of pride and despair.

He's thinking how he'll never be able to tell me that he is so proud of how well I shot.

Dad walks away from the major. He doesn't want him to see his tears. So Dad pretends he wants a closer look at the observation and command post.

"Jack, I had no idea how far five hundred yards is," Dad whispers.

"Help him, Lord," I say. "His heart's broken."

"Tough shit!"

God can be such a hard-ass.

35

0230 Room 17 Osprey Inn—the major said Dad will be up all night at the receiving center watching new recruits arrive. Dad tries to take a nap and can't. He can only think about what happened the day after he abused Mom.

Dad hid in the studio after the big fight. Next morning he took Mom to the hospital.

Mom wasn't really badly hurt, not in her body. But she was feeling diminished, so small and abject, as if she was shrinking down to nothing.

I asked God to do something to help her and he only laughed and said: "Let the chips fall where they may."

"You're no help!" I said.

I only get short answers and most of the time he doesn't seem to care about what he calls the "minor annoying shit." To give you an idea, these "minor annoyances" God refuses to do anything about include sick and dying children and old people begging for forgiveness.

God takes what he calls the "long view." Anyway that's his excuse.

"It all has a happy ending," says God. "Not 'happy' the way you Americans think of it, rather happy the way Shakespeare understands things, dramatically satisfying if somewhat dark."

Hopeless!

Does anyone know or care that a wannabe theatre director is in charge of the universe?

• • •

When they got back from Mass General, Mom went into the house without speaking to Dad.

Dad crept out to the studio.

About an hour later he came in to take a shower in the guestroom bathroom because the water heater in the studio was broken.

After big fights Dad always slept in the studio, sometimes for several days. Mom and Dad used to ignore each other till they made love. There was a pattern: the move to the studio then the reconciliation, then the fabulous sex—a nice ritual. Mom once called their fights "foreplay."

But those battles were only verbal. I know all the juicy details because they both replay their memories incessantly. He slapped her once when they were young. That picture is constantly popping up in Dad's brain. I can't help swimming in my parents' sexual history too. Sex and fighting is really a huge deal to them.

Dad's shower was interrupted.

Mom stormed in screaming, not words, just shrieks. She had been in the shower too so she was dripping and naked. She knew

Dad was back in the house because when the downstairs shower is used the water pressure on the third floor drops to a trickle.

She took a detour through the kitchen and was clutching a butcher knife. When she burst in Dad jumped out of the shower without turning it off.

"GET OUT!" Mom screamed. "Look at the bruises on my shoulders where you grabbed me! LOOK!"

She hadn't noticed the huge bruises till after stepping out of the shower moments before. There were large handprints of discolored flesh where had Dad gripped her shoulders to slam her against the wall.

Dad didn't know he was gripping her that tight. He got faint at the sight of the bruises. He would have gladly killed himself to be forgiven. In fact he was thinking about grabbing away the knife and plunging it into his chest.

As Dad backed out of the guest bathroom he was thinking that he should draw Mom like that. It was his first thought about making art since I died—streaming water, hair plastered to her breasts, wielding a knife. Dad stumbled to the stairs and fell down them backward. He wasn't hurt.

She walked down to him—knife held in front of her like Lady Macbeth making an entrance and stood, legs apart, over Dad as she screamed, "GET OUT!"

Water dripped off her pubic hair onto Dad's face while she bent over him waving the knife.

There was a faint white puckered scar on the left-side fold of her outer labia visible through the pubic hair. They stitched her. I was a big baby.

It was the first time Dad felt sexually aroused since he learned I was killed. He saw the scar and suddenly I was swimming through images of my birth that flooded Dad's brain: Mom splayed, pushing, screaming, the flash of the scissors as the doctor made a cut, more blood, the top of my head, bloody and wrinkled, Mom stretched wide, the sudden slither of water, a wet head, shoulders, legs, a baby, a cord, and there I was.

I wanted to see more but the image flickered, got confused and petered out into some sort of haze where all I saw was a half-remembered pretty nurse, then a snippet of a gallery opening, then a church basement in Maine, then me lying in Dad's arms a few hours after my birth, then nothing.

With memory there are these big gray patches that roll in just as it gets interesting. It's shocking what everyone forgets. You don't realize how pathetic your brain is, and how much is missing till you die. Then every memory gets literal, perfect, sharp as the view of the ocean after it rains. This happens because you suddenly have access to God where everything is stored exactly as it is, was and will be.

It's scary! Who wants to remember *everything*?

Speaking of memories, I asked God if there was going to be a judgment.

"Yes and no, but not the way you mean," he said. "Why bother when everyone recalls every moment of their lives, every thought, every breath and will for eternity?"

Before I could ask he answered my next question.

"There is no heaven, or hell," God said, "just now, but as you've discovered now isn't so bad, unless you have too many regrets, so maybe it's heaven after all, for you anyway."

I asked him what *that* meant.

"You were in boot camp. How did you feel on the first day compared to the last? Give it a million years or so. You learn only what you need to know on any given training day. We'll break you down shotgun style then build you back up. Boot camp, life, death, it's all the same, but you're going to learn! And that goes for everyone!"

"Learn what?" I ask.

"To know yourself, schmuck!"

There is no way to change anything. Even God won't mess with memory. "No one fucks with my hard drive," is the way he put it. Actions and thoughts are no longer filtered through self-justifying ideology, prejudice, religion, or self-protective lies or self-pity. So the crazy shit and the angry shit and the misinformed shit and even sincere but wrong shit is clear. And since you're in the river not only do you remember *everything*, eventually *everyone* swims in *your* memories. And so they learn what an asshole you were and probably still are. And you swim in *everyone's* memories too so you know how every action of yours affected everyone you ever met and how their actions shaped other lives. A ringside seat till the end of time was not what I expected, though that's not right either, because there doesn't seem to be any end in sight.

Jean-Jacques Rousseau, Mohammad, Luther and Marx are some of the sorriest souls. They've been swimming in millions of people's minds who got massacred, burned at the stake, beheaded, stoned to death, gassed or shot and who come roaring into the river to ask them what the *fuck* they had in mind.

"Hell" is watching all the unintended consequences of your

best intentions unfold forever. "Heaven" is realizing that you have eternity to try and understand what happened. Reality is what is still there when all your ideas about what *should* be there fade away. Most days you're just going chow to chow.

I complained to God about having to remember everything forever and all he said was; "Tough shit! Now you know what it's like for me!"

• • •

Dad was driven out of our house stark naked, balls flopping from side, the knife pricking his back. Mom: a bird swooping at a cat, driving the marauder from her nest. She chased Dad through the kitchen door, locked it after him. He was huddled on the back lawn when Mom appeared on the wrought-iron bedroom balcony three floors above him. She towered naked and terrible hurling curses and his belongings.

Mom was beautiful, her hair backlit by late-morning golden winter sun, wisps beginning to dry enough to fan out behind her in the breeze à la *Birth of Venus*, her torso thrust over the wrought iron rail, her waist sharply defined against the red brick—large breasts hanging down as she leant far out to take aim at Dad, nipples wide and pink, "so changed" Dad thought, "from the little rosebuds I first touched but no less lovely."

Looking at my naked mother and hearing Dad's sexual thoughts isn't as sick as it sounds.

I'm *dead* and have no cock!

I miss my cock!

I ask God about the resurrection of the body.

"Will it happen?"

"You just wanna get laid!"

"Sure, and what's wrong with that?"

"Sex leads to trouble."

"And all the good things."

"Maybe, but it's more trouble than good."

"Are you saying you fucked up when you created fucking?"

"*Virgin birth* ring a bell?"

"Who gave us dicks?"

Nothing.

God is good at clamming up when it suits him.

"Who invented sex?"

He won't say a word.

"I thought so! You won't take responsibility for your actions!"

A silent God in a silent universe when it suits him, though he once admitted he *could* resurrect our bodies any time he wants. But he won't say if he ever will.

• • •

Dress-shirts floated gracefully in their gossamer plastic cleaner bags; shoes and toiletries pelted Dad—

"Pig," hissed Mom.

"Sarah, please I'm *so sorry*!"

"All I hear is grunting!"

"I admit everything. '*In the greatness of his folly he shall go astray!*' "

"And shut the *fuck* up with your goddamned bible verses! I'm sick of the sound of your voice! You tried to kill me!"

"*Please*! This is all because of Jack's death. You know I never would have hurt you!"

"*No!*"

Fistfuls of family pictures glided toward the river on the breeze. A Great Blue heron squawked and flapped away on huge gray wings over the marsh. Dad and Mom were both freezing but didn't seem to notice.

It was at that moment I realized that this was my fault.

I'm not sorry I joined the Marines or even that I was killed. I *am* sorry for the way I left home.

Dad did the best he could, so did Mom, and I repaid them by feeling morally superior, by storming out, by knowing my father so well that pushing his buttons was as easy as making a three-year-old cry. I've been a self-righteous prick.

36

2150 Receiving Center—a spare low red brick building. The new recruits are so young—stand trembling in the dark, feet placed carefully on the rows of yellow footprints. They look as if they're twelve years old. Did I look this pitiful?

They're awake after bedtime.

Children just a few years younger are having stories read out loud to them while these new recruits are screaming, "Yes, ma'am!" "Yes, sir!"

Young Americans are asleep or watching TV or having sex in their college dorms. The new arrivals will be awake for the next seventy hours. They won't think about sex or TV for the next three months. They will be purged of the passions of the flesh.

As each busload arrives what God calls "the liturgical ritual" unfolds. A DI tears into them, hustles them onto the yellow footprints in tight rows.

Dad is thinking:

Which footprints did Jack stand on?

What was he thinking about?

Did Jack feel as frightened as these recruits look?

Did Jack know that someday I'd wait in darkness so I can slowly walk along and look at every single set of footprints to be sure that this faithless father sees the actual footprints my beloved son stood on?

Does Jack know I'm saying, "I love you Jack" over each footprint?

He does.

"Give him a break," I pray. "It was my fault. I'm sorry."

"No!" says God. "They're willing to die for strangers. What did your father ever do for anyone?"

37

aby Jack is on his changing table. Jessica is talking to us. My son is so beautiful. I wish I could hold him. His favorite moment is when he can grab some part of Jessica's face, a nose, lip, ear, cheek. He gets so excited and kicks furiously. He smiles as soon as he focuses on her face. I wish I could just once see him catch sight of me.

I'd cry if I had eyes.

Even though Jessica is complaining she keeps her voice cheerful, though the words are sad. He doesn't understand. All he hears is her sing-song, talking-to-the-baby tone. He's smiling.

"Being a single, young mother, living with your parents is anything but easy, and it doesn't matter how much you love your child. You're sore, tired, sleep deprived; none of your friends are going to understand what you're doing. Your parents are going to be just as tired as you, sad for you, angry with you; trying to help and pissed off as hell they can't take vacations, and generally going crazy while trying to be supportive.

"Fuck!

"But you make it better too because you can't be put on a shelf so I can't curl up in a ball and quit.

"Your good grandmother gave you a mobile that had pictures of pink and blue bunnies and puppies and crap like that. Well, I got a copy of *Leatherneck* and went through and cut out pictures of Marines and glued them on the blocks. I glued copies of your daddy's Parris Island portrait on the blocks too. So when you lie on your back and look up what you see is lots of Marines and your daddy floating over you slowly spinning in the air.

"Jack, I still listen to your favorite CDs, and I hope *Kind of Blue* is good for baby development, because your son is being raised on it.

"Mom says your jazz is fine for him. I told her that when he grows up, he'll say, 'Green as a Marine's uniform' instead of 'green as grass' because of all the pictures of Marines I have all over the crib.

"I'm kissing Baby Jack for you so you can taste his sweet skin. I love you. I AM SO TIRED! I wish you were here to help me!"

"Help her Lord!"

"No! I like her, I really do but lots of mothers cry."

38

January 22, 2005, 0930—The gas chamber is a concrete shed about the size of a three-car garage. It stands in a field next to a forest of oaks and pines. Recruits learn to face CS gas and not panic as they take off their masks, choke, and sob, burn, clear their masks and put them back on.

Recruits wait in the sun standing at attention in rows platoon by platoon. It's more like an August day than winter. There are three male and one female platoon getting ready to go through. DIs shout commands—male platoons answer—a thunderous choir. The female platoon also sounds off—a higher pitch but no less thunderous a piercing siren call to break your heart.

Little girls putting on gas masks, some are smaller than Amanda was when she was fifteen. They're only thirteen days into training raw and green. They remind Dad of Amanda's high school friends—girls headed for art school, intelligent, sensitive faces, pretty, feminine—lovely even in cammies, even with tears on their cheeks, even screaming "Yes, Ma'am" to their female DIs till the veins stand out on their graceful necks as they spray spit into the hot air, even sweating till the fronts of their cammies cling.

Dad's nose burns from a whiff of tear gas that floats out of the gas chamber when the door opens.

Dad is thinking:

I'm one hundred feet away and the gas is choking me. I wonder what the men who must have ogled these girls a few weeks ago would think of these warriors-in-training as they file into a gas chamber.

The male platoons are getting ready.

Dad's chest burns.

The DI's are herding the recruits into the chamber screaming:

"You will live!"

"You will survive!"

"I will not let you die!"

The recruits file into the chamber at a trot. Five to ten long minutes later they stagger out blinded and each must grasp the shoulder of the recruit in front of him or her or fall.

They're led to a vat of water that they dunk their masks into to cleanse.

They puke, cough, cry as mucus pours from their noses and mouths.

They are led to nearby bleachers.

The recruits waiting to go into the gas chamber look on terrified at the screaming, groaning, blinded recruits emerging from the smoke-belching dark door of the chamber.

The bleachers are under two huge old live oaks. Spanish moss hangs from thick gnarled limbs above the dazed platoons as they pack the tiers of aluminum benches feeling their way along with trembling hands. Snot pours as they shout, "Morning, sir!" or,

"Morning, gentlemen!"—Good manners under extreme duress—as they pass the DIs and my dad.

One recruit is so confused she screams, "Good morning, sir!" to the trunk of an oak. Her DI, Sergeant Mary Ortiz, smiles then quickly puts her game face back on and begins to curse her recruits.

Mary Ortiz loves her recruits, the Marine Corps, and her mother in that order. She's from the Dominican Republic, moved to New Jersey at the age of fifteen, and was an electrician before she joined the Corps.

She is saying:

"You're putting your whole squad in jeopardy. You know that?"

"Aye, ma'am!" screams the tree-greeting female who struggles to get to the bleachers while puking.

"Any day, squad leader! You gonna be last again?"

"No, ma'am!"

"That was absolutely hideous!" screams Sergeant Mary Ortiz, while thinking; she's the best recruit I've ever trained . . . Just to know I made some kind of change to make a better qualified Marine . . . the females want to be taken care of where I come from. But you gotta stand on your own two friggin' legs if you want to survive! They need to be better Marines and not need anybody. I need to set the example."

An unconscious convulsing heat casualty is carried off on a stretcher. He's stripped naked and a sheet soaked in ice water thrown over him with ice dumped on top. Two DIs grab a stretcher and race through the crowd of recruits.

I swim into the heat casualty, say a prayer for him and swim out. He'll be okay. He's already regaining consciousness.

39

My sister wrote this in her diary at the very moment Dad was watching the recruits at the gas chamber:

We of Letters are pretty much isolated, except for afternoon visits from the art department. They send ambassadors up from ninth floor with the little graphic we run on our page. Jason is trying to be kind, trying to get me out of myself.

The only time I've ever seen our publisher—God—was today when Jason brought me along to the fourteenth floor executive boardroom—wood paneled, with pictures all over the wall signed by presidents, even one of Churchill.

Jason figured a visit to the boardroom might cheer me up. There was some meeting with visiting Democratic Party leaders who were to be interviewed. I started crying when I saw Churchill's portrait. It happened to be the same picture Jack had in his room. He kept it next to his Buddha. Jason saw the tears and stepped in front of me to shield me from curious eyes.

40

Mom is thinking:

I'm going through the motions of the abused wife who is taking charge of her situation.

One foot in front of the other—I eat, I breathe, I call Amanda, but nothing feels immediate.

I feel like a piece of paper from which a story is being erased.

My to-do list:

Get dressed

Remember to shower

Eat

Sleep

Call my lawyer

Divorce Todd

Call HLS to ask about registering again after a thirty-year hiatus

Call Amanda

I'm looking up at my invisible life through a thick layer of dirty water.

When he banged my head, I was saying to myself: *Oh so now*

he's snapped. I wonder if he'll kill me? But it was nothing personal. I might as well have been observing a fly struggling on its back in the jam while idly wondering if I should throw the toast away.

I guess this is how it ends. How strange he beat me because of just another argument. What if he knew about Rubin? It makes me laugh—Todd beat me for no reason when he had a real reason he'll never know.

"Why did you create humans?" I ask God.

"The Brooklyn Botanic Garden."

"That's it?!"

"And I like William Wegman's large-format Polaroids of his dogs."

41

January 23, 2005, 0330 Hotel Company Platoon 2098, Third Recruit Training Battalion with SDI Staff Sergeant Baker.

The major tells Dad, "This is the seventh cycle Baker's taken through as an SDI. I arranged for you to go lights-to-lights with him because he's so experienced. This platoon is early in the training cycle, so you'll be able to see the change when you watch another platoon later in their cycle."

The major leaves. His parting instruction: "Don't ever get between the platoon and their DIs. Never stand or walk between them. Think of the platoon as a baby tiger and the DI as the mother tiger and you'll be fine."

"Why?" Dad asks.

"No one gets between a platoon and their DI. Even a general wouldn't. That's just how it is."

SDI Staff Sergeant Baker walks into the DI House from the exterior landing. Baker is thirty-three, shaved bald and six one with barn-door wide shoulders, intense blue eyes, an ironic expression, and a jutting jaw. He loves his recruits, his junior DIs, his daughter, his wife, winning platoon achievement awards, and hunting deer with a bow in that order. He shakes hands with Dad and rattles off the basic schedule for the day in a low rasp:

"We're on TD fourteen, lights 0500. Except today, today is linen so it's lights at 0400. Chow, 0600, PT, clean house, MCMAP—Marine Corps Martial Arts Program—afternoon chow, drill, haircuts, 2030 lights out."

Dad glances out the door of the DI house into the squad bay.

"Go ahead," says Baker, "take a walk around before the recruits wake up. Lights aren't for another half an hour."

The farther Dad walks into the squad bay the darker it gets.

Musty sweat and dirty-laundry smell—air is warm.

Dad is thinking:

When Jack was little he didn't like sleeping alone. Sometimes he crawled into our bed. Other times he only made it to our bed-room door and I'd find him huddled asleep at the foot of our door when I got up to paint. I'd pick him up and lay him next to Sarah. I'd have a hard time leaving. I wanted to stay and watch Jack curled next to his mother. They were lovely in the dawn's light. Jack was cold. The feet of his pajamas were always worn through and his toes were like little blocks of ice. Sometimes I'd smell his diaper was past the point of no return and change him then tuck him into bed with Sarah. It always amazed me how one little diaper could reek like all the toilets in Paris . . .

Dad studies a sleeping recruit and is overwhelmed by the desire to kneel.

He does.

The sleeping recruit—a tall white farm boy from Vermont—doesn't feel my father's arm laid over his back. He doesn't feel tears soaking into the plain wool blanket. He doesn't know that at that very moment his mother is awake and praying for him.

Dad closes his eyes—

"Lord Jesus, please have it be Jack!"

Dad opens his eyes.

No miracle today.

God is laughing.

Dad gets to his feet.

The next rack has a short black recruit from Detroit stretched on top of the cover in the lower bunk. Dad bends over him and listens to his steady breathing. A recruit on fire watch shouts out the time and pounds on the designated spot on the DI house wall next to the door. Dad stands, then walks out of the squad bay to the quarterdeck. The recruit is still pounding. He has a question for his SDI. SDI Baker ignores the recruit. And moments later Baker enters the squad bay after kicking the DI house door open with a loud bang.

"*What are we doing*!" Baker screams at the recruit pounding on the wall.

"This recruit is . . ."

"LIGHTS!" screams Baker.

Lights on—

Bedlam!

Dad backs into the far corner of the quarterdeck next to the head door and watches the chaos. Recruits wearing boxers, and T-shirts leaping to get online—screaming "Aye, sir!" in response to a barrage of bellowed instructions. Recruits pull on cammie uniforms in less than one minute.

"Linen!" screams Baker.

Everything must be done just so—fold sheets just so—

Dad has no idea how the recruits understand the rapid-fire screamed instructions—

Racks stripped—

SDI Baker counts down—Sends the recruits into a panic by skipping numbers: "Thirty, twenty-nine, twenty-eight, twenty-seven, twelve, eleven, ten, nine, eight, four, three, two, *one*! Fold sheets! Pillowcase! *Put it down*!"

"Aye, sir!"

"*Pick it up*!"

"Aye, sir!"

"*Put it down*!"

"Aye, sir!"

"*Pick it up*!"

"Aye, sir!"

Recruits back on line—bed linen folded and held in front of them in trembling hands. There is a correct way to fold dirty linen; a Marine way and wrong way. SDI Baker sends them back to do it again.

Baker is never silent—screaming instructions with every breath—perpetually furious with his recruit's many failings. Recruits flinch in unison at every command—linked by some invisible force—

Where do sheets go?

Where do the pillowcases go?

Recruits desperately urge each other on.

"Let's go! Let's go pillowcases!"

0416—Lined up outside the barracks in the dark—

Baker paces in front of the platoon. Dad is careful to stand off to one side, not get between the SDI and his recruits. The terror is infectious.

0417—Marching to chow.

0420—Baker calling cadence—marching—Dad is shedding tears in the dark. He had no idea cadence is so beautiful—ringing out from many platoons in the deep stillness before dawn. The DI calls out the line and is answered by the recruits.

SDI Baker: "Everywhere we go-HO!"
Recruits: *"Everywhere we go-HO!"*
"People wanna know-HO!"
"People wanna know-HO!"
"Who we a-ARE!"
"Who we a-ARE!"
"So we tell them"
"So we tell them"
"United States Marine Corps!"
"United States Marine Corps!"
"One! Two! Three! FOUR!"
"One! Two! Three! FOUR!"
"United States Marine CORPS!"
"United States Marine CORPS!"

Dad is thinking:

Jack's voice joined to so many!

0421—They stop to practice drill on the way to chow—

"You're right next to the sand pit!"

"Aye, sir!"

"Do you want to play in the sand?"

"No, sir!"

"Then smack your heels down!"

"Aye, sir!"

"Squeeze those elbows!"

"Tight! Tight! Tight!" answer the recruits in a high-pitched scream.

Dad is thinking:

I've been asleep my whole life.

42

Subj: How am I?

Date: 1/23/2005 7:53:51 AM Eastern Standard Time

From: SarahRutherford@aol.com

To: AmandaOgden@NYTimes.com

Jack died a year ago today. I'm glad Todd smashed my head. For one golden moment I felt alive again. He gave me a mission: get rid of Todd, divorce Todd, punish Todd, hate Todd!

I try to bring one happy memory to mind, test it against the present, and see if it's powerful enough to burn brightly. I try and remember any day when I felt anything but grief. I can't. Todd is violent guilt. And you are just smoke blown away by the hurricane of Jack's killing.

There is a "yes but" that eviscerates meaning. "How are things with your job?" Yes but does it really matter? We live in a world where a mother holds a folded flag with the hands that held a son.

I feel better with Todd away. I'm so angry with him,

not because he tried to kill me but because he killed Jack. Todd sent Jack to his death borne on the wings of Todd's spiteful behavior. Your father is not the first genius monster. We all know about Picasso and Jack Kennedy was well, "another Kennedy after all," as my father used to say.

Isn't it odd how so often it's these "humanist" leaders who are the world's leading scumbags to the actual human beings in their lives? But pricks have facilitators. I was Todd's. I've half a mind to go to his studio and deface his paintings while he's on Parris Island.

The stupidest cliché: "Well, at least they can never take your memories away." Yes, they can my dear! There is no memory so sweet that it can stand up to a young Marine breaking bad news with tears in his eyes.

They said they were sorry. But if they were so sorry why were their uniforms so perfect? How could they be so clean in such a dirty world?

Mother

Subj: Re: How am I?
Date: 1/23/2005 10:31:20 AM Eastern Standard Time
From: AmandaOgden@NYTimes.com
To: SarahRutherford@aol.com
Mother: There is no way to reach into the little

private hell you and Dad have made for yourselves and save you. So I won't try.

Some of us think that our short lives are long enough to unravel or even answer these questions. Others of us look at the desire for meaning as reason to look for a truth beyond the realm of day-to-day experience. We call this religion, but in the end a better word for it might be humility. Jack was right, without sacrifice there is no meaning.

Mother, don't mourn Jack's selfless death.

Love, Amanda

43

I swim with my sister. The first sweep of letters is complete. Amanda trembles as she takes the elevator.

At the main entrance, between the revolving doors is a bronze bust of Adolph S. Ochs publisher 1896 to 1935. Next to him is a bronze plaque memorializing the victims of 9/11. Amanda tapes my boot camp graduation picture to the plaque and my citation for the Silver Star along with this note:

> To my friends at the *Times*:
>
> This is my brother Pfc. Jack Ogden USMC. He died trying to protect you. He was not a Republican or a Democrat but an American. The war he died in may be wrong. I don't know. I do know that he was not a victim but a hero. Altruism should not be met with silence or pity, let alone condescension. My brother's willingness to sacrifice, and the selflessness of tens of thousands like him, is a bigger story than what our politicians, courts, media, social and artistic elites say or do.

Amanda Rutherford Ogden,
News Assistant
Letters to the Editor

44

Jessica talks to me out loud. It's snowing and she's wrapped in a long black wool coat. The baby is with Jessica's mom. There are snowflakes clinging to Jessica's long lashes. Her breath is making a cloud in the frosty air. She always straightens the American flag the Legion guys from the Newburyport post keep on my grave.

She used to cry at every visit. Today she doesn't. She steps behind the headstone and takes off her gloves, brushes off the snow and places both hands on the frigid stone.

The amazing thing about Jessica is that what she says and what she's thinking is usually the same thing. With most people there's an internal conversation that's different than what they're saying. Swimming in them is like watching a 3-D movie without the glasses. Thoughts and words overlap but not exactly. But with Jessica her thoughts and words are in sync.

"Jack, I don't know if you played with play clay when you were little. When you open the new packages all the colors are bright. The red is red and the blue is blue and the yellow is yellow and you make dolls and dogs and dinosaurs and try and break them apart so as to put all the colors back in their packages.

"Jack, no matter how hard you try the colors mix and after a while you have this big lump of clay that's just gray. Well, that's what I'm worried about. I take out all my memories and they start out bright and clear. But after a while things get mixed. Even the feelings get confused."

Anne Bradstreet's poem crashes into Jessica's thoughts:

By duty bound and not by custom led

To celebrate the praises of the dead,

My mournful mind, sore pressed, in trembling verse

Presents my lamentations at his hearse . . .

"Jack, what is duty bound and what is custom led? Dad's saying it's been a year and that it's time for me to move on. When he started talking that way I got mad and yelled. Then Mom said, 'Jack wouldn't want you to be alone raising a baby.' Dad said, 'You can't spend the rest of your life sitting on some dead guy's grave.'

"And it's a weird thing that Dad brought this up now because there is somebody I like. He was one of the recruiters working at Andover when you volunteered. Jack, nothing has happened with Patrick. And it won't till I'm sure about how I feel about the idea of somebody else. When I go there to help with the poolee functions we just talk and he likes to play with our baby.

"Patrick is from Boston so that's why he asked for recruiting duty here so he can be near his mom because she has MS. His dad is a cop. He had a girlfriend since junior high but they broke up. He said she couldn't take the idea of being with someone deployed. And when he came back from his second deployment to Iraq she asked him to get out of the Corps. But Patrick re-upped because we're at war, and when his three years at the recruiting office is done he's headed back into the infantry and will be deployed again he thinks.

"Patrick asked me how I feel and I said that I'll be very sad to see him go but very proud of him. And I told him that I want us to win over there, otherwise you were killed for nothing. I told him I worry it won't work out.

"Patrick said any Marine killed doing his job never dies in vain because by doing your job you pass on the tradition that keeps the Marines ready. He says that all the battles you Marines fought during the last two hundred years are really just one long war: the fight to keep America safe, to let everyone know that, 'If they mess with us there are these badass Marines who they'll have to deal with.' He says a Marine's job is to, 'Always be ready for the call.'

"Yesterday he asked if I'd like to go out and not just to a another poolee function, but where he'll come by and pick me up and take me up to Portsmouth to dinner while Mom baby-sits.

"I told him I need to think it over and I asked Mom what she thinks and she told Dad and he said, 'You can't cry all your life.' Mom said, 'You like Patrick and he's a Marine so he's Jack's brother.'

"So I called Patrick and asked for a little time to think and he said fine, that he understands. And he said, 'I like you a lot Jessica and I'll wait till you want to go out and I want you to know that meanwhile I'm not going out with anybody else.'

"I almost believe him. But what I worry about is how to remember our time Jack. We didn't have very long; just two years in high school then the last summer and ten days after you came back from MCT. I think Patrick would make a good daddy. He said he would like a big family.

"So he isn't just fooling around and we haven't even been out yet and he's talking about kids.

"He's twenty-five, which for a Marine is old, and he made sergeant in three years which Master Sergeant Dubois said is fast for infantry.

"But Patrick doesn't read much and is into sports so if we're together I'll have to be the one to read to the baby, and I promise I will. And he'll listen to your music too.

"But there will never be anybody I love like I love you Jack and it might not be fair to Patrick because I'll always be comparing.

"I think that the really sad part isn't just that you're dead but that everything you did is in the past. And every day that passes means there are more things we don't share.

"The past just keeps getting further away.

"And the bright colors are going gray.

"The thing that I'm saddest about isn't that you're gone but that life has gone on without you. Something besides you should have stopped. That's how I feel, that the most unfair thing is how everything just went on.

"And I can't even stop my feelings from moving on!

"I can't pretend that I don't like Patrick even though I went up there to begin with to find out things about you.

"The last thing I was looking for was some other guy!

"I can't keep the memory of anything alive the way I'm supposed to. I think that if I say I'm going to remember forever it's just a lie to make me feel better. So the only way I can stay connected to you is to love our baby the way you would love him. It's like taking fire in my bare hands and passing it on."

"I'm sorry for not taking better care of her," I say.

"Everyone leaves somebody. Suck it up!" says God.

45

Subj: Mom

Date: 1/23/2005 9:28:34 PM Eastern Standard Time

From: AmandaOgden@NYTimes.com

To: SarahRutherford@aol.com

Mother: You know perfectly well Dad is no habitual wife abuser. You admit that he flipped out once because of Jack's death. And I don't think you'd be having sex with a kid in the office under other circumstances! So you may be justifying what you're doing—and your friends will be on your side—but I *know* you know Dad doesn't fit the abuser profile and you said yourself he is so sorry it's pathetic. So you can fool everyone else but not me. If you want out just say so but don't try and justify yourself.

Jack was a bigger person than the rest of us. I think he was willing to go with the flow of being an ordinary human which is quite an achievement for a Rutherford. He didn't sit there sneering at everything but became what your generation always talked about but never was: authentic.

Are you going to honor Jack by allowing your life to disintegrate just because you and Dad are spoiled rotten? Is this what Jack died for?

Amanda

Subj: Your attack on me
Date: 1/23/2005 11:40:56 PM Eastern Standard Time
From: SarahRutherford@aol.com
To: AmandaOgden@NYTimes.com

Amanda: You have nerve! I don't have to justify myself to you! But I will because I love you and you are my friend, and by the way, you're the only person I confided to about my idiocy at the office. It should mean something that I trust you.

Fact: Our marriage won't survive Jack's death.

Fact: The people who used to live in this house are gone.

Fact: Who Todd is, is a mystery to me now.

Fact: What I am or will be is also a mystery.

I don't seem to have any way to pin things down. I certainly don't have the energy to answer your tidal wave of hostility.

Get off your high horse!

The head-smashing incident was merely the last straw. I've been strong for Todd and you and Jack too. You are an ingrate if you can't see that.

Do you have any idea how hard it's been trying to keep a semblance of continuity and normality around here? Do you know what a towering egomaniac Todd has been? Do you know that on 9/11 what he was worried about most was losing those pictures?

It was bad enough baby-sitting a grown man. I can't be the keeper of a ghost.

Sorry, I know that makes me seem monstrous. Perhaps I am, but there it is.

And you may not believe this but I still love Todd. And I have forgiven him and will tell him so. It's just that I can't abide him. I can't abide anything.

It turns out that everything that makes civilization civil has been invented out of thin air. We've been playing dress up and let's pretend for our whole human history. We have perfected self-delusion.

I won't abide the charade. I am alone. So I will be what I am.

Mother

46

Amanda sits in Jason's office. She stares at the fading stack of the newspaper's letters pages piled on the little table next to the door.

"Tell me more about the circumstances of Jack's death," says Jason.

Amanda hands him the copy of my citation. He reads then reaches over and pats her shoulder very lightly and tells her how very sorry he is.

There are tears in his eyes.

For a nasty civilian Jason is a sweet guy.

He loves the *New York Times*, his job and his daughter in that order.

"I got a call from security, then another one from the publisher's office. That notice you put up really made people quite uncomfortable."

"Am I fired?" asks Amanda.

"No, but you're going to have to get some help. And let's just say please don't do anything else out of the ordinary."

47

January 24, 2005, 01037 Hotel Company Plt. 2098, with SDI Baker. The platoon is marching into the squad bay with their DIs. They're back from a clothing issue. Dad is tagging along. He's drained, mind empty.

The major has left Dad alone with the platoon since lights. He comes back and tells Dad that he wants to take Dad over to another platoon further along in the training cycle. Then he says: "Staff Sergeant Isaac Jackson is that platoon's SDI and wants to meet you."

"Who's he?" asks Dad.

"Your son's SDI, sir."

1304, Bravo Co. Plt. 1077—Staff Sergeant Isaac Jackson is stamping up the DI highway in the center of the squad bay. My old SDI is black as Africans are black, true ebony, not African-American milk chocolate. SDI Jackson is five feet eight inches tall. He radiates terrifying power. His shoulders seem as wide as he is tall. You could slice bread on the three regulation creases ironed into the back of his blouse. Under his DI campaign cover his face disappears into a shadow impenetrable as the shade in the mouth of a cave.

Dad is frozen. His heart is beating hard. The idea of meeting my SDI makes Dad feel as if he is about to get as close to me as he ever will. And there is something else: Dad senses a threatening presence he doesn't understand, like the foreshadowing of an earthquake that makes dogs howl.

The platoon stands silently on line on either side of the squad bay rigid in the position of attention.

Dad is a good six inches taller than Jackson, but Dad feels as if he is looking up at him when they meet. Jackson nods and doesn't shake hands and points to the DI house. He marches in. Dad follows. The Greenbelts are all in the squad bay so we're alone.

Jackson is the first Marine Dad's met who has not shaken his hand when Dad offered his. Dad's heart sinks. So does mine.

"So you are Pfc. Jack Ogden's father?" asks Jackson in his low raspy voice.

"Yes."

"Sit down."

Dad perches on the edge of a metal chair. SDI Jackson is sitting at his small desk across from Dad. He gives Dad a hard stare. Dad lowers his eyes.

"Thank you for meeting with me," Dad mumbles.

"I heard you were visiting us to see how a platoon gets trained."

SDI Jackson stares at Dad steadily. I'm scared shitless. So is Dad. Why am I scared? I'm dead, what can Jackson do to me?

"I wanted to see what my son went through."

"Is that right?" asks Jackson in a disinterested monotone. Then he starts to rattle off facts as if he's reading from a list and keeps his eyes on Dad the whole time—no expression—as if he's watching an insect. "Your son was fast, loud, intense and had leadership skills. A leader like your son sets the example for others to follow. He was my guide and honor grad. Where the fuck were you?"

Dad's head jerks up. Jackson's expression doesn't change.

Words are truth now, not hidden. At last somebody has come to the point.

"Where the fuck were you?" Jackson asks again.

"I let my son down," Dad blurts.

"Too bad,"—no emotion.

"My marriage is falling apart."

"Happens a lot after a KIA,"—flat, as if commenting on the weather.

"I abused my wife."

"Shit happens,"—bored.

"I'm trying to reconnect with my son."

"I heard how you screamed at the Marines at his wake. You showed disrespect for your son and his uniform. I heard you spit on the flag,"—deadpan.

"I lost it," Dad whispers.

"Your son got up at lights and gave one hundred percent. Your son was fast, always sounded off at the top of his lungs. Any kind of correction seemed not to faze him. Then we fired him from squad leader just to see how he'd take it. Then this other recruit fought back from a case of pneumonia, and I made him squad leader. By grad your son was the guide again."

"I wish I had been there."

"Too late for wishing,"—disinterested.

"I wish I hadn't lost it at the viewing."

"We DIs keep each other from going over the edge. We can pick up the signal that a DI is about to flip out before he starts to reach for recruit to do bodily harm. Who the fuck are you accountable to?"

"Nobody," Dad whispers.

I'm looking out Dad's eyes. Jackson has never taken his cold gaze off us.

"When your son got down here you could tell he came from a well-off background. His attitude was that he could do whatever he wanted without comeuppance. I almost dropped his ass when I found out he was keeping a journal. But I didn't take it away from him even though I knew what he was doing. I didn't let him know I knew. I remember watching him scribble fast while he was in the head. He believed he was fooling me. I remember bringing him into my office and asking him if he wanted to call home, figured I'd reward his bad behavior, just like God does with all undeserving nasty fucks, give him all the rope he needs to hang himself. So I figure, make him cocky so he'll shit the bed and I can kick his spoiled little ass off my Island. I was looking for what button to push. And I remember looking into your son's eyes and they were vacant like 'where's home?'

"Most recruits would've jumped all over it but he was nonchalant about making a call home. Most recruits would have done anything to hear a familiar voice in the middle of the chaos we create around them. And I couldn't figure it out. All I knew was his father was some rich shit. I figured your son was on my island trying to break free of his father's dreams for him. I started pushing those buttons. I told recruit Ogden he was never going to be a Marine. I made him feel like his dad was going to win. That's how I motivated him. I said anybody can buy a uniform but it's what's inside that makes you a Marine. I said, 'You are too fucking spoiled to make it. I'll break you.'

"Training Day twenty-eight he's pounding on the DI House wall asking to see the senior drill instructor. I make him wait there a long time before I say, 'What?' And he comes in with these scraps of paper he's been keeping and hands them to me and says, 'This recruit has been keeping a journal and this recruit understands it's against the rules. This recruit wants to be a Marine.'

"So I take him out onto the quarterdeck and tell my heavy hat to thrash his heart till we have him crying, until he collapses and has to be carried back to his rack after he pukes. And he didn't know it but the way I showed him respect was that I never read a word of that trash.

"I knew from that moment your son was going to be a great Marine. I can tell you this: the kid who graduated was not the little shit who first came here.

"As SDI my job is to know my recruits. Your son got no letters from his dad. I had to pit him just to get it out of him. I knew something was wrong just by watching his face at mail call. He told me about you. I made him write to you anyway, even though you're a turd. So he did but you never answered. He was more at eighteen than you are at fifty-three. It's more than you fucking deserve but no matter what you can always say, my son was a Marine."

Jackson stands and strides into the squad bay.

48

Amanda rides the elevator to the newsroom. My sister hesitates at the security desk; nervously picks up a *Union Times* flyer from the Newspaper Guild of New York, and glances at it: ". . . . Represents 1,500 *Times* employees. . . . We have just completed our first full year under the new eight-year collective bargaining agreement . . ."

Amanda takes a deep breath and walks into the newsroom passing cubicle after cubicle each holding a journalist.

"They actually think they're indispensable," God says and laughs. "This isn't a newspaper it's a family-owned theocracy."

Amanda walks to the row of clocks and reaches up and rips down the handwritten Baghdad sign taped under Moscow's clock.

The journalists nearest her look surprised. She turns and drops the ripped sign in front of a bearded man. He hangs up his phone and recoils. He loves the *Times*, taking out-of-town friends to the Harvard Club, and his summer home on Deer Isle Maine in that order.

Many journalists are slouched below the level of the dividers; others are blocked from seeing Amanda by a row of big square columns down the center isle. It will be necessary to shout to be heard by the whole congregation.

"JACK WASN'T A VICTIM!" my sister shouts.

How do monks react to a heretic who defiles the holy of holies? They wait for security while hoping she's not a suicide bomber.

Security—a large black ex-cop—is about one hundred yards away. Amanda figures she has less than thirty seconds.

She clutches the little piece of the newspaper with my name on it as she clambers up on a desk kicking aside a Rolodex. A young Asian man in a white shirt and red tie—who a moment ago was on the phone to his source in Sri Lanka—retreats to a safe distance several cubicles away. Others in the far distance stand up to see what all the fuss is about.

"Why is Jack's name only in this shitty box?" Amanda yells, as she waves the clipping. "Why do you piss yourselves every time Tony Kushner farts but you can't be generous to one American hero? Why is a Pulitzer a big deal but not a Silver Star? Who makes those rules? Does anyone in this room have a family member in uniform?"

The security guard takes Amanda's arm and gently helps her off the desk. He loves his little brother, his mother, his son, the Yankees, and his wife in that order.

As the guard leads her out Amanda yells her question again with her voice breaking, *"Does anyone in this fucking room have a family member in uniform?"*

"My little brother's in the Navy ma'am," the security guard answers.

Amanda bursts into tears.

49

January 25, 2005, 1323, Plt. 1077—Recruits are sitting in small groups working on two life-sized rubber dummies practicing first aid. They're rehearsing for their final Knowledge test.

SDI Jackson is in the DI house. Dad is standing by the head door on the quarterdeck. DIs are walking between the groups of recruits coaching their test practice. Dad is shook up from SDI Jackson's in-your-face attack. I still can't swim in Jackson. And God won't explain anything.

1329—March to chow. Jackson is ignoring Dad. Dad barely knows where to walk.

1335—The 1077 don't need the DIs to chase them out of chow. They are seasoned, cool, calm and collected. They eat in less than six minutes and begin to stow their trays without being told then head out to where their rifles are stacked in perfect rows on the sidewalk. While they wait for their DIs most hold Knowledge sheets studying for the final test under a sky that is lead-gray with low dark clouds.

1341—"Put that crap away!" shouts a junior DI. Knowledge

sheets are stowed. The platoon forms up. The junior DI is still perfecting the platoon's marching even though they have already won the award for drill.

"Align your left!"

"*You*, you come with me," says SDI Jackson.

Dad was watching the recruits pick up their gear. He jumps when SDI Jackson speaks inches from his ear and the brim of his campaign cover brushes Dad's shoulder. Dad spins around. SDI Jackson strides away. Dad hesitates.

Without turning SDI Jackson shouts, "Follow me!"

Dad does. He has to run to catch up.

Five minutes later we pass under a cluster of overhead steam pipes and cross the road to the parade deck. The stands are full of several thousand parents watching a graduation ceremony.

To our right is the Iwo Jima Memorial. Parents pose proudly in front of it getting their pictures taken. The 3rd and 4th Battalion platoons are on deck. Six male platoons and a female platoon will be graduating. DIs and SDIs lead them, swords in hand.

The wind is beginning to blow carrying fat raindrops. A Marine band is playing.

"Let me explain it to you," says SDI Jackson without looking at Dad. "Pfc. Ogden was in admin, not infantry, and the only training he got for combat was here on PI and that shit they teach at MCT. You have to ask yourself, if you were as honorable as your son what would you do now?"

Parents are cheering and rushing out of the packed stands embracing their sons and brothers.

SDI Jackson strides off in the direction of the squad bay.

50

1430, Plt. 1077 Squad bay—Instructions for stripping everything out of their pockets are being given to the recruits. They must go to the final Knowledge test with nothing but their cammies, boots and pens so they can't be accused of cheating.

On line holding their pens in front of them:

"Everybody has a black ink stick?"

"Yes, sir!"

1455—Plt. 1077 marches to the test. SDI Jackson is ignoring Dad again.

1501—Lined up for the test in front of a large round one-story brick building. SDI Jackson shows the recruits how to fold their newly-issued all-weather raincoats.

"Now you will just have to walk yourself through the test as if I was walking you through it."

"Aye, sir!"

"Mouth to mouth resuscitation, chin lift: look, listen, feel, finger sweep."

"Yes sir!"

"Remember that trash!"

"Yes, sir!"

"Lock your knee out. That will give you a proper about-face. Did you hear Martinez?"

"Aye, sir!"

"How many breaths per minute?"

"Twelve, sir!"

"Then what do you do?"

"Check for pulse, sir!"

"After that do you go right into the twelve breaths?"

"Aye, sir!"

"Martinez lock your knee! Are you retarded, son?"

"Sir, no sir!"

A recruit requests permission to pray.

SDI Jackson: "You want to pray? Why?!"

"It helped on the rifle range, sir!"

"Pray damn fast."

"Yes, sir!"

The recruits huddle in a circle and pray.

SDI Jackson: "In the friggin test don't friggin look around, or they'll assume you're cheating. Don't look around!"

"Yes, sir!"

"The sand pit made you a team! Unity through hardship!"

"Aye, sir!"

"If you tie a knot on top of a field dressing, what is it?"

"A pressure dressing, sir!"

"All of you already know this trash!"

"Yes, sir!"

"So apply what you know!"

"Aye, sir! Stop the bleeding, start the breathing, check the wound, treat for shock!"

"This recruit requests Knowledge."

"What?"

"What is the fourth step for treating shock, sir?"

"Martinez, you're retarded son!"

"Aye, sir."

"You already know all this crap!"

"Aye, sir!"

"You ALL know this crap!"

"Aye, sir!"

"Lock it up."

"Aye, sir!"

1522—Exam papers handed out—

SDI Jackson: "Shut your fat mouths!"

"Aye, sir!"

"That's the last time you say anything till the test is over."

"Aye, sir!"

"I just said shut the fuck up!"

"Aye, sir!"

"You must all be from West Virginia! When I tell you to shut the fuck up, SHUT THE FUCK UP! And that means you don't say another friggin word! And I tell you to *shut the fuck up* and you all say 'Aye, sir!' Now I'll say it one more time: SHUT THE FUCK UP TILL THE TEST IS DONE AND NOT ANOTHER WORD!"

Silence.

1603—In the test hall for the practical exam, recruits line up with life-sized rubber dummies.

"Go to cubicles four, five, six. Your victim has been shot in the right leg," barks the DI assigned to run the test.

Each recruit must demonstrate how to treat the wound—Tie on field dressing and apply pressure—

"The bleeding *didn't* stop, apply the next step."

"Yes, sir!"

"The bleeding *did* stop, apply the next step."

"Aye, sir!"

A recruit applying the field dressing in front of Dad is tying it on with his web belt. He works quietly, gently as if on a real wounded Marine. This is what they did for me. And the bleeding did not stop, and all the first aid in the world couldn't stop it.

Dad is crying again.

1930—SDI time in the 1077 squad bay—SDI Jackson passes out letters, some of the recruits have to do push-ups to earn their mail, either because they get so much or because someone has written something on an envelope such as "Go Army!" SDI Jackson considers an insult.

SDI Jackson sits on a locker and the recruits sit cross-legged around him on the floor.

SDI Jackson is talking to his platoon in his conversational fatherly voice.

"So when I made SDI I told Kramer—that was my old senior when I was a junior DI—it would be tough for me to compete against him because I respected him so much. He answered; 'You're not competing against me but for the Marine Corps to put the best Marines out there.' And that said it all.

"The ultimate club in the Marine Corps is the Blackbelt SDI club. You've got to be able to relate to that kid from Troy, Michigan, or from some fancy neighborhood. And you flip that angry kid or that stuck up kid. They might start out in racial cliques, with the black kids hanging together and the white kids hanging together but here you figure how to level it all out. What you do is you have to destroy all those differences. And they change because they see the example of their DIs because when we put on a campaign cover we are either a Greenbelt or a Blackbelt or 'Nick the new hat.' Those are the DI's only 'races.'"

"Aye, sir!" bark the recruits.

"When I had my first conflict it was with DI Lussi. He was motivated more than anyone I ever knew. He would even come in at 0200 dressed like a recruit and low crawl into the squad bay in the dark and pretend he was a recruit and wake up recruits and say things to them like 'don't you just hate DI Lussi?'"

The recruits laugh.

"And they thought they were talking to the recruit in the next rack and would tell him everything. And then the next day he'd incorporate his inside knowledge into training. He had those recruits doing everything double-time and thinking he was God."

"Aye, sir!"

The recruits hang on every word. They know that this intimacy is a rare reward for having fought their way to the threshold of graduation.

"Well, I'm sitting in the DI house and all of a sudden I realize things are too quiet in the squad bay and I look through the blinds in the DI house window to check what's going on and I see that DI Lussi has got his hands around this recruit's neck and is choking him. I was on the deck before I knew it. And I hit Lussi in the side and knocked him down. And I said in front of everybody; 'You get your shit out of my house and go home and don't come back till I call you!'

"Then I called his wife and told her why I sent him home. And I told her; 'Your husband jeopardized my recruits, you keep him there till I call.'

"Then I ordered the recruit who had been choked into my office and I told that recruit; 'I will not tolerate my DIs putting their hands on a recruit.' Then I asked that recruit what he wanted me to do about this and he said; 'Sir, I don't want to get my DI in trouble.' So I looked at the recruit and he seemed okay and I said to him; 'I'll see what I can do.'

"Then I called DI Lussi's wife again and asked to talk to her husband. But she said he was still at the emergency room because when I punched him I broke two of his ribs. Now I'm out on a limb too because I broke his ribs. So now we have a DI who assaulted a recruit and an SDI who has assaulted his DI. So I called up my first sergeant and told him that there was a DI that might be pressing assault charges.

"Aye, sir!" murmur the recruits. They scarcely dare to breathe.

They don't want to do anything to stop SDI Jackson from finishing the story.

Dad is taking it all in, mesmerized. It's the first time since he got to the island that he's not been completely absorbed with his own suffering. Jackson never even glances at Dad but Dad can't take his eyes of my old SDI.

"A few minutes later Lussi called me and he was apologetic and seemed to be okay with me breaking his ribs. So since no one was pressing charges after three days DI Lussi was coming back to the platoon.

"When he came back I said; 'DIs don't ever apologize to recruits but that's exactly what you're going to do.' I got all my recruits in a school circle sitting on the deck just the way you are now. Then I came into my DI house where I had Lussi waiting, and I told him I didn't want him to apologize to the individual recruit but to the whole platoon for letting them down and for not being a professional. So then we walked out to the platoon.

"Lussi says: 'Okay, THINGS, your drill instructor did something wrong you understand that?' 'Sir, yes sir!' 'We're not going to have a problem with this right?' 'Sir, no, sir!' 'Good to go! Now get out to the pit!'

"And we all went to the pit and thrashed their hearts for an hour to make them understand they were still just nasty recruits. So they were down in the pit pushing and doing mountain climbers and I told them; 'We will not tolerate weakness or mistakes.' And of course Lussi was right down in their faces and they responded in a way that was unbelievable. They seemed to understand that the only way to get our family back on track was to work even harder."

"Aye, sir!"

"After that the cycle was just spotless. We won everything. Because sometimes you've got to pay for something once and for all, clear the air, make a new start and the fact I broke his ribs told those recruits that I cared about them. And the fact he got back to work and we kept it all in the house told them that we could settle it right here."

"Aye, sir!"

Jackson sits still for a moment looking at his recruits. No one dares to move so much as a finger. Then he slowly spits his tobacco juice into his ubiquitous Dr. Pepper can.

"Who hasn't told his story?" asks SDI Jackson.

Hands go up. Jackson barks out a name.

A recruit stands.

"This recruit was bouncing around in confusion. His MOS is infantry. And he joined the Marines because of the war."

"Aye, recruit," murmur the other recruits.

Another recruit stands.

"This recruit is from Guatemala and moved to New Jersey with his mom when he was twelve, and this recruit is 0-300, infantry— he joined because his friend was killed in Iraq and this recruit went down to the recruiting station the day of his friend's funeral. This recruit hopes to soon become an American citizen."

"Aye, recruit," from all the other recruits.

"This recruit joined to see the world."

"Aye, recruit."

"This recruit joined to show my friends I had bigger balls than they do."

"Aye, recruit!"

"This recruit joined because his dad's a Marine."

"Aye, recruit."

"This recruit joined because he wanted to be proud of something."

"Aye, recruit."

"This recruit joined because he loves America."

"Aye, recruit."

"This recruit wants to get all his bad habits out."

"Aye, recruit."

"This recruit wants to protect his family."

"Aye, recruit."

"This recruit will be the happiest person alive in just one week, because he will be a Marine!"

Thunderous: "AYE RECRUIT!"

"My son was a recruit. I never wrote to him. He died in Iraq before I could say I'm sorry. Forgive me!"

The words pour out of Dad's mouth before he can stop them. Dead silence.

The recruits stare then look away hurriedly. Dad is sobbing.

Up to that point they have paid little attention to Dad, assumed he was just some civilian, maybe like the civilians who work at the chow hall, maybe an electrician come to do repairs.

"GET ON LINE!" SDI Jackson bellows.

Recruits scramble to their feet and race to their positions at the foot of each rack, toes on the line, hands at their sides, each at a perfect position of attention, recruits seven days from earning the eagle globe and anchor, a platoon of Marines in all but title.

SDI Jackson stamps up the DI highway. On the way past Dad he grabs Dad's arm and pulls him along.

Once we pass the door of the DI house SDI Jackson slams it shut and turns. He looks furious.

"Don't ever say anything in front of my recruits again! You will *not* fuck up their concentration. Get out of my squad bay!"

"I'm sorry," sobs Dad.

SDI Jackson gives Dad a look.

There is a long moment of silence.

"You owe me a drink," SDI Jackson says.

51

January 25, 2005, 2100—Mandy's Bar, Beaufort SC off Route 802—SDI Isaac Jackson and Dad have had three beers each.

SDI Jackson is dressed in a gray T-shirt and sweat pants. Out of uniform he looks smaller. They drink in silence for about fifteen minutes. SDI Jackson drinks another beer. Dad drinks another beer. SDI Jackson orders ten more and tells the waitress to bring the beers at the same time, unopened. He arranges the bottles in a line in front of him. Every time he finishes one he puts the bottle into the empties row and takes another and also hands one to Dad.

Two patrons are watching TV at the bar. We're the only people at one of the six tables. Marine memorabilia cover every inch of the walls and low ceiling.

SDI Jackson can hold his liquor. Dad is getting drunk.

Dad's legs have gone to sleep but he doesn't dare move. SDI Jackson has not taken his eyes off Dad's face since we sat down.

God says to me: "So don't say I never do anything for you!"

"Okay," I answer, wondering what he's talking about.

"Ask and you shall receive."

"All right," I say, still not able to figure out what he means.

"So quit your whining!"

"Fine."

It hits me:

God is speaking to me through SDI Jackson, literally, mind-to-mind!

Then God speaks in SDI Jackson's audible voice to Dad. His tone is conversational, friendly, unhurried.

"I didn't find the Marine Corps till the tenth grade. My sister was dating a Marine. My brothers and my sister thought that I was crazy—they wanted me to stay in New Orleans."

Dad nods. He's feeling numb. I'm stunned.

"My mom and dad were separated," God continues, "but they never lived more than five miles apart and saw each other every week. My father had a drinking problem. My mom couldn't cope. We were poor. My mom worked for the Navy as a mess hall manager. Dad was a cook at the Fourth Naval Air Reserve. He drank up all he made. Then they fired him.

"I was sixteen when I went down to the recruiter's office. I never got recruited. I went after them. I had never met professional men before, men who treated everyone with respect. I was what they call a Category Four so they never wanted me because I tested so low. I remember when I finally got a phone call to come in after I retook the test. The guy on the phone said, 'This is Gunnery Sergeant Brian. I want you to come down and do some paperwork.'

"I got sent to boot camp in San Diego because we lived on the west side of the Mississippi. If I'd lived on the east side I would've got sent to Parris Island. When I got to San Diego I was stranded in the receiving barracks because we still didn't have enough recruits to fill out a whole platoon. So there we were as recruits but housed in the same barracks with the kids who were getting sent back home. They were being processed out for drug pops mostly. And they sat around telling us how to pop a drug test or fake heat exhaustion so we could get back home too. And I looked at them like they were crazy. The last thing I wanted to do was get dropped. I had spent two years dreaming of being a Marine. I had just about killed myself trying to become what you disrespected, what you hated your son becoming. It was all I ever wanted."

What God told Dad was mostly things I knew because SDI Jackson had told us about himself in the last days of training at SDI time when he'd kick back and play father and we'd sit in a circle at his feet. I already knew how he'd tested low on the ASVAB and how he struggled in infantry after he blew out his knee and all about how Jackson became a Marine prison guard then a DI.

God drained a last beer and stood. He put his hands on his hips and looked down on Dad.

"Now," God said to Dad, "I think about you and I figure, okay this asshole came down here so maybe he deserves a second chance but he needs a new start. So what shall I do with you? Who will set you free, Todd?"

Dad had no answer.

"Your real loss is you'll never get to know your son as a Marine. But your son accomplished what he set out to do. Your son accomplished one of the greatest things he could have done no matter how long he had lived."

God puts his arm around Dad and we stand. A host of dead Marines is watching. The usual chatter in the river is dead silent.

Every time Dad stumbles God tightens his grip around his waist to guide him.

We drive in God's pick up back to PI.

We park in front of God's house, a one-story ranch smaller than Dad's garden shed, in a row of other houses, each one identical, each small, each shabby but spotlessly neat.

Dad can smell the muddy low-tide flats. The scent reminds him of Joppa Flats when the tide is out. It reminds me of taking long walks with Dad, reminds me of the night I first arrived on the Island, reminds me of how I failed my Dad.

We walk under oaks hung with moss then up a couple of streets. Fra Angelico is there. Duccio is there. Lots of dead Greek monks and nuns are marching around. Fra Angelico's painted angels are holding hands and dancing into the distance ahead of us. Duccio is carrying one of his Madonnas over his head as if he's in some sort of procession. And then Sister Gertrude flies past in her plane and, sure enough, Jesus is the pilot and she's wearing her bride-of-Christ white dress and her veil is flying out behind them.

The full moon casts Dad and God's shadows in front of us making hard black patches. God guides us along the back of the bleachers until we come to an open space in front of the Iwo Jima Memorial. By moonlight the bronze looks gray, the Marine's faces are in shadow invisible under the rims of their helmets.

God pushes Dad to his knees at the foot of the pedestal.

Nothing left to hide—no point to Dad's idle thought about the fact that he's bigger and heavier than God, maybe has a good chance of holding his own if he wanted to.

Dad thinks:

Can't fight God.

He doesn't know that tonight the expression is literally true.

"How did it work out for you after you assaulted Sarah? She call the cops?" asks God.

"No," Dad mumbles.

And he's too fucked up to wonder how SDI Jackson suddenly knows Mom's name.

"If she called the cops you would have had to pay."

"I did pay. She won't touch me."

"That's not paying."

"I love her."

"Doesn't your wife have brothers?"

"No."

"What about her dad?"

"He died"

"Where I come from a guy beats up on his lady and her brothers beat his ass. Only cowards beat their ladies."

"I went over the edge."

"I bet no matter how much I piss you off, no matter what I do you won't go 'over the edge' with me."

"People behave worse to the ones they're close to. You're a stranger."

"I'm your son's SDI. I'm his brother Marine. I'm closer to you than your heart. I trained him to die. I *am* my brother's keeper."

"I snapped because he died."

"And maybe you don't like it that she's getting old. Does she look like her mom yet?"

"No."

"You're saying nothing changed? Tits? Pussy? All just as fresh and perky as the day you met?"

"We're both getting older."

"Does that piss you off?"

"No."

"I bet you'd rather be fucking her when she was eighteen."

"Shit."

"Am I pissing you off now?"

"Yes."

God lets go of Dad's hair and yanks him to his feet by his belt.

"Take a swing at me punk!"

"No."

"You afraid?"

"No."

"Then try."

"No."

"How'd you bang her head on the wall?"

"I placed my hands on her shoulders and pushed her against the kitchen wall."

"Show me."

"No."

God grabs Dad's wrists and places Dad's hands on either side of his face. An instant after Dad's palms touch God's face he smashes Dad's hands away, spins Dad around and puts him in a chokehold.

"I bet she didn't do this."

"No," Dad gasps.

"This is a blood choke. You'll be out in nine seconds. Pfc. Ogden would know how to do this. He'd know how to break my hold, too."

"Are you going to kill my dad?" I ask.

"Shut the fuck up, Jack!" God barks.

We regain consciousness thinking about our sailboat, feeling as if she's half over in a storm. God pulls us to our feet with his hands clasped around our chest.

"That was for the mother of a Marine you abused. This is for spitting on the flag your son died for."

God punches us in the side. We hear Dad's ribs crack. When Dad tries to breathe we feel a stab of pain. Dad falls to his knees.

I'm so happy to feel something physical again, even pain.

Then I'm kicked out of Dad, just watching, swimming in his thoughts but feeling nothing physical.

"Say you're sorry!" God commands.

"I am sorry, sir," Dad whispers.

"I'm sorry too," I say.

"Open your mouth, YOU!"

"*I am sorry, sir!*" we shout.

"I want to hear you sounding off like you mean it!"

"I'M SORRY, SIR!" We scream.

God helps Dad to his feet. He's gentle. Then he hands Dad an envelope. Dad is bent double clutching his ribs. God holds my long lost letter under Dad's face. At last I understand.

"Pfc. Ogden sent this to me before he went over to the big sandbox. Your son told me to get it to you if something happened to him. When I heard you spit on the flag I said fuck it. But it's yours now."

52

January 27, 2005 1730: Jessica's giving our baby a bath and talking to me. He's kicking up a storm in the kitchen sink and waves his arms whenever the water splashes into his face.

"Jack, today your dad met our son. It was about four in the afternoon. I was so scared when I saw who was knocking. And he looked terrible. He wasn't shaved, had lost a lot of weight and was sort of bent down because he was in pain from some kind of accident. I wouldn't have opened the door but he saw me. The front door was open and he knocked on the glass storm door.

"I had opened the door to let light into the hall where I was vacuuming. I heard the knock and turned around. I was holding Baby Jack on my hip and vacuuming with the other hand.

"When your dad saw our son he sank to his knees on the outside steps. Then he pitched forward till his forehead was touching the ground. So that kind of changed everything because when you see your son's grandfather on his knees and his shoulders are shaking because he's sobbing you can't just leave him there.

"I opened the door and knelt. Baby Jack was in my arms. Then your dad sits up and there he is face to face with his grandson. I'm kneeling on the stoop and he's kneeling facing me. Baby Jack is between us.

"Your father is crying and I am too. And I put my arm around your dad's shoulders and he sobs. Of course Baby Jack is freaked out because we're crying. So the baby wails and that snaps your dad and me out of it and we have to smile because Baby Jack is really going nuts.

"I need to sit down," says your dad.

"'Come in,' I say.

"Your dad sits at the kitchen table. He's never been in our house before. And he looks around and sees your boot camp graduation picture on the mantel. And I know he knows that Baby Jack is your son by the way he's looking at him. Your dad has tears running down his cheeks and says: 'Will you forgive me?' 'Yes,' I say.

"For a while we're quiet but the baby is still crying so I say, 'May I feed your grandson?' And he says, 'Yes.' So I do.

"A few minutes later Dad came home and then Mom came in. At first no one said much. They just passed the baby around. Your dad would kiss Baby Jack, cry some more and sometimes laugh till he had to stop because his side was hurting so much. He has broken ribs he said.

"Then he read some of your letters. Then everybody started acting the way people do at a wedding after a few drinks when they loosen up while two families start to kind of mingle.

"Your dad apologized to my parents for hanging up on Dad and for the way he acted at the funeral. And he said he was sorry for ignoring me. And Dad said, 'If I lost a child I'd go nuts too.'

"And your dad held our son for a long time until our baby fell asleep in his arms.

"Then he whispered, 'Thank you Jack.' And I don't know if he meant you or the baby. Then he thanked me for keeping the baby. No one has ever done that. He called me brave. He was really sweet. And then Mr. Ogden asked if he could bring over your mom. And of course I said yes, even though the idea of sharing you with them makes me really nervous.

"And your dad gave me your letter to him that someone on Parris Island gave him. And he said I could make a copy so Mom scanned it. And I read it as soon as he left.

"Jack, I'll always love you. And I'll call Patrick today since now I know its okay with you."

53

From: Pfc. Jack Ogden USMC

To: Todd Ogden

C/O Staff Sergeant Jackson USMC

12/27/03

Dear Dad,

Tomorrow I leave for Camp Lejeune where I did MCT—what a shithole that was! Actually I'll be going to Camp Johnson next to Lejeune for my MOS school.

I'm looking out of Jessica's window and can see our house across the water. I haven't had the guts to drive over the bridge and see you during the last 10 days. I see why the night before grad SDI Jackson told us that a lot of Marines feel isolated from the civilian world right after boot camp.

Dad: do you know how much time I wasted in high school at St. Martin's and Chandler? Do you know that I was just cruising along? Did you want me to do that for four years in college? How much wasted time were you okay with? How much weed was I smoking? Did you know or care? I wasn't working hard. At St. Martin's no one gave a shit as long as I won track events. And those nice teachers at Chandler were suckers. There were no grades—"too competitive"—and as long as I figured out how to stroke them in class discussions they loved me.

Okay, so bullshit aside, why did I join? I still don't have "the" answer. Here's my best shot:

1) I wanted to stick it to you. You were right about that.

2) When I saw the Twin Towers fall it pissed me off.

3) Freedom is precarious and I want to be more than a bystander.

4) I read a letter when I was researching a humanities paper at Chandler. My paper was on women in WWII. I was pissed off with Cassie for making us write such a politically correct bunch of crap, you know women in WWII, even though men did the fighting. I changed my mind after I happened to pick a nurse called Frances Slanger to write about.

Slanger was a Polish Jew who came to America as a little kid and grew up in Boston. She became a nurse in spite of lots of anti-Semitic shit from some people who didn't want Jews in the nursing school. She loved America anyway, faults and all. She believed she owed her new country something.

Slanger got sent to France right after D-Day. She wrote a letter to the *Stars and Stripes*. The next day a

German artillery shell hit her field hospital. The letter got to the paper after her death and was published November 10, 1944.

Her mom didn't want her over there. Are you sorry she went? Are you sorry we won? Do you think we still need a military?

Please read this copy of Lt. Slanger's letter.

STARS AND STRIPES

It is 0200 and I have been lying awake for one hour, listening to the steady, even breathing of the other nurses in the tent. The fire is burning low and just a few live coals are on the bottom. With the slow feeding of wood, and finally the coal, a roaring fire is started. I couldn't help thinking how similar to a human being a fire is: if it is allowed to run down too low and if there is a spark of life left in it, it can be nursed back—so can a human being. It is slow, it is gradual, it is done all the time in this field hospital and other hospitals in the ETO.

We had read several articles in different magazines and papers sent in by grateful GIs, praising the work of the nurses around the combat areas. Praising us—for what?

We wade ankle deep in mud. You have to lie in it. We are restricted to our immediate area, a cow pasture or hayfield, but then, who is not restricted? We have a stove and coal. We even have a laundry line in the tent. Our GI drawers are at this moment doing the dance of the pants, what with the wind howling, the tent waving precariously, the rain beating down, the guns firing, and me with the flashlight, writing.

Sure, we rough it, but in comparison to the way you men are taking it, we can't complain, nor do we feel that bouquets are due us. But you, the man behind the guns, the men driving our tanks, flying our planes, sailing our ships, building bridges to the men who pave the way and to the men who are left behind—it is to you we doff our helmets. To every GI wearing the American uniform, for you we have the greatest admiration and respect.

Yes, this time we are handing out the bouquets . . . but after taking care of some of your buddies: seeing them when they are brought in bloody, dirty, with the earth, mud and grime, and most of them so tired. Somebody's brothers, somebody's fathers and somebody's sons. Seeing them gradually brought back to life, to consciousness and to see their lips separate into a grin when they first welcome you. Usually they kid, hurt as they are. It doesn't amaze us to hear one of them say "Holy Mackerel, an American woman!" or most indiscreetly, "How about a kiss?"

The soldiers stay with us but a short time, from ten days to possibly two weeks. We have learned a great deal about our American soldier, and the stuff he is made of. The wounded do not cry. Their buddies come first. The patience and determination they show, the courage and fortitude they have is sometimes awesome to behold. It is we who are proud to be here. Rough it? No. It is a privilege to be able to receive you, and a great distinction to see you open your eyes and with that swell American grin, say, "Hi-ya babe!"

Dad: put it this way: If two lines were forming, one to those "prestige" schools and high paying jobs Chandler kids think they're entitled to and the other line was forming to be somebody Frances Slanger might respect, I suddenly knew which line I wanted to be in.

And if this woman—who stood all of five one and who could've stayed home and who had to wear thick glasses and who was afraid of the obstacle course in her military nurse boot camp—volunteered for front line duty, why can't I?

Is America worth defending? I think so. If that is right then aren't we all somehow responsible?

Dad: just for the record I want you to know that you are still my friend who trusted me to keep watch when we sailed. And you let me paint next to you. And even though I'm angry with you I know you love me.

Please show this letter to Mom, Amanda and Jessica. And please tell Jessica to live her life. Tell her that if I'm gone the last thing I want is for her to be alone. Please go see Jessica! Please be kind to her! And please hug Amanda and Mom for me. And Dad, remember what Lao-tse said: "The net of Heaven has wide meshes and yet nothing escapes it."

I love you Dad.

Author's Note to Book Clubs

I would like to show my gratitude for your book club's consideration of *Baby Jack* (and/or my novels *Portofino*, *Zermatt* and *Saving Grandma*), by making myself available to answer your questions. If your book club contacts me through my Web site (FrankSchaeffer.com), I'll set up a time when we can talk. (All you need is a speakerphone.) My only request is that your club have a minimum of six participants, and that you give me adequate prior notice.

Meanwhile here are a few questions about *Baby Jack*. Please don't read these notes until *after* you read the book! I hope the questions will be helpful in stimulating your club's discussions.

To set up a time to talk to me, please contact me at FrankSchaeffer.com.

Book Club Notes—Suggested Discussion Topics

1. Whose voice in the book best represents you: Todd, Sarah, Jack, Amanda or Jessica?

2. When God shows up did you take this as a theological "statement" or is God just another character in the book?

3. Is *Baby Jack* "anti-Christian" (or even "anti-religious") because God is different than the Sunday school teachings about God you might have received?

4. If the "greatest generation" was so great how come they had so many selfish "boomer" children?

5. If you are someone who has no loved one in the military, and did not serve yourself (like me until my son volunteered), do you feel my novel is "attacking" your values?

6. If you have or had a loved one in the military or serve[d] yourself, do you feel that *Baby Jack* "validates" some of your own experiences?

7. Have you lost a loved one? If so, does the novel resonate with the emotional trauma you experienced?

8. Do you think this statement true?—"We have come to the

inevitable dead end of the rights-centered quest for meaning as an 'I want' society. The formulation of individualized 'I want' leads to alienation. This alienation is at odds with everything that human beings are and need. There is an unexpected way out. Serve others and serve the community and you will be truly happy."

9. Is Jack Ogden a "Christ figure?"

10. Did God change his mind about helping Jack and Todd?

11. One person said *Baby Jack* is making the point that "The problem of our culture is that the class discontent in America pervades everything from peoples' personal lives to the national political sphere." What do you think?

Acknowledgments

I thank my wife Genie. Without her love I would have no reason to write. And Genie's excellent notes are always my first line of defense against "inspiration."

My agent Jennifer Lyons prevents my writing from gathering dust. Her friendship, advice and professionalism are the foundation upon which my writer's peace of mind—such as it is—rests.

I want to thank my very dear friend and publisher Will Balliett. Will read the earliest rough drafts of *Baby Jack* and gave me notes that resulted in a better book. More than two years later Will helped me fine-tune the final manuscript. His editorial work was inspiring. My editor Tom Dyja shared ideas that were immensely helpful. The fact that I admire Tom's books meant that I had the privilege of being edited by a writer I trust. Tom asked me to write new scenes and trim others. And he provided me with long detailed editorial letters full of wise advice. I am very grateful. I am also grateful to Keith Wallman who gave *Baby Jack* a careful line-by-line going over and to Jay Boggis for his copy edit. I also want to thank Callie Oettinger for her creative and outstanding work as the publicist for this novel.

I wish to thank Bing West, Carolyn See, Kimberley Patton, Charlotte Gordon, Nate Fick, Max Alexander, and Cathy Franks for their gracious pre-publications endorsements, encouragement, and suggestions.

I never served in the military. My son John served as an enlisted Marine from 1999 to 2004 and was deployed twice to

Afghanistan, as well as sent on other missions around the world including Iraq. He taught me about Marines by example. Without John's grafting me into the military community I would not have written about the men and women who defend us or those who love them. Moreover John has encouraged my writing ever since he was a child when he read my first novel *Portofino* a chapter at a time as I wrote it. There is also an overlap between *Baby Jack* and *KEEPING FAITH: A Father-Son Story About Love and the United States Marine Corps*, a nonfiction book I co-authored with John soon after he got out of boot camp. I borrowed some of John's material from *Keeping Faith* and used it as part of Jack's "voice." My love and admiration for John motivated this book.

My daughter Jessica and my son Francis have encouraged my writing. Jessica is a terrific mother, scholar, writer and friend. She read *Baby Jack* in an early draft and was most helpful. She then read the final draft and made some important suggestions. Francis' ceaseless encouragement has always sustained my work. And his skill as a high school teacher is humbling. His dedication to his students inspired a great deal of Jack's character. And Francis has spent a lot of time listening while I read my writing to him out loud. His advice is always good.

My sister Debby read *Baby Jack* in an early draft and made helpful comments. My friend Elizabeth Keefe made helpful suggestions and was encouraging as well. She helped develop the notes to the book clubs section.

While I was working on *Baby Jack* I was also co-authoring a nonfiction work with Kathy Roth Douquet: *AWOL: The Unexcused Absence of America's Upper Classes from Military Service And How*

It Hurts Our Country. Her friendship—not to mention the way she supported her Marine husband Greg, when he went to war in Iraq—provided a lot of inspiration for *Baby Jack*. And some research we did together for *AWOL* was helpful in writing *Baby Jack*.

Several books were vital to this project including *My Old Man and the Sea*, by David Hays and Daniel Hays. It is about their father–son sailing adventure. Their book inspired two scenes in *Baby Jack*—fixing Todd's boat and sailing it. I know very little about sailing. Most of what I wrote about Todd's sailboat and the sailing trip I borrowed from the Hays' wonderful book. I was also helped by reading *Holy Tears* edited by Kimberley Patton and John Stratton Hawley. One essay therein was particularly helpful in gathering material for Jack's comments on Buddhist and Hindu philosophy, *The Poetics and Politics of Ritualized Weeping in Early and Medieval Japan*, by Gary L. Ebersole. *Dietrich Bonhoeffer* a book by Dallas M. Roark, was helpful and related to Jack's comments. I also used material borrowed from *One L* by Scott Turow for Sarah's back-story at Harvard Law School. Speaking of HLS my very good friend Frank Gruber sent me various HLS alumni publications to help me better understand his (and thus Sarah's) Harvard Law experience. He also very kindly read a final draft and provided me with some helpful notes.

Thanks to Adrienne Rich for her essay, "Anne Bradstreet and Her Poetry," found in *The Works of Anne Bradstreet*. I paraphrased several lines from it as the basis of Jessica's "essay" on Bradstreet. I would also like to thank my friend Charlotte Gordon whose outstanding book *Mistress Bradstreet* introduced me to, and helped me understand, America's first poet.

In writing the *New Yorker* "review" about Todd's work I was helped by reading critic and art historian Edward Lucie-Smith's catalogue copy from a show of Steve Hawley's paintings. And Steve Hawley—one of the great contemporary neo-realist painters—also let me interview him in his studio. Many thanks.

In writing Jack's "citation" I was assisted by reading many similar items in *The Boot* (the newspaper of Recruit Training Depot Parris Island), as well as *Leatherneck* (the excellent and indispensable publication of the Marine Corps Association). My "article" about Jack's death relied heavily on several pieces in *The Boot* and *Leatherneck*.

The "flyer" Amanda leaves around the offices of the *New York Times* is about actual events (other than the part about Jack Ogden). I took those reports from the *Jacksonville Daily News* (the newspaper that serves the Camp Lejeune area), and *Leatherneck* magazine. I contemplated inventing fictitious accounts of heroism for Amanda's flyer but wanted to celebrate actual events. (This was one place where the work Kathy did for *AWOL* was used herein and I thank her.)

The mother's lines quoted by Amanda, wherein the mother says, "I don't know if my son was a 'hero.' He did what he was asked to do, and he did it without hesitation. Maybe that's heroic . . . ," were taken from a letter that Mindy Evnin—mother of Mark Evnin, a Marine killed in Iraq—wrote to me. (Her remarkable letter is in *AWOL* in full.) Similarly, Lt. Slanger's letter, though somewhat shortened, is real. Her letter to the *Stars and Stripes* and the biographical information about her life Jack puts in his letter were taken from *American Nightingale*, Slanger's biography by Bob Welch.

During my extended stay on Parris Island gathering material for *Baby Jack* many Marines and recruits helped me by their willingness to talk to me while allowing me to observe the training cycle. Amongst them (listed in the order I met them) were, Major Ken White, Major Keith Burkepile, First Sergeant Lawrence Finneran, Staff Sergeant Elliot, Sergeant Guerrero, Staff Sergeant Maynor, Staff Sergeant Itnalia, Staff Sergeant Coons, Sergeant Silva, Staff Sergeant Potter, recruits Torres, Petersen and Jackie Allberty, Staff Sergeant Timothy Soignet, Colonel Kevin Kelley, Sergeant Major John Wylie, Staff Sergeant Sherri Battle, Sergeant Tammy Shelton and Sergeant Ortiz.

I'm sorry that I don't know these Marines' current rank or even some of their first names. I was jotting names as best I could while trying to keep up with hard-charging Marines and recruits during hectic days and nights as I went "lights-to-lights" with various platoons.

I am particularly grateful to the SDIs and DIs. They kindly let me intrude into the intense training cycles of their platoons. And I am most particularly grateful to Staff Sergeant (retired) George Henderson USMC. He was my son's SDI on Parris Island in 1999.

Staff Sergeant Henderson kindly took the time to let me interview him. We sat in the library at Camp Lejeune and talked for two hours. He was very helpful and I thank him for his generosity in volunteering information about his path to becoming an SDI, and his life in the Corps. His insights were invaluable.

I am grateful to Lt. Col. Greg Douquet for specific information related to the Bell 402 helicopter and most of all for being so kind as to support his wife Kathy's writing while we've worked together on *AWOL* and other projects that had such a positive impact on this book. And thank you to Linda Kosarin for a splendid cover. And thanks to Robert Walters for creating and maintaining my Web site. Thank you to Sue Canavan for the design of the book. And thanks to Jamie McNeely for her editorial assistance on the final draft.

I would like to thank Tom Feyer, the editor of the Letters to the Editor page of the *New York Times* as well as Mary Dorhan. They generously took time out of a very busy day to talk with me in their office and let me observe their work at the *Times*.

I would like to thank Seleno Clarke, jazz composer and B-3 Hammond organ maestro extraordinaire for inviting me to his jam sessions at American Legion Post 398 in Harlem. This inspired a scene in *Baby Jack*.

Headmaster Peter Smick and the teachers and students at the Waring School (Beverly, MA), were kind on my many visits to the campus. The high quality of the Waring students and staff inspired me to try to create Jack and Jessica as kind, intelligent, well-read and articulate high school students.

Last but not least, I humbly thank every man and woman who has earned the eagle, globe and anchor. Without you I would have no story and much more importantly, our country would not have its first line of defense. I also thank every family member who supports and loves "our" Marines.

And for those readers who have lost a loved one while he or she was wearing the uniform of any branch of our military, thank you for your incalculable sacrifice. And for those of our warriors who have been injured defending us I offer my humble thanks and prayers for you and your families.

I hope some little glimmer of the respect I have for those who serve has come through in these pages. And please forgive me for any part of my novel that might have offended you.